Relating To Michael

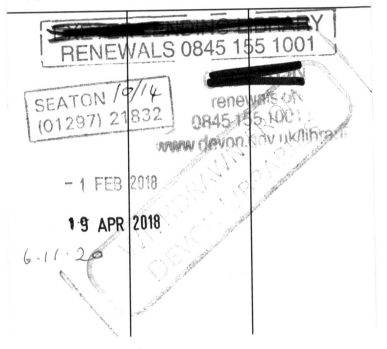

chipmunkapublishir
the mental health publisher

Published by
Chipmunkapublishing
PO Box 6872
Brentwood
Essex CM13 1ZT
United Kingdom

http://www.chipmunkapublishing.com

Chipmunkapublishing gratefully acknowledge the support of Arts Council England.

Note

The characters, school and respite centre in this novel are fictitious and any resemblance to actual persons, living or dead, or to actual establishments is purely coincidental.

Acknowledgements

I would like to thank Karen Hayes for her unwavering kindness and insightful questions. Her tact and enthusiasm were beautifully measured.

For attention to detail when using an editorial eye my thanks go to Marge Franklin. Her close reading of the final draft was particularly valuable.

To writers Liz Shakespeare, Alison Harding and Shirley Cowling who listened to chapters from an earlier draft of the manuscript, my heartfelt thanks. And to Sal for her patient help with the cover image, my love and thanks.

Mary Maher

Description

'Relating To Michael' is a work of fiction. Michael is Robin and Tamsin Cooper's beautiful autistic son. Robin has left Brock Cottage, their home, and moved to a room over 'Coopers and Son', the family antique business in nearby Linbury. He and Tamsin strongly disagree about how they should treat Michael. The continuity of the family as embodied in the image 'Coopers and Son' is very important to Robin but Michael offers his father no real acknowledgement. This distresses Robin. Nursery rhymes are Michael's main vocalisations. Playing one note, D flat on the piano, and running water are other obsessions.

Tamsin, who has problems with dependence, is pulled in all directions by her love for their son and her wish for acceptance and normality. She works from home as a potter. Harvest jugs are her speciality.

'Relating To Michael' is about a family's struggles and frustrations as it journeys towards a different understanding.

Mary Maher

About The Author

Mary Maher has had four collections of poetry published, and many short stories one of which won a SW Arts Award. Her poems have appeared in the first Forward Anthology, on TV and have been used by The Hospice Care Trust, the UCLA Writing Programme and Exeter Health Care Arts. When the scheme was running she was a W H Smith Poet in Schools. She enjoys editing as well and recently edited two art books.

Yorkshire born in 1937 to a family of miners, Mary has had manic depression several times and believes this is why she felt 'at home' working in Special Education where there was a lot of honesty, a lack of social inhibition and where life was vivid, never humdrum, on a daily basis.

For Sal

Mary Maher

Chapter One

Tamsin glanced back at her son's bedroom window before slithering down the overgrown grassy slope to the kiln shed, thus avoiding the thirteen steps. Nine years ago when Robin had been building them she had asked him to make one more. At the time she had been standing on the top path patting and contemplating her pregnancy while Robin prepared the foundation for the thirteenth step.

"But we don't need another one, Tams."

"It's not about need."

Before Robin could retaliate with some quip of his own, as Tamsin knew he would, she'd swept down the twelve cobbled steps and planted a kiss on her husband's lips while he hastily raised and held a cement-ladened trowel away from her face.

Today the sound of a tractor wafted from a far field across the valley. It was early. Their beautiful son was still asleep and with luck might not stir for another hour or so, giving Tamsin time to check the kiln's contents and get back before he woke and panicked.

Tamsin needed time to herself before Michael's day began. It was a breathing space in which she could root the day ahead.

After last night's rain, wisps of steam rose from the wet grass. She lingered for a moment outside the door of the kiln shed, scanning the green, undulating countryside which sheltered her home.

At the top of the slope, to the right of the cottage, a recently converted granary, one up, one down, was also still asleep, blinds closed. Tamsin smiled as she thought of John, her tenant, getting ready for the day behind those closed blinds. Her tenant? Hers and Robin's to be legally accurate, even though Robin now no longer shared the family home with her and nine year old Michael.

She entered the shed with apprehension. Inside she was enveloped by the kiln-toasted air. Eagerly, fearfully, she removed the bung from the kiln door. How had the jug fared this time?

Last month the first jug had been blown to smithereens by a random bubble of air left in its base. It was a special piece, a harvest slipware jug, a centre piece for her forthcoming exhibition. An exhibition to test the market, bring in commissions and set her on the road to independence. So for this second attempt she'd kneaded and slammed down the clay with even more determination than usual, to get rid of any wanton air bubbles.

She stooped to peer through the hole and there it was. Hot,

pink, incandescent. Apparently complete. The proud specimen of a harvest jug. She placed the bung on the stone shelf where it glowed like a fat cigar. The temperature in the kiln would now begin to fall. With a mixture of relief and anxiety Tamsin stepped back outside and into grass that was still glistening with rain. Of course she would not know for sure if the jug was safe until later, when it would be cool enough to open the kiln door.

The stream, which wound its way around the bottom of Brock Cottage's garden, Robin and Tamsin's half-acre, was rushing after last night's heavy showers. Deep in thoughts and hankerings, contrary and contradictory, Tamsin obsessively matched her path to the water's river-bound meanderings. Out of habit she longed to tell Robin about the jug. After all, it had been one of his many ideas that she look for exhibition space. He was good at ideas, planning, delegating, and she still prized and needed the approval and understanding he gave her for her clay work, if not for her attitude towards and treatment of their son. She kicked out at the grass, soaking her clay-stained trainers.

By the hedge bordering the garden, where the stream dashed away under the lane and into her friends' field, rich ferns feathered up and over the lichened stone arch of the bridge. Foxgloves sprouted at its base and then soared, vivid with health. Their petals were velvety, dusty with pollen. Digitalis, good for the heart, Tamsin murmured, picking one for the kitchen. She also rescued a lager can nestling among the lower leaves. A local must have chucked it on his way home from Linbury. Tamsin absentmindedly read the label and turned it over before glancing up the slope at the cottage. Her eyes lovingly swam over its flaking white cob walls to settle and linger on Michael's window, dampened by the beading of a night's condensation. The yellow curtains, not drawn, were an inlaid square of peace in the white. Michael's room, Michael's home. But when they had diagnosed Michael seven years ago, Tamsin's rosy daydream of becoming a happy family had faded, and when she and Robin had split, it had slowly morphed into mockery. Robin now lived a spartan existence in one room above the family antique business in Linbury, 'Coopers and Son'. On his own. But for how long would he remain on his own?

Tamsin's musings were suddenly interrupted when the door of the granary flashed open and framed its tenant, yawning and stretching in Speedos and T-shirt. He blinked in the swift flood of sunlight. Just off for his morning run, he stepped outside and started to bend and flex his muscular legs, and then he saw Tamsin and grinned. "Hi-ya Tamsin. Okay?"

"Yeah. Just checking my jug." Tamsin waved the foxglove at him and then she continued climbing the slope. Having John around made a world of difference to her mornings. Usually launching her and Michael's day required mammoth concentration, but for these last few months things had at least been a little lighter, a little less lonely, warmer, more real. If something went wrong she could call on John to help out. He was her neighbour, next door and, as a classroom assistant working at Michael's school, he knew how to deal with her son's needs and difficulties and was not fazed by them.

John jogged along the top of the paddock to the top gate. Then he slowed down and halted abruptly as if he had forgotten something. He ran backwards and then on the spot, marking time. "Don't forget, Tamsin Cooper, to sign the form for tomorrow's meeting. Applied Behaviour Analysis."

"Applied what? Oh right. Thanks." Bugger, she'd forgotten to unpack Michael's school bag last night. Bad mother. Inattentive to detail. Again. Tamsin dreaded the condescending disapproval of Michael's young teacher and the school's headmistress, Mrs Green.

By the back door she stopped to collect a few logs from the pile. Newly stacked, it smelt strongly of resin. John must have been sawing and splitting again. Good for him. Good for Michael. Her son loved the flicker of flames.

Before Brock Farm Estate had been divided into lots and sold, the cottage and the granary had been part of the Estate. Prior to the sale, Tamsin's grandfather, Brock Farm's retired dairyman and sitting tenant, had bought the cottage and granary for a nominal price, leaving the farm with a viable number of acres and its immediate outbuildings, and on the death of her grandmother Tamsin had inherited the two buildings.

If she had already been inside and upstairs with Michael this morning, when John started out for his run, there would have been a peppering of pebbles thrown at the bedroom window accompanied by a raucous "Wakey, wakey!" Later, obviously showered, his hair wet and spiky, his olive skin blooming, he would appear at the kitchen door ready to pick up Michael and take him to school in the minibus. John's youth, although he was not that much younger than her, made Tamsin feel less burdened, more hopeful. There was an infectious alertness about him.

The logs were not for heat, it was already July, but for the drama of flames which Michael, hands clasped as though in prayer, revered as he gazed deeply into the kitchen's cavernous fire while Tamsin made toast and tea. Dressing her struggling son was another of her morning dramas.

The back door was solid and heavy. A safeguard. Tamsin loved it. The security it offered. Standing on the threshold she often felt her grandmother was there with her, holding kindling, hugging it into her wrap-around floral apron. Tamsin lifted the wooden latch with her elbow and then, pressing with her back firmly against its weathered oak, she swung slowly into the kitchen where she stood balancing for a moment and listening to each sweet tick of the grandfather clock as it dispersed into the pure anticipation of silence.

The clock struck seven. Tamsin held the logs close before suddenly abandoning them to drop them noisily into the hearth. Immediately she regretted it. Had she woken Michael? She cocked her ear. No. All was well. This time.

John would need a drink when he returned from his run. As she opened the fridge door she reflected on the subtle contrast between the warm, life-affirming rituals John was adding to Brock Cottage and the restraining routines which occupied much of her time with Michael. She filled a grey, stoneware tankard with orange juice and ice, flung wide the kitchen window and placed the tankard on the cob sill ready for John's return.

The fire in the wood-burner leapt into life. Tamsin knelt and contemplated the flames before she closed the little cast iron door. Later she would open it for Michael's gaze and delight.

She couldn't imagine her days now, her nights and days, difficult though they were, without Michael. She thought about how each waking hour she floundered, an explorer in unknown territory, never knowing what she might encounter and where child development charts were an enemy. But she also knew she had to go on. And needed to. They'd coped. That she and Michael had got this far was a miracle. And they'd coped latterly without Robin, who'd finally given up on them because she adamantly refused to consider future life options for their son: a residential school, a care community.

"It's not about the bloody future Robin. It's about now. Our lives now. And what do you want? You want him to go away. We need to sort us out. Be together as a family. He's our life."

"He is part of our life, Tamsin. An important part, but our life together is not just about Michael. And we do need to plan his future. For his sake. Work out what is best for him."

"You mean what is best for you."

"That's not fair. If you are not careful he will become an obsession. Your reason for living. A mission. A project."

She'd been angry. Scared. How dare he say she was obsessed? Obsessed with her own child. Her skin prickled. She'd wanted to hit out at him, hurt him. Michael was different and because of his difference he, their son, was special. She'd hoped that one day it would dawn on Robin that Michael had his own unique qualities to offer to the world and to his family. Family to Tamsin meant closeness, love, loyalty through thick and thin. To Robin it also meant continuity. Father and son, Robin and Michael Cooper. 'Coopers and Son', the family business.

On the other hand, she could see dear John really enjoyed Michael's company. She could see it in his face. It shone with pleasure and affection, and this gave Tamsin such a warm feeling in her gut each time she saw them together. And the feeling grew and secretly blossomed. John reminded her of a dolphin as he gently nudged Michael in the right direction.

Recently, late at night when she was sitting alone in her kitchen, Michael in bed, Tamsin had allowed herself to fantasise about a life in the future. Not the future Robin had envisaged, but a life in which people recognised what Michael had to give and welcomed it. A future in which Michael played football with her on the level by the stream, had friends, parties, sleepovers. There would be bright days with blue skies when he would call out to her from across the garden and laugh. His laughter would rock the valley. And crucially it would be about something funny. Something that she could understand. Then she visualised Michael answering the phone and saying "It's daddy." And then she saw Robin on the other end gob-smacked with happiness and pride.

But Michael still hadn't uttered the word 'daddy', and this was the image that brought her fantasising to an end each time. The vision was too achingly lovely, too painful. Michael saying daddy. And Robin hearing him.

Tamsin put the foxglove in water and slipped her finger inside the hooded petals and rubbed the pollen as the kettle came to the boil. She poured steaming water into her stoneware mug, dunked a teabag and sat at the large kitchen table to think some more. The fire crackled. She opened the fire-door and put on another log. Challenging Behaviours, High Dependency, Severe Learning Difficulties: what term would the so-called experts come up with next? Each new term seemed to go round the houses to suggest positive discrimination and in Tamsin's view, failed. It was only a matter of time before each new term became a term of abuse, like *idiot* or *imbecile* which she'd read online, had once been specific indications of I.Q. And what was it John had just said? Applied Behaviour Analysis?

Her son was unusual. Michael was destined for something. He had shown her such pleasure: light that drifts, that glitters, and movement so fast the eye catches only its tail. It passes the eye and is gone. But not without Michael jumping and clapping his hands. The joy, the intense joy. His acknowledgement of the moment. How in a pause and a look he could turn something ordinary into something extraordinary.

Only two days ago he'd been mesmerised by the flame on the taper as she'd lit the kiln. He'd grabbed her wrist and waved it. Ecstasy so elusive and temporal it hurt him, she could see, with a satisfying pain crinkling the skin around his eyes before he leapt into the air with a release of delight. He loved the drift of smoke from chimneys, candles, the shattered light on rushing water, dew on cobwebs in the hedges like diamond necklaces. He had given her such wealth; shown her a different way of looking. Maybe he could show others. Why couldn't Robin see this?

And Michael's voice: It had an indefinable quality as though it had been filtered through ancient stone. His renderings sometimes transported the cottage into another consciousness. His voice when he said 'mummy'. So seductive, like the voice of an angel.

Her son was not a resource for research or experiment. He was not material or territory for all kinds of therapy experts to work on or fight over. He did not need life options. He needed recognition.

Tamsin put her head in her hands, for she knew there were other things, actions she wanted to hide from, close her eyes and ignore. Disruptive behaviours she wanted to say were a 'stage', believe he would grow out of. Head-butts when desires were thwarted. Floods when he left the tap running, unaware, as his fingers flicked and his gaze concentrated on the flashing stream.

And the constant sound of D flat, the one and only note Michael played on the piano. On and on. These things were not so easy to live with. Or love.

But John seemed able to focus fully on Michael: attentive to his physical needs, making fruitful observations from a distance or listening closely to mumblings and odd words. And John was so patient. "No Michael," he would say, taking Michael's arms, stroking them and diverting his attention from the piano and D flat or a running tap. And on her visits to the school Tamsin had noticed how well John worked with Ginny Smart, Michael's teacher. Classroom assistant and teacher, they were like brother and sister. Tamsin envied them their benign, easy arrogance, their youthful confidence. Ginny newly qualified and newly married had replaced old Doris Nokes whom Tamsin badly missed. Ginny Smart's bouncy tendency of always looking on the bright side however grey the day irritated Tamsin. It was patronising, but so far, Tamsin, sensitive to the underpinning nuances of conversations, had not detected anything flippant or cynical about this attitude. If anything Ginny was too earnest. She was ambitious and it showed. Optimism grew on her like a second skin. Like armour.

At the school barbecue when she had handed Tamsin a hot dog she'd said, "Michael gave me really good eye contact today. Must have been at least three seconds. I feel I am getting somewhere."

Tamsin was flummoxed. Ginny must be grabbing at straws. So far, sight gave Michael sensory pleasure: a flame, water, rather than aiding his communication. His eyes would flicker to avoid contact or suddenly pin you with a wide-eyed frantic gaze.

But it was Ginny's unfailing zealousness to correct Tamsin's oversights which sought and found Tamsin's weak spot. It went to the heart of her fragile confidence. Tamsin dreaded sorting the school bag in case she came upon yet another condescendingly chirpy little note informing her that she had forgotten to include this, that and the other for Michael's day. Behind the note lay the true message: judgement and disapproval.

Tamsin had been surprised when John asked to use her wheel. He wanted, he said, to renew his relationship with clay. A relationship begun at college. This meant him using her favourite place where clay abounded like a muddy womb and her treasured wheel spun like the earth. She had expected to feel proprietorial, for her sheds and wheel had been a haven, especially during the dark days of her split from Robin. It was here that she found peace in times of stress. Her sanctuary, her resort. But instead she found she had taken pleasure in sharing it with John.

But what of his other relationships, apart from clay? John; who was he?

Before John had taken over the tenancy of the granary and agreed to help with the finishing touches of the restoration for a reduced rent, Robin had given him a thorough interview and was "wholly satisfied". The references were excellent and the police checks, according to Michael's headmistress Mrs Green, were in order. But why wasn't Robin just a teeny weeny bit jealous of another man about the place?

This was John's first non-residential job. He'd told Robin he was worried about getting too institutionalised. He'd worked in a couple of Supported Living establishments and had nursed his father, who'd suffered from premature dementia, in his final days. But to Tamsin he'd spoken little about his past. Not a word about other family members or friends. Maybe he was getting away from a bad marriage. And divorce? Or a toxic relationship? She would have to ask him. Invite him over for supper. Probe a bit.

What Tamsin did find sweet was what John said one day, while engrossed in centering a ball of clay on the wheel. "Michael is the reality between my two new worlds. Work and home." A role for Michael. What a notion, and she had waited for John to say more, but he hadn't. Instead he'd bitten his lip and resumed concentrating on a wide, flared studio bowl before it flopped and collapsed onto the wheel and they'd both laughed. The exchange though had left Tamsin happily mystified.

She went outside to get a couple more logs and then remembered the school bag. She found and signed the form about the coming meeting and made a mental note to check Applied Behaviour Analysis on the jargon busting section of her favourite website. When she double checked the contents of the bag she came across more folded pieces of paper in the front pocket. Oh no, not more forms. The paper was so precisely folded that the creases were knife-sharp. There were in fact two pieces of paper, one folded inside the other, a note in Ginny's writing and a photocopy of an article on Respite Care. *You forgot Michael's spare shorts again Tamsin.* Motherly Doris Nokes had had a pile of spare clothing in the stock cupboard. She had never made Tamsin feel small or inadequate unlike her young replacement. Tamsin had found the changeover of teachers hard and had wept when Doris retired, on behalf of what turned out to be her, and strangely, not Michael's, bewilderment.

The article was from a magazine on Mental Health. Were the note and article related? Did Ginny think Tamsin could not cope? Needed Respite, Respite Care? A night, a week, two weeks away from Michael, or did Ginny Smart think Michael needed a break from his mother? Had Robin been talking to her? Influencing her?

She steadied herself. She did know she got things out of proportion sometimes. She took a deep breath and exhaled slowly. They were just pieces of paper, it was just another day. And the jug, the jug looked as though it was going to be okay. She glanced at the clock. Its face was bigger than hers, ticking and looking down at her. A clock she had lived with all of her life. When she was six she had stayed on with her grandparents when her own mother, single at the time of Tamsin's birth, had married and gone to live with her brand new husband in Brazil. Nowadays when Tamsin looked at the dial on the clock she often saw the nodding face of her grandmother merge and tick with her grandfather's.

Seven thirty; the clock chimed the half-hour. Not a stir from the room above. Tamsin went and stood in the shadowy back hall where the glittery piano lived secreting its predatory D flat. A high window, no more than a foot square and offering no view of the sky, only a view of nettles and brambles on the steep bank, peered down at the piano. She put down the piano lid quietly and then climbed the bare wooden stairs. Her head ducked familiarly under the beams as she climbed to the sunlit landing and then listened outside Michael's door before unlocking it.

Michael was still asleep. He was very beautiful: blond hair, rosy cheeks and his skin was creamy, uncreased. A peachy child - voluptuous.

The warm smell of urine in the room was not unpleasant. Even so she opened the window and leaned out into the fresh air. John was below, standing, stooped with his hands on his knees and breathing hard. His dark hair, usually carefully spiked, now was wet and tangled, heavy with perspiration. Before he looked up at her and smiled she noticed the logo on the back of his T-shirt; 'HANG ON'. "Thanks," he said, nodding at the empty tankard by his feet.

"It's a pleasure. I've signed the form."

"Good girl. Oh, and don't forget his shorts."

"Sod off." It made her feel better, took away the tension when he teased her.

Strange he hadn't mentioned the Respite Care article. Tamsin withdrew and returned to the bed where she stroked the roundness of her child's face and hard skull, the juxtaposition of the firm bone and soft flesh giving her palm sensual comfort.

Michael opened his eyes. They were like intense, vivid blue marbles and she was aware of herself shrinking under his unseeing but penetrative gaze. He was the image of Robin. She felt as though he were trying to pin her to the wall. Common sense told her he was frightened, that he didn't seem to know where he was. Each time he woke must, for him, be the equivalent of a waking nightmare. Did he dream, have bad dreams? Tamsin wasn't sure if he had a memory in the usual sense: detailed, specific. Sequential memory, making sequential links with time and place, as Ginny put it. John said he did but Tamsin had no idea. She tried, as always with great effort, to accept her son's long gaze dispassionately. It was her only way of dealing with it. And his. He rarely recognised comfort for what it was and would often hit out and panic in her embrace. In the mornings her arms ached to hold him but she had to wait for him to come to her. She rubbed the bruise on her cheek: last week's punishment for pulling him away from the piano when the constant sound of D flat had started to feel like a tin-tack being hammered into her temple.

Michael shivered suddenly and began to sing softly, "Mummy, mummy." And then he sat up and his voice soared, echoing in and out of the upstairs rooms and along the landing of the cottage. "Mummy, mummy!"

"Darling. It's all right." So then Tamsin began to sing, her voice low and gently laboured. "Mummy, mummy quite contrary how does your garden grow? With silver bells and cockle shells and pretty maids all in a row o, o, o, and pretty maids all in a row."

"O, o," sang Michael and crept, sighing, into his mother's arms and lay there, curled like a pink and white satiny shell, her prize for the morning.

Chapter Two

"I'm going to open the kiln soon. And the jug looks okay, fingers crossed. In fact it looks absolutely fabulous," Tamsin shouted to John from the top of the steps as the minibus headed out of the drive and up the lane on its way to its first pick-up. He wound down the window. He was happy for her. She could see it in his shining eyes when he smiled and stuck a thumb up in the air.

She had decided not to question him this morning about the article on Respite, in Michael's bag. She'd wait until the meeting and then have a word with Mrs Green, the Head.

Now she was free for six hours and still itching to share the news about the jug. Somehow the need to share good news, brag, was always more pressing than the need to share bad stuff. And who better to brag to than a loyal and understanding husband? Once Robin had been there for her in all her moods. She missed him. His congratulations or consoling hugs. His pride or concern for her, close by. But not his aloofness from Michael. And if Robin didn't want Michael then he couldn't want her.

Not really want her. Surely?

She released the catch on the kiln door and, with her eyes closed for a second, bathed her face in the sudden whoosh of warmth. The contents were revealed in all their glory: mugs, bowls and the jug. Yes. Perfect. No cracks. No cracks around the handle. But she would still need to check the base. The jug stood boldly like a champion at the front of the kiln. It was still too hot to touch but she could go over to Brock Farm and tell her friend, Anna. Yes she would go and tell Anna.

Tamsin ran across the lane and pushed open the gate into Brock Farm. A heron swooped up the valley, its gangly legs trailing. It flew as if after some memory and slowly came to earth like a waking dream to stand and peer into the water weeds of the shallow stream. Tamsin also stood for a moment, deeply breathing in her familiar surroundings: the evergreens on the other side of the valley and the dark shade they offered, the hill behind her work sheds rising steeply to a thicket of hazel, the white of her cottage and her friend's solid stone farmhouse. The cottage and farmhouse stood rather like a parent and child in the landscape.

The light was already peeling away the cool of the morning. It was going to be a hot day. Tamsin moved quickly through the stone arch into Anna's walled vegetable garden and up the pebble path lightly crushing rosemary spears and sage leaves on her way. As she entered the porch she called through the open front door, "The heron's back."

"Heron? What heron for God's sake?" Anna's voice, trained by the seasons' storms and restraints, withheld any surprise.

She sounded distant, absorbed. She must be at her computer. Tamsin felt a moment's disappointment. She needed to talk, but if her friend was deeply involved it wouldn't be kind to disturb her. Anna worked from home, running a small accountancy business for farmers, but apart from the demands of her work she was, at the moment, prey to another preoccupation which put a strain on her days and left her and Joe in limbo land.

They had lived at Brock Farm for about five years and Anna and Tamsin had got on like a house on fire right from the start but were still discovering things about one another. Joe was more difficult to get to know. He was gruff and frightened Tamsin a bit.

"You couldn't put the kettle on and call Joe from the yard could you Tamsin? I am up to my eyes with the Sandy Farm accounts. You heard the news about Simon Platt?"

"Simon Platt?"

"Well Joe'll tell you. It's awful. Must just finish this bit and then I'll be with you both."

What did Anna mean about Simon Platt? He was a young local farmer, recently married to Sarah. Tamsin didn't know them that well but was used to seeing them around Linbury, especially on market days.

Tamsin rounded the imposing farmhouse by the narrow path to the back and went in search of Joe. While scanning the grainy depths of the barns with screwed up eyes, thoughts of her harvest jug returned: the coiled plait along the handle, firm as ripe corn. Maybe she could arrange for the jug to stand among sheaves of corn at the coming exhibition which was to be held at The Harrow, Linbury's Arts Centre. A harvest jug was a bountiful thing. She imagined taking it to the fields brimming with cider after the great machines had stopped for the day; cider to slake the thirsts of the farm labourers, a crop's dust spotting sweat on their brows. It would be great if she could persuade Anna and Joe to have the cider and harvest tea in one of their fields like they used to in the old days. Now that the jug looked as though it had come safely through its first firing would be a good time to approach them with the idea. Robin had suggested it months ago, before he'd left, and it was he who'd spoken enthusiastically about making it an occasion, a celebration as a follow-up to the exhibition, for family and friends. Who was he sharing his ideas and enthusiasm with now? Mollie from the auction rooms?

She didn't see Joe at first. Then she heard rustling and saw his shadowy shape at the far end of one of the barns criss-crossing spills of sunlight as he struggled with sacks of feed. His prim steel, seriously rimmed glasses glistened as he twisted and turned.

When he saw Tamsin he carefully lowered a sack to the ground from his shoulder and then came out from the shadows to join her. "We need some more rain. Last night's was not enough…" he muttered accusingly. "It must be coffee time soon. Are you coming in? Anna's in the office."

"I know. I've just spoken to her. She'll be with us in a minute." Tamsin decided not to ask about Simon Platt. She'd wait for Joe to tell her in his own time.

Two long, sinewy bodied tabbies and Rocky the sprightly, compact wire-haired terrier appeared from nowhere and positioned themselves close to Joe's heels as the five of them ceremoniously strode down the concreted slope to the kitchen.

"Joe, the heron's back." Tamsin's tone was both false and placating.

"The heron? What do you mean, the heron? The water'll be glutty I expect," he said swiftly and dismissively. "Anna tell you about Simon Platt?" Since Robin's departure and John's arrival as a tenant in the granary, Tamsin had noticed an even greater wariness in Joe's tone and manner towards her, but today it was more than that. He seemed tense, angry.

"No Joe. What's the matter with him?"

"Dead. Yeah, dead." Joe looked away from the house and towards the horizon of trees.

"Dead?"

"He shot his calves and then turned the gun on himself."

"No?" Tamsin's mouth gaped.

"And just as things were looking up. We can sell our beef cattle abroad again."

In the sunshine the kitchen window appeared black and the closed dark green back door forbidding. "It might not have anything to do with the calves." Tamsin spoke quietly.

"What do you mean? He shot his calves, Tamsin. For God's sake."

"You know. Sometimes we take out our anger on

something else. Something not connected… " Tamsin was thinking of Michael and his inappropriate outbursts.

"Huh, who said he was angry? I think it was despair. Well past anger."

Tamsin pushed open the door as Joe took off his boots and left them outside tipped and balancing against the scraper. "Sorry." Tamsin changed tack. "What about Sarah?"

"I only heard at six this morning."

"Poor Sarah. How absolutely dreadful."

Tamsin had originally thought that Joe's edginess was due to her presence, but obviously it was the news about Simon Platt, and then she remembered that it was also around that time of the month when Joe's and Anna's hopes would either be dashed yet again or hopefully realised.

They had been trying for a baby for a while now but without success, and were planning to see a consultant at Linbury General. Obviously not a good morning then to gloat about one of her own creations, the jug, or seek comfort and reassurance by whining about Ginny Smart's notes and articles. All trivia compared with the news about Simon Platt, and Anna and Joe's worries. Thwarted, Tamsin conceded she would have to put her frustration on simmer.

Inside Joe crossed the kitchen and flopped into an easy chair which sagged and creaked in a torn and faded loose cover. A grubby blue hand towel was draped across its back. Rocky sat panting and claimed one of Joe's stockinged feet with a paw. The cats curled up by the old, cream enamel stove but their eyes remained coldly open: two pairs of stone-green orbs roamed around the kitchen, widening into bright black globes each time they alighted on Rocky.

Tamsin put on the kettle, reached for the mugs from her friends' dresser and then stood with her back to the old porcelain sink, praying for Anna to hurry up and relieve the tension.

Joe humphed as he got up and went to the sink. "Excuse me." Tamsin shuffled to one side. He washed his hands and dried them on the blue towel before reaching for the newspaper.

"Anna okay, Joe?"

He gave the newspaper a shake. "You've just spoken to her haven't you? You know I only saw Simon last market day. Having a drink in the Black Swan. Actually your Robin and that woman from the aucton rooms were there as well."

Tamsin's expression tightened as she swallowed an

unasked question.

"In fact, come to think of it, I wondered then if something was up because Simon was just sitting there in silence, staring into his ale. I feel bad now. I should maybe have made more of an effort. Got him to talk, but…"

Tamsin could not see straight and bitterly tried and failed to imagine Joe successfully persuading anyone to share their deepest feelings with him. Except maybe Anna.

"I dunno… " Joe pondered. He lowered the paper to his lap. "You've no idea what's going on in people's heads sometimes, have you? Though I wonder Sarah didn't see it coming. I've sent Sam over there, to see if there's anything we can do."

"Maybe Sarah did see it coming but couldn't do anything about it. Not all couples are like you and Anna," Tamsin said, struggling.

Anna flounced into the kitchen. Tamsin jumped, startled.

"The sparrow's back Tamsin! Tamsin, what are you like? You old romantic. Sorry, I shouldn't joke. Not today." Anna looked at their sombre faces. "Oh, he's told you has he? It's dreadful, isn't it? Poor Sarah." Anna reached for a mug of coffee. "Biscuit?" She opened a battered old floral tin and shook it half-heartedly in Tamsin's and Joe's direction before putting it down on the table, neither of them having accepted her offer. An uncomfortable silence followed before Anna shrugged and pointed at the baggy T-shirt Tamsin was wearing, "Eh, what's with that? It's John's, isn't it? Is anything going on with you two?"

"Yes it is John's, and well spotted." Tamsin brushed at the streaks of red clay slip on the front of the white shirt with its blue LET GO logo on the back. "And nothing's going on Anna, as you put it."

"Wearing a bloke's shirt looks like the start of something to me…"

Tamsin blushed. "They were just there, hanging behind the door in the shed. Anyway … "

Anna wasn't listening. "All right my lovely Joe?" She went round the table and put her arms around her husband's neck and kissed him. Instead of responding, he winced and glanced over at Tamsin with embarrassment. He then went back to holding his mug with two hands as if he were comforting himself with its warmth.

"Any dough cake left? I fancy a bit with some butter."

Anna let Tamsin get it from the enamel bread bin and cast around for the butter which she eventually found in a dish at the back of the stove. She placed them both firmly on the table in front of Joe while Anna remained at his side.

"Thanks," Anna said, stretching across her husband while attempting to cut and then butter him a piece of the dough cake. "John is very good though with Michael, isn't he? I saw them this morning, driving up the lane, singing away they were, together. You should have heard them! I'd be jealous if I were Robin …another man in my place and seeing more of my wife and son than I do."

"Yeah?" said Joe, appearing to wake up from his private world and come back to the kitchen table. He looked over his glasses and fixed Tamsin with a stare. "You two need to get things sorted."

"He doesn't seem to be. Jealous, that is," Tamsin stammered and felt guilty and confused again because even she was puzzled by Robin's lack of resentment towards John. Or had Robin actually installed John as organised protection for her? Was he paying him? John did seem very protective and did do a lot around the place for both her and Michael. She wouldn't put such a patronisingly devious tack passed Robin.

"But what about the land and all the work Robin has done about the place? Restoring the granary. Your sheds. It doesn't make any sense to me. Leaving your land. Your property." Joe still with his questioning eyes on Tamsin leaned towards her. He was fractious. Tamsin tearfully turned away.

Joe noisily cleared his throat and sat back. "Sorry Tamsin. It's the Simon Platt thing. It's got to me. I have no right to interfere in your… But I do really hope you two can sort things out."

Tamsin felt overwhelmed. Out of her depth. "He's got the shop, Joe. The family business. It means such a lot to him. More than Brock Cottage ever could." She wished they would both shut up about the situation. They were always probing, hinting instead of accepting the situation like she had to.

"But not more than you and Michael, surely? Sorry. Joe's right, Tamsin," said Anna. She shoved Joe's arm. "It is not our affair. I expect it's complicated." Anna put her head on one side and smiled sadly at Tamsin.

Joe got up and grudgingly gave his wife a peck on the cheek. "Yeah. Anyway, some of us have got work to do." He opened the back door and stretched for his boots with one hand.

Tamsin got up to leave too.

"No, no, don't you go," Anna smirked conspiratorially. "Stay for a bit."

Joe looked back at the two friends. "I thought you were up to your eyes in accounts."

"Oh, piss off you… " Anna waited for Joe to reach the top of the slope before she said, "Old Grouch," and stuck her middle finger up in the air. "He's taken this Simon Platt business to heart, naturally, rocked his world a bit. Sam's shaken up too and I think that's why Joe's sent him across to Sandy Farm: to see if he can be of help in a practical way. I think something similar happened in his own family. Sam's. Suicide. But of course that's left Joe out there on his own with all morning to think about it, mull it over and over and fret… Come on Tams, sit down for a minute. He's a straightforward man. What he can't understand has to be wrong. You know…like what has happened to you and Robin. Sorry to go on about it. But I just wish, we both do…" She broke off mid-sentence and drew Tamsin to her and gave her a hug.

"But you do understand your Joe, don't you? He's a lucky man, Anna. I don't understand poor Robin at all." And yet Tamsin had to admit Robin often did seem to understand her. He'd share her elation about the jug. And it had been his idea, the cider and harvest range of mugs and jugs.

"I s'pose I do. Thanks." Anna let Tamsin go.

Tamsin sniffed and smiled while pulling out the sturdy wheel-back chair with its moulded seat from the table. She sensed a belated opportunity and began to describe her jug, caress its invisibility, run her fingers round its rim, the rim that had no refinement of a lip, this being one of the medieval features she had incorporated into the design of her jug. Her friend listened attentively, so Tamsin continued and elaborated about the handle and its weight which she could feel again in her palm as she relaxed and felt the sombre, stilted mood of the kitchen roll over into easy intimacy. Her smile brimmed with enthusiasm and only when the air tingled with sudden silence did Anna thump the table, frightening the tabbies, and say in a thick Devon accent, "A jug big enough to bring cream up to your nose eh?"

"Cider," Tamsin corrected wryly.

"Course, silly me."

"Come on. Enough of me. What's your news?"

One of the tabbies climbed first onto a chair and then stretched up and onto the table, slinking round and round, her brindled fur flicking dust motes in a shaft of sunlight coming from the small window above the sink. Finally the tabby sat with a celebratory purr and curled into the empty space which had only recently belonged to Tamsin's invisible jug .

Anna was looking through the small window, apparently checking Joe's whereabouts.

"Oh well, I suppose I'd better get back if you've nothing to tell," Tamsin teased. "Thanks for listening to me." Tamsin leant forward and lightly stroked the tabby with her finger tips.

"No. No, you don't have to go. I have got a bit of news myself." Anna was whispering as she came back into the centre of the kitchen. "But I don't want Joe to know yet, build up his hopes... you know... but, but, but... I have to tell somebody, or I will burst." Her voice crescendoed.

"That would not be a good idea in your condition!"

"What do you mean? How do you know?"

"It's written all over you. Go on then, tell." Tamsin's face was eager with expectation and the hope that her guess was right.

"I'm late." Anna took a deep breath. "Nearly a week, in fact. Oh maybe I shouldn't say anything. Tempt fate. I dunno. Actually it's only a couple of days. But then I am rarely ever late. I suppose I am lucky that way. At least we've never been kept guessing. Before."

Tamsin hugged her friend and gave her a kiss. "Till now. Hasn't Joe guessed? He must know what time of the month it is."

Still in Tamsin's embrace Anna whispered into friend's hair, "If he has, he's not asking."

For a moment as she continued to hold Anna, Tamsin wished Michael was back inside her own womb and they were starting again, her and Robin. She remembered how thrilled Robin had been when she'd told him she was pregnant. He'd been combing her long, sun-streaked hair with his fingers at the time, as she'd sat rocking on her childhood swing by the stream.

She let her hand linger on Anna's arm and gave her a final squeeze before she left and slipped back across the lane.

Tamsin didn't go into the cottage but went straight to the kiln shed and lifted the jug carefully from the kiln. It was warm, like a new loaf of bread. She caressed it, the tips of her fingers searching meticulously for imperfections. None. Now she held its full red body to her breast and breathed a sigh of relief.

Chapter Three

Robin was not surprised to see Tamsin draw up outside the shop in the red mini he'd bought her for her thirtieth, and reverse into a parking space.

He was chatting with Mollie at the time while studying on screen a catalogue of lots for sale at Lindon's next auction.

At the sight of Mollie, Tamsin's smile faded and she stood still, half in, half out of the shop. The old doorbell clanged back and forth. "Oh. Oh hello Mollie. I didn't see you there. You haven't got fifty pence for the meter have you, Robin?"

Robin leaned across Mollie. The time worn wooden till opened with a ring. "Sure." He got up and fiddled with some coins. "Yeah. Here we are." He came towards Tamsin and, stretching across an old chest which had patches of veneer missing, handed her a fifty pence piece.

It was dark in the shop except for a pool of light from the angle-poise over the roll-top desk at the back where he'd been sitting at the computer with Mollie. His eyes followed his wife out into the sunlight and watched her feed the parking meter. Her long hair, determined to have a life of its own, had escaped from its band and was getting in her eyes. He felt a sudden tenderness for her. He missed her. She still was his dawning vision each morning as he woke.

"What's brought you into Linbury at this time, Tams?"

Tamsin wriggled her way nimbly between the crowded antiques, her fingers sliding smoothly over walnut, oak, mahogany, desks and table tops as she went.

"I was just passing and saw a parking place, so I thought, well you know..." She spoke slowly and smiled stiffly as her quickly scanning eyes came to rest on Mollie's slim feet shod in red high heels and tucked neatly under Robin's desk .

Tamsin was not just passing. She either wants or needs to see me, thought Robin. It was a comforting thought.

Mollie looked quizzically from Tamsin to Robin, then she briskly shrugged and got up from her chair. Slowly, elegantly, she stubbed out her cigarette in a porcelain pansy ashtray and slipped the lipstick stained ivory holder neatly into her purse. "I think I'll nip out and get a spot of lunch."

"Don't go on my account." Tamsin drew back into a narrow gap between an old oak settle and the patchy chest of drawers to let Mollie by.

"Gosh, no." Mollie ostentatiously looked at her watch. "Is it that time already? How time flies… See you later then, Robin." She nodded at Tamsin.

Robin waited for Mollie to leave. "Has anything happened? Is Michael all right?"

"No of course nothing's happened. I would have rung. Not to us anyway. I am glad to see you care though."

"Of course I care. I worry about both of you. And what do you mean, 'Not to us.'?"

"Sorry. But you know about Simon Platt? Committing suicide? Joe told me."

"Oh yeah… I heard it on the local news… Terrible. And I only saw him…"

"I know," Tamsin quickly interrupted. "Joe said he saw you. Joe's pretty shaken up… "

"Why do you think he did it? Did he leave a note?"

"I don't really know any more than you do." She put a greasy paper bag down on the desk. "I did get a couple of pasties, just in case … "

Robin murmured, "Well done." But he was picturing Simon Platt's wife. Lost. Robin felt the big, uncomfortable balloon of space he'd grown accustomed to, momentarily inflate and sigh inside his chest. Poor Sarah Platt. Unimaginable, what she must be going through. Loss. Robin knew loss, a different kind. The son he'd wanted but lost. Still alive, but trapped in a shaky, lawless world of his own. And bearing no relation to anything Robin had come across before. A world in a minor key. The son he'd never know. Michael was the image of him, people said. A guilty chill ran over Robin's flesh every time he thought about it. The family face. What a sad mockery of the sign, 'Coopers and Son' he could now see in reverse, arcing the darkly tinted plate glass window etched in black and gold script.

The pasties had leaked circles of fat onto the paper bag. He would rather have had a pint with uncomplicated Mollie in The Black Swan. He liked to get out at lunchtime, away from the shop for a while. And it was just so easy with Mollie: a pint, a smooth chat about which lots to go for at the coming auction, and they usually managed a sort of in-house laugh or two about well known bidders and their quirks. Nevertheless, it was always a relief to see Tamsin, and she looked lovely today, girly and athletic, in her casual way: a baggy T-shirt hanging over her shoulder and tight pink vest, cropped jeans and muddy trainers with no socks. Her legs were tanned and shapely. She propped them up on the chair beside him, casually brushing his thigh. He got up and went into the room behind the shop. He wished she wouldn't do that; act as if they were still naturally close. He couldn't believe she was unaware of what she was doing. "Coffee?"

"No, just water please. I had a coffee with Anna and Joe."

He came back in with some tomato ketchup and took down two Wedgwood blue and white plates from a dresser behind the desk. He dusted the plates with his shirt sleeve and removed Mollie's ashtray containing several crushed cigarette ends from the desk and then sat down. "I'll try and come over at the weekend and give John a hand with the staircase in the granary - the banisters - before he has an accident."

"Robin, are you coming to the school meeting tomorrow?"

Ah, so that was why she had come. "About?"

"Applied Behaviour or something... Oh, and Respite Care? I'd appreciate some support. You are still his..."

He caught her narrowing pressured look and groaned. "Do you mind? You understand what they're going on about. You can tell me about it later." It wasn't good enough, he knew, but... It got him down. All this intense worthiness. He wouldn't care, in fact, to be honest, he'd back it one hundred percent all the way if any of it helped, but as far as he could see it only seemed to contain the situation as it was. Dish out patronising false hopes rather than make things better. Head towards a cure, a resolution. There was a lot of talk, bigging it up with brash terminology, and very little real action as far as he was concerned, which had the effect of excluding rather than including him.

Tamsin looked at Robin. He knew she wanted to say something that would change his mind, but she'd said it all before. Too much. And she never said what Robin wanted to hear... Let's plan. Let's really help him. Let's think ahead. Be practical. Realistic.

When they had slept under the same roof the gap between them had become disfigured, bloated with their misunderstandings and consequent rows. It bred dissatisfactions in all corners of their marriage until not only did Michael's difficulties seem without hope, but so too did those of his parents.

And yet Robin could see that behind his wife's eyes today there was a mind like a search engine, searching for the trigger words which would trip and trap him into joining her at this meeting.

"I can't Tamsin. Come on, tell me how the jug is instead… Have you fired it yet?" Things were more bearable now they lived apart in that they could avoid, with effort, and distance themselves from their problems. The dailiness of life outside the home and school diluted the strength of their differences. And every now and then one of them would experience a re-tuned perspective. Like now, when Robin looked at his wife and saw the young beautiful woman, he used to love, start to smile.

"Yeah. Yeah. Took it out of the kiln this morning. It's going to be all right." She beamed. "Perfect." She shaped the outline with her hands.

He wiped flakes of pastry from his mouth. "That's a relief, eh? After the other?" He felt disappointed that he'd had to ask about the jug: that she'd not been bursting to tell him as she would have done a year ago. "Can I see it at the weekend?"

Tamsin shrugged.

Was he was trying too hard? But then he had another idea. "How about one for in here? Later. After the exhibition. When you're churning them out. Commissions from farmers flooding in…? "

"Well, Luke was going to sell them at The Cider Mill for me with my other kitchenware… coarseware, I suppose he'd call it."

"I know. But harvest jugs, especially copies of nineteenth century decorated slipware, should do well in here. Collectables do better than antiques, on a weekly basis anyway."

"Do you think? What, next to porcelain, Worcester, Derby and stuff? All those delicate breakables. Are you sure?"

"Yeah… The originals fetch a bomb at auction. And now I come to think about it… " Robin got up and went into the back again. He returned, flipping through a huge book. "Here, see… " He pointed to shiny coloured photos of beautiful amber harvest jugs. "And what about the odd baluster copy and posset pot?" He was excited.

Tamsin hesitated. "I dunno, Robin. Luke's been good to me so far and the jugs - and the mugs, litre ones - will complement The Mill's cider sales."

"I know, I know. But why not sell your stuff here *and* at Luke's. Be flexible? Double your market potential?"

"I," Tamsin glared at Robin, "am flexible."

"Look, here." Robin showed her the book again while ignoring her self-deluding jibe. "These inscriptions are delightful: *Once a pip and now so fissy;* and this one; *Pour a little for your slake."*

"I have inscribed an apple tree in fruit, through the slip on the body of the jug. Sgraffiato?"

"Is it? Great, but think of it with an inscription as well. Say, underneath the tree. *Once a pip and now so fissy...*You could incorporate it with its next firing, the glaze firing*?*"

"Yeah, I could actually. I'll think about it. Yes, it is a good idea."

Robin was pleased. It was good when they got off the subject of Michael and meetings and school, about which he could apparently do or say nothing that was useful. But now he badly needed something less intense: a pint and some small inconsequential chat.

Tamsin got up to go. Robin felt a guilty wash of relief. "I am really delighted about the jug. Well done."

Tamsin smiled weakly. Suddenly she looked lost. He wished he could put his arms around her, but all she had left for him was a husk of the love she once had. She used to give him the heart, the sweet nut of her heart and their love had been a romance with letters - *my dearest, darling* - poems, trysts, picnics under willows by rivers, even carving their initials on trees and surprising one another with apt gifts. Gifts which showed they had been listening and knew one another's longings by heart. Now the feeling between them had withered to a sliver with sharp, defined edges.

Before he'd left Brock Cottage there'd come a time when he could take no more. Ashamed and humiliated by their cold embraces and rushed, rare sex he had watched his wife stroke their son's face, listen out for him from their bed, dote on him. Robin knew fathers were supposed to be jealous of their newborn children. The love intruders. It was a cliché. But it wasn't like that for him. He had been at the birth for God's sake, even cut the cord. And the first year had been wonderful: watching Tamsin, her hair falling over this new baby as she'd cradled him. His baby. And Robin had looked forward to the future; not so much playing with his son, as later, talking man to man, in the shop, at auctions. 'Coopers and Son' . Maybe he wouldn't want to follow his father into the business. That was all right. Robin had even started to prepare himself for this. Sons were less inclined to do so nowadays. Look at the sons of farmers. But he and his son would still banter about the business, wouldn't they? Robin had imagined them doing this, much as he had done with his own father. But then came the blow, the odd behaviour and the diagnosis and suddenly there was no meaningful future any more. No normal son for him. Tamsin's focus switched; seemingly inward. It was as if she was still pregnant. Pregnant with a cause, and would be for ever. And when she doted on Michael it was as though she was loving his neediness, trying to encompass it, hold it steady and firmly in place. Sometimes Robin thought she was flaunting Michael, provocatively, as though she had something to prove.

For a time Robin felt he could wait if there was light at the end of this dark tunnel in which they might revert to their old and tender ways. But life at Brock Cottage grew worse instead of better and now the future loomed large for him like a dumb, accusing shadow.

"I'll see the jug at the weekend then. Come and tell me about the meeting if you want. I just can't hack it. All those bossy women."

He really couldn't stand their knowingness, the concern in their eyes, especially the knack Ginny Smart and Mrs Green had of maintaining doleful eye contact and letting it linger. It was a pity Doris Nokes had retired. She and John would have made a good partnership. John was down to earth like Doris. And safe. Robin had meticulously checked him out, followed up his references and made phone calls. John was good at his job, the references said: solid, got on with things, a valuable team member. And Robin approved of all that. He himself didn't know how to handle Michael, how to relate to him, but he liked to do what he could for his wife and son. He liked to anticipate snags, stop the gaps, make arrangements. And delegate where necessary.

Tamsin broke into his thoughts. "I'll see you then? At the weekend?"

Robin's mobile trilled loudly and by the time he had confirmed to Mollie that, Yes he was on his way, Tamsin had stalked out of the shop.

Robin rushed out and caught up with her on the pavement. "Would you like to borrow the book?" He held open the car door as she took the offered tome.

Tamsin took the book and stroked its shiny cover depicting a red and amber glazed earthenware harvest jug coated here and there with white slip and decorated in sgraffiato. "Great," she added. Her face softened with relief and belated pleasure as she clumsily stretched up to kiss Robin on the cheek. Then she got into the mini and placed the book carefully on the passenger seat and patted it before driving off. If she had looked in the rear view mirror she would have seen Robin still standing on the pavement with a bereft expression on his face.

Chapter Four

Why did she always feel like a truculent, bolshie school girl every time she entered the school? Think calm, she told herself. Think positive.

"Hi Tamsin." Penny Simpson, Kylie's mum, waved madly from the other side of the hall. Roger Simpson put up his hand, it was a slight gesture, and smiled. The young couple looked good together, their legs like two alive isosceles triangles in matching white jeans. Penny was slim, girly with a cloud of brown hair. She wore a tight belt at the waist and extremely high heels which brought her head level with her husband's shoulders around which he'd loosely tied a soft grey sweater. Tamsin thought of joining them until she saw Mrs Green heading in their direction and then engage them in conversation. Tamsin watched as they nodded frequently and emphatically. Roger slipped his arm around his wife's waist and squeezed it while giving her a look as if to coincide with one of the points Mrs Green was making.

Kylie, their daughter, had Down's Syndrome. People only had to look at her to understand, whereas with Michael, Tamsin often thought, it was more difficult. It was his actions that gave him away. Nobody knew he had problems, big problems, just by looking at him. This made new situations, Tamsin had to admit, more nerve-wracking for her although she would never wish away his beauty. Kylie's perky nature Tamsin found attractive, and the way she would keep saying "hello" all the time however inappropriately. It was sweet and made you warm to her.

Michael's quirky behaviour unsettled people in the street, the shops, in the outside world as Tamsin tried not to say. People did not warm to him or his mother. She would have welcomed some sympathetic gesture, however patronising. Initial, spontaneous acceptance she knew was too much to hope for without some form of introduction or preparation.

Last year in the gardens by the River Lin, the horror on a man's face as Michael flew at him, not to tell him excitedly about a toy boat lost in the weir or about the swans' nest – no, Michael flew at the man only to finger the pile on his brown corduroy trousers. He did not even look up at the man - so obsessed with line and texture was he, and the man stood fixed to the spot, petrified and helpless, his arms slightly flapping from the elbows as though he were trying to fly away. Tamsin rushed forward and plucked Michael from the man's trousers while apologising profusely. The man said it was all right, but backed away, brushing himself down in a brisk and agitated manner.

When Tamsin told Robin about the incident he had winced but clasped one of her shoulders as though he were glad she had handled the situation and was saying, well done.

Later Tamsin was to remember this occasion in the gardens, when she went to see a Mirtez photographic exhibition at The Harrow and saw his landscapes which she'd always loved, in a new way. His lens seemed to seek out and capture related forms - the line that swung and veered from established form. Her favourite was of a photograph taken in Granada. The furrows and new growth in the orchard grove, alongside the pressure of the cypresses in the courtyard, led one's eye upward and into the shadowy castle windows and the stubbed castellation fingering the sky. In the centre a hatted gardener in baggy trousers relaxed, leaning on his hoe. Corduroy and the furrow, texture and line. Corduroy meant something more than just material to Michael. He saw form differently and with a passion, too. But now, looking at Roger and Penny Simpson together, Tamsin remembered Robin's pedantic reaction to her sudden joyful realisation and comparison. "The way Michael sees, Tamsin, isn't anything to get excited about sweetheart. It isn't normal." And on announcing this he'd turned away and left the room.

Through the school hall window Tamsin took a sideways look at her blurred reflection. Sometimes she could feel her face slipping into the expressions of her grandmother. These moments were as fleeting and elusive as the silverfish which scuttled to the back of the cottage hearth. But, except for the blond hair they shared, where was the gift of her own imprint on Michael? She could see the image of Robin in Michael's face or rather *on* Michael's face, benignly lying there like a dust sheet. Did Robin see this likeness too? And how did he really feel about it?

"Food for thought?" John was at her elbow with a tray of coffee and biscuits.

"Thanks," she said. She was grateful for the interruption to her thoughts. "John, did you know about the article on Respite Care? In Michael's bag? Put there yesterday?"

John frowned. "Sorry?".

Obviously not. "Never mind. It's nothing. Who's that?"

John followed Tamsin's gaze. "Susie Barmouth, the

Behaviour Consultant."

"I thought she wasn't one of the parents." Susie was wearing a navy suit with a pencil slim skirt. She wore the jacket open over a white blouse and this gave her an informal but authoritative air.

Tamsin nodded to John indicating the approach of Mrs Green. He scuttled away and began to circulate with his tray of coffee and biscuits.

"Hello Tamsin dear. How are you are bearing up? Managing to divert Michael away from the wretched D flat?"

"I am fine. I have got … " Tamsin was going to mention the jade soup bowls Mrs Green had ordered.

But Mrs Green interrupted, "Robin not with you?" As she spoke she continued to look around the room in an obvious effort to keep tabs on all her parents.

She knew Robin and Tamsin were not together any more. Why did she have to ask?

"I think you are going to find this evening very worthwhile, Tamsin. Did you come in with John then? What with living so near… How's he getting on in your granary?"

"No. We didn't come in together." What was this, an inquisition? Mrs Green's tone had a sort of innocent sing-song quality to it and she never seemed to forget that she was a professional working in Special Needs, paid to care and glossed with status. She approached people as if they were problems, encircled them with concern, not getting too close but in gentle control of their escape.

"That was thoughtful of you dear. To come in independently. Some of the parents can be a bit sensitive and might imagine," Mrs Green chuckled, "that Michael was getting preferential treatment when we know he isn't, don't we?"

Tamsin cringed.

Mrs Green cast another brisk eye around the assembled parents. So far only Ginny Smart's class had been included in the project for modifying behaviour. "Ah, I think we're all here. Better make a start. Now if you could each collect a blue chair and come as near the front as you can manage. Without crowding Susie of course." She smiled at Susie.

Tamsin glanced around to locate John. He was standing at the back, arms folded, whispering to Ginny. Penny and Roger Simpson sat close together, shoulders touching and Penny, Tamsin noticed, had got out a pen and paper. To bring a pen and paper had not occurred to Tamsin.

Susie Barmouth spoke in an enthusiastic manner about behaviour and used the phrase "our children" a lot, underlining it with a lingering and reassuring smile. Tamsin's eyes narrowed and she had to renew her effort to relax.

"Stimulus, response, reinforcement. We must reinforce appropriate behaviour."

It sounds as though she is planning battle tactics, Tamsin thought, but it would be good to get Michael dry. So far, strict time routines and a picture programme hadn't had the desired effect.

Penny, Tamsin saw, was scribbling away. Roger had a hand on his wife's shoulder and was reading as she wrote. They were obviously of the same mind, and both keen to help with their daughter's echolalia. Would Robin have felt differently if Michael had been a girl? There was a sort of protective streak running through his nature for her if not for Michael.

Suddenly from the back of the hall a sharply raised voice punctured the air. The seated parents turned around en masse, with a shuffle. Tamsin felt a surge of relief as the tension in the hall changed gear. Mrs Green looked annoyed and was holding up her hand like a policeman on traffic patrol.

The shout had come from Mrs Dixon, a small, big shouldered woman of about fifty wearing a short denim skirt and a white shirt with the sleeves rolled up to her elbows. She was standing up, shaking her fist in the air. Into the stunned silence she shouted again, "Every time Brian screams, I scream right back in his flipping ear."

Good for you, thought Tamsin, envious of this mother's assertive behaviour. She herself had been wondering how she could broach the subject of the Respite Care article, and the shock of finding it. She was still quietly fuming, but was aware that if she tackled it badly with either Ginny or Mrs Green she might influence their handling of Michael in the future. Only in little but erosive ways, maybe. After all, they were only human and would surely hate, like anyone, to be made to feel guilty. It was the fact that the article had appeared out of the blue with no accompanying explanation that annoyed Tamsin so much.

Susie Barmouth was trying without success to rearrange her fallen expression of confidence into a sympathetic smile. "Do you find it helps, Mrs uhh?"

"Dixon," Mrs Green interjected.

Susie flicked through her papers. "Ah yes, we do have a

programme for Brian related to his… "

"Helps? It makes me feel better, I know that much."

"Good. Good. Now Brian's programme is to do with his screaming, isn't it Susie? Mrs Dixon? Mrs Dixon, are you with us?" Mrs Green shrugged her shoulders with irritation and waited until there was a lull in the kerfuffle. "Now, with regard to all the individual programmes, we'll get them processed for the rest of you so that when we meet here a week today, we can all get started and with the six weeks' holiday ahead you can really then give them your full focus."

There was a sigh from the back of the room. It was Mrs Dixon again. "I thought we'd come here tonight to be told more about the Respite Care, not about screaming and whatnot. To arrange for Brian to go away for two weeks to that Respite Centre, to give me and me husband a bit of a break. We could do with a holiday, we could."

So Tamsin wasn't the only one to receive a photocopy of that article. That at least was a relief. She must watch her tendency to jump too quickly to conclusions. She was getting paranoid. Tamsin studied Mrs Green's reaction.

"Respite Care? Whatever gave you that idea, Mrs Dixon? We spelt out clearly what the meeting was about in the form you had to sign, didn't we? Programme Planning for Inappropriate Behaviour?"

Ginny Smart rushed forward to the front of the hall and whispered to Mrs Green, who then frowned heavily at the newest member of her teaching staff. Rather sheepishly, head down and tip-toeing, Ginny Smart retreated to the back of the hall again.

"Respite Care is an excellent service, don't get me wrong about that, and some of you may wish or indeed be advised in the future to make use of it, but unfortunately… " Mrs Green looked pointedly at Ginny Smart and sighed. "The information was inadvisably… It was just for your interest this time. In a general sense, so to speak. Not meant to mislead or confuse you. Mrs Smart was trying to be helpful I believe, weren't you Mrs Smart? If any of you have got any further questions regarding it, or indeed about Susie's actual programmes - the real reason we are here tonight, then please come and see us." Mrs Green cast a strong dallying look around the hall, imperceptibly drawing the strings of her control. "Have I forgotten anything?" She looked over at John and Ginny who both meekly shook their heads, and so Mrs Green let her authority rest in a moment of silence before concluding. "In that case can I have a quick word with Mrs Dixon?" Mrs Green went and stood by the hall door. As she passed Tamsin's chair, Tamsin heard her whisper to Ginny, "Do not, until further notice, send home any notes etc to parents without running them by me first. Consult, consult, consult... "

And Mrs Dixon was not going to be allowed a quick escape either. Using one arm outstretched to guide but not to touch her, Mrs Green led Mrs Dixon up the stairs to her office.

John started to stack the chairs while Ginny came over to Tamsin. "I am sorry, Tamsin. I was only trying to help. Let people know what's available."

Ginny Smart was going to go on putting her foot in it, for quite a good few years to come, Tamsin guessed. People with a passion usually did. But Tamsin was not sure what Ginny's passion was. Was it the children in her care or was it ruthless ambition? "All these notes get very confusing Ginny... There were three yesterday." She wanted to add that it was not like this in Doris Nokes' day, but she curbed her tongue.

"I know, I know. I am going to be on the carpet either tonight when she has finished with Brian's mum, or tomorrow morning. But as I was saying, look at Michael. He's probably going to need full-time care for the rest of his life and it's not fair on you without you knowing what's out there for you."

Tamsin flinched and shrank back. "I want to concentrate on the here and now. I like Susie Barmouth's programmes..." she muttered in a small voice, clipping each word defensively.

Ginny's attempt at a smile tightened into a grimace.

"We didn't get that Respite Care thing, did we Roger? Should we have done?" Penny and Roger Simpson had joined Tamsin and Ginny.

"No, no." Ginny spoke slowly, lazily, benevolently, her head on one side. "I don't think you will need Respite Care in the same way. If at all."

"Are you sure?" Penny looked rather petulant.

Tamsin was fit to explode now, but still aware that she didn't want to jeopardise Michael's days by giving his teacher cause to hold a grudge against his mother. So again she bit her tongue.

"As long as we don't miss anything," Penny persisted with a dogged smile and turned to Tamsin. "Bye Tamsin. See you next week."

Tamsin turned her back on both the Simpsons and Ginny Smart and went and had a word with John.

"Do you want to come in for a coffee or a mug of cider when you get back? Anna will be there, babysitting."

"I'd love to but I can't. Paper work and a de-brief with Greeny and Co. It's never ending but thanks anyway, Tamsin. Talk about crossed wires. What was that all about?"

"Grr... Ask Ginny!" With that Tamsin left and purposely forgot Mrs Green's heavy, breakable soup bowls lurking in the boot of the mini.

Chapter Five

Clutching tissues and both a little misty eyed, Tamsin and Anna walked out through the church door together.

"Thanks for not letting on, Tamsin. Joe would be pretty miffed if he got to know I'd told you first," Anna whispered. Joe and Anna had given Tamsin a lift to the church and on the way Joe had announced quietly, almost reverently and without smiling that he and Anna were going to have a baby.

"Well, you only suspected then, didn't you? You hinted. That was all, so it wasn't really telling," Tamsin whispered back. "And it's great news. Really it is." She sniffed hard and wiped a damp nose. They stepped up onto the grass to allow space for the funeral party: close friends and family, to huddle like sheep, with the vicar around the porch entrance to St Andrews, Linbury's parish church. Joe, Tamsin noticed, was standing tall, shoulders back, while talking to two other farmers, with Sam at his side looking lost and shocked. All four men gave the impression of being very uncomfortable in their sober suits. Tamsin could almost smell the mothballs and thought how huge and raw their hands looked, unoccupied, empty and hanging from dark, shiny cuffs.

"Hi Luke. You all right? I must come and see you soon with some more stock for The Pound House. And the harvest jug is fine. How's… "

"I'll look forward to it Tamsin." Luke's greying beard was lush compared with his thin, mousy pony tail held back by a rubber band which curled shyly on the collar of his navy suit. He looked doleful and hurried by. He obviously did not want to stop and chat, maybe because being a widower he would know a little of what Sarah Platt was feeling today. Although his wife had died of natural causes. Jessica, the daughter Tamsin had been going to ask after, was presumably at college. On her visits to The Mill, she had seen Jessica fuss around and worry for her father in a very solicitous manner and give the impression that she was older than her eighteen years.

Neither Joe and Anna nor Tamsin were going on to the crematorium as they were not close friends of the grieving family. But Sam had made arrangements to go.

Six bearers adjusted the weight of the coffin on their shoulders and then walked slowly under the giant yew outside the porch and then through an avenue of lime trees heady with pollen to the shiny-as-a-cockroach hearse. Two of the younger bearers bore an unnerving, brotherly resemblance to Simon. Joe together with the other farmworkers went forward with bowed heads and touched the coffin out of respect.

Anna looked proudly on at her husband.

"Those farming hymns, do you think Sarah chose those?" Tamsin muttered. The two friends gazed, not at one another, but over the heads of the slowly scattering congregation and into the distance. Many of the mourners seemed to be maintaining raised eyebrows as if about to query something.

"I dunno. At least they were hymns and an appropriate ones. You ought to hear what some people choose. My cousin for his dad wanted anything by the Beatles except 'Help!' At the wake afterwards that was, not the church. But somebody at this church, St Andrews, last year had 'I Did It My Way' blaring as the congregation came out. Did you hear Joe singing?"

"Couldn't fail. Powerful voice, hasn't he? Very deep."

"Yes it is, isn't it?" Anna allowed herself a small smile. "It's still very early days but I've taken the test and booked a doctor's appointment. Poor Sarah. Her mum's coming to stay for a while." The two friends paused and looked anxiously at Sarah being gently jostled and bundled into a waiting car by a solemn group of older mourners.

"I dreamt about my mother last night."

"Really?"

Last night Tamsin had dreamed her mother was on a train waving goodbye again. Long, luminous silk scarves undulated in the current of air as her mother wound down the window and reached out of the train as it gathered speed. But the child she was leaving on the platform was not Tamsin. It was Michael dressed in black shorts and T-shirt and calling, "Mummy, mummy?" She'd dragged herself from her bed and gone into Michael's room. He was calling softly in his sleep, "Mummy, mummy?" over and over, pleading for something. But for what? Mother and child, question and answer: that was not their way of life. "Don't worry, I won't ever leave you. There will never be windows full of our goodbyes, Michael."

He was usually calmer at night, in the dark. Daylight on the other hand offered him a galaxy of visions. Things sprang at him, drove him into corners or attracted him, pulling him like a magnet. Daylight did not bring him the comfort of a reality he could cope with.

Tamsin stroked her son's forehead and, moving her fingers

and thumb to his closed eyes, pressed them tenderly but firmly, letting her hand bob up and down. When she went to take her hand away, Michael grabbed her wrist and placed her fingers back on his eyes. She dozed by his side and dreamed again. This time her grandmother's head was swinging like a pendulum and she was muttering, "Tch-tch, tch-tch, tch-tch" just like the kitchen clock.

"Have you heard from your mum lately? It would be nice if she lived in this country, was a bit nearer. She could give you a some support. Help you out now and then. Babysit." Anna knew a little of Tamsin's story.

"Last time I heard was about six months ago. She emailed from a bar in Rio. Sometimes she sends me a text but when I try to text her back I find I don't know what to say. So I end up saying something bland and boring. I hear about once a year if I am lucky. Some years I don't hear at all. She's so unpredictable."

"Do you ever wish she'd made a clean break when she went?"

"Oh no. No." Tamsin frowned. "Like this, at least I can live in hopes … "

"Ah, Tamsin. Yes of course." Anna put an arm around her friend. "What about your father? You've never mentioned him."

"No. My grandparents didn't know who he was. My mother wouldn't tell them apparently. A bit of a mystery. A blank."

Anna squeezed Tamsin's shoulder. "I don't know about you Tamsin, but I am knackered now. Blow the farm accounts. I can't do any more today. How about we go home, change and go for a lazy walk in the woods? Take a sandwich. Joe's going to The Black Swan for a drink with some of the other farmers. And we'll be home in time for Michael."

They walked towards the car behind Joe. Only a straggle of funeral goers now hung around the churchyard in their dull clothes, reading epitaphs, kicking up gravel on the paths, not knowing quite how to leave.

"Yeah, okay. I know what you mean and I've got that fucking meeting tonight. You still okay for babysitting? Again? Sorry."

The two women reached the car and Joe must have overheard Tamsin's query and turned around. "No, she isn't Tamsin."

"But Joe… " Anna protested.

Joe put a foot inside the driver's side while holding on to the door and speaking over the roof of the car. "I'm sorry, but we can't risk Anna getting hurt. And the baby. If Michael hits out or has a tantrum and needs restraining, I'd never forgive myself … "

Tamsin winced.

"But Joe." Anna looked surprised by her husband's forthright announcement. "Just this one last time. I can't let Tamsin down, especially at the last minute. Michael will be all right." She slid into the passenger seat.

A sudden wave of grief engulfed Tamsin. That she should have a son whom people feared. He wasn't dangerous. He didn't mean it. It was just that you couldn't always anticipate his reactions… which on reflection, she had to concede, could cause harm, if indirectly and definitely unintended.

"Maybe Robin could… " She hesitated. "John can't because he has to be at school too, like me." She wanted to show she could cope without Robin on the home front, so she wasn't keen to ask for his help. Especially if he wouldn't come to the school meetings with her, which was where she really needed the kind of support she knew Robin was capable of giving. Professionals would not intimidate him.

"No. I'll do it." Joe said firmly. "I just don't want Anna to put herself at risk."

Tamsin was stunned. "You, Joe?"

"I will. I will do my best. We won't let you down. I just don't want Anna… "

Tamsin flinched again. "I know, I know. Thank you Joe. It won't be for long. I'll be home as quick as I can."

"Are you ready then? I'll take you girls home first before meeting up with the lads."

Tamsin got into the back of the car and shrank into the corner of her seat. Joe drove off and a disturbing and swollen silence unsettled the car and its passengers.

They were sitting on a grassy hummock among overgrowths of beech roots which had once been a hedge. They'd stopped for a bit of lunch along the bottom path which was a hazy green tunnel with a circle of light at the end. Tamsin was taking alternate bites from a bar of chocolate and an apple while Anna hungrily tackled a heel of bread and some ham and blue cheese.

Tamsin threw her core into the undergrowth. "I keep eating junk food at the moment. Anything sweet or salty."

"Well as long as you're not turning veggie."

"Mashed potato and onion gravy. I love that. Toast.

Comfort food."

"What, no meat?"

"Bacon sandwiches. Lovely."

"Joe is touchy about veggies. Farmers are." Anna screwed up some silver foil and put it in her small backpack.

"I can't fathom your Joe out."

"*You* can't? *I* can't and I am married to him. He broods a bit. Spends too much time on his own, thinking. When he goes out to the field his head must be like a rabbit burrowing down its hole, and then when he comes in at night it takes him all evening to scramble out again. Bless him. Sorry about tonight. Are you okay with it?"

"Yes, of course. It is really nice of Joe. And he's got Sam, hasn't he? To talk to, I mean. In the fields."

"Sam? He's a good worker but he's only eighteen and he needs a bit of listening to as well at the moment. This business with Simon Platt is reminding him of his own family's tragedy I think."

"Yes. He did look very strained, I must admit. I'll leave some chicken and salad out for Joe."

"That's settled then. Oh thanks Tamsin for being so understanding."

Tamsin prayed Anna's baby would be all right. She wondered if that niggling thought had wormed its way into Anna's consciousness yet. The one thought that seemed to occur to all mothers at some stage in the pregnancy. Didn't it? It had to Tamsin, but then Michael's problems did not show up on the scan. And so she'd been mistakenly reassured and had dismissed the thought of anything being wrong with her coming baby. Feeling safe, she had bloomed and got on with being happily pregnant.

"Look." They were walking now on the upper path with the wood below on one side and a field on the other. Tamsin pointed to two tiny blue butterflies towing one another hither and thither, flitting in and out between red campion and cow parsley along the bank. "They look as though they are being chased by the butterfly police."

"Beautiful." Anna bent forward to stare absentmindedly at the butterflies. "Did you and Robin ever think of having another baby? Tell me to mind my own business if you want to."

Tamsin tried to scoop the butterflies with her hands but without success. "No. Yes. Well, Robin I know would have wanted to try. He was once the son in 'Coopers and Son', as his dad was before him. Perversely, I think it would have been easier if Michael had been a girl, you know. The trouble with the Coopers and the business side of things is sons have had such high expectations laid on them for generations. And family is important to Robin. I think that is why he stayed with me so long. Hoping."

"What happened then? Why didn't you have another?"

"I wanted us to be settled as a family. With Michael. I wanted some togetherness. We needed to come together over Michael. Anyway, we hardly ever had sex towards the end. That was why Robin went really. It got… "

Anna stopped and looked at Tamsin, "Didn't you talk? And sex isn't the be-all and end-all is it?"

"No, but it helps keep you together. And Robin not making more of an effort with Michael seemed like a rejection of me somehow. He doesn't seem to accept him. And we rowed. About Michael, and Michael was there, hearing it all. Things got so tense. Robin's proud."

"Maybe he doesn't know how to accept him."

"What do you mean?"

"I don't know really. But don't *you* miss it? Sex?"

"I miss the comfort, the affection, the warmth, the friendship. He's still a good friend, but when it turns into something else I sort of… I dunno… a horrible hard shiver like wire runs through me… I clam up."

"You were once good together though, weren't you? Have you thought of getting help? Counselling?"

"Yeah, we were. Before Michael. Robin wanted me to but do you know what they used to say about autism in the sixties and seventies? That it was the fault of middle class mothers. They were cold, distant. I don't think I could handle therapy if that's what you mean. And look at my mother. Left me when I was six. Therapy always seems to be about mothers. Say if I had to go into all that. And I bet I would. Well I couldn't. I just couldn't. It would be asking for more trouble and I have got enough as it is."

"But the thinking has moved on. It is not like that these days. They haven't thought that it is somebody's fault for years. But going back into the past… you and your mother and that… could be painful. I see what you mean. You want to concentrate on the present." They were on a steep bit of the path now and both puffing hard. "I can hear my heart beating. But what if he finds someone else meanwhile?"

"What can I do? I know I just couldn't cope with any therapy stuff right now. I want to get on with life. Get Michael's toilet programme underway. It looks really promising." Tamsin enunciated every word precisely while at the same time picturing Mollie at Robin's desk in 'Coopers and Son'. "Anyway, enough of me. You wait till you have your scan. Talk about hearing your heart beating. You'll see another little heart beating. Inside you. It'll be amazing." Tamsin's tone was overly reassuring. She changed the subject. "Do you think we can just make the chapel before we turn around? Have you been there yet?"

"No. I've heard about it though. Yeah, we've got plenty of time. There are still lots of places I want to see around here."

They crossed a field and with a clang opened a five-bar metal gate into a dark, shady copse.

"I can't see any chapel… "

Tamsin laughed, "There are only the ruins left. It was a chantry chapel for the big house, over there see, through the trees. A priest used to live here and say prayers at intervals during the day for the souls of those up there." She pointed again through the trees to the house.

The outline of the chapel showed itself in the remains of a stone wall about a foot high plumped out here and there with cushions of moss. At one end two larger stones jutted out. "I think the altar was here." The web of leafy beech branches above diffused the light. Tamsin felt a sudden peace descend and she welcomed it.

"Robin and I used to come here a lot. We were church crawlers. In fact that's how we met. In a church the other side of Linbury. Robin said he never thought he'd meet a girl who loved churches like he did and that he'd have to marry a prim, old woman instead. It was fun. We studied pew ends. Robin loves wood, especially old oak, and we searched for Green Men on pew ends and roof bosses. We'd picnic in the churchyard. Use a tomb as a table. Sometimes there were primroses, snowdrops, bluebells. Many churches leave the first mowing until after the spring flowers have faded. It was lovely."

"It sounds idyllic."

"It was. Michael was conceived here." Tamsin looked across at her friend, checking her response before going on. "By the well over there. It's a natural spring really. It was a morning. We'd come to record the dawn chorus."

"Maybe that's part of the problem." Anna sat on a cushion of moss.

"What you mean ?" Tamsin bridled and then went to sit by her friend. Together they looked up at the canopy of beech.

"Maybe it was just too idyllic. Once." Anna put her hand on top of Tamsin's and leaned towards her until their foreheads touched.

"Maybe it was. Maybe it was," said Tamsin thoughtfully.

Chapter Six

Tamsin drove fast and the lane's blue asphalt appeared to rise up and meet her. On the right a forest of larch and spruce loomed high and caused her to lean very slightly to the left. May's green in the hedges and fields, no longer gloating with newness, had settled into July's dull jade. She braked. One of Joe's tractors was ahead. Sam was driving. She put the mini into reverse and smoothly slid back into a field gateway. They nodded at one another each mouthing "hello" in an exaggerated manner to compensate for the heckle of their engines.

At the top of the hill Tamsin turned left. Here the lane levelled out and along its middle was a raw edge of grass which Tamsin imagined she could feel brush the bottom of the mini. She raced along, tapping the steering wheel with one hand in time to a drumbeat on the radio. She was in a good mood and something so simple had caused it. Anna had come across with Joe to babysit.

"We thought we were a bit over the top worrying about what Michael might do, Tamsin. Sorry. We're getting everything totally out of proportion at the moment. You know, we're just over the moon, scared and happy all at the same time. So we thought what if we both came across? Joe could deal with Michael if necessary… "

"And it might not be… hopefully… " Tamsin butted in.

"And," said Joe, "I can get in a bit of practice. Listening out. Worrying… I bet you do a lot of that."

If they were getting things out of proportion then Joe's admission meant they had something in common. It wasn't only her always overreacting, and this link gave Tamsin such a warm feeling that it nearly made her cry. She was astounded that such a little thing, a throw away remark, could have such a huge effect.

"Thanks Joe. And I do understand your concern for Anna. And the baby."

It was still light, early evening with long, thin, creamy clouds stretching across the sky. As usual Tamsin was drawn to look at stone linhays crawling with ivy and dotted randomly about the landscape. They appeared as focal points, almost iconic, their entrances black and gaping. John said her interest in them had sexual connotations but Tamsin thought it depended on the person.

Some people saw sexual connotations in anything and everything. The number of ordinary words that had double meanings in the sexual sense could deflect even the simplest of exchanges.

She swept down the hill past fields of ruminating Friesians, their mouths sliding from side to side in time to their slow steps forward. It was only four miles from home to Michael's school at the other end of Linbury. In the valley she could see the small town and St Andrew's where she had been only that morning. The River Lin, formalised by granite parapets on the three arched bridge, was home to The Black Swan's ferry, *Pen-Ultimate*, a drift of willows and a pair of locally well known swans. Early evening traffic was weaving a strict dance as it circled the small roundabouts, one at each end of the bridge, and then crossed and met over the middle of the water.

On the outskirts of town was Luke's mill. She needed to call in some time soon and restock the shelves of the gift shop, a converted pound house, with mugs, soup bowls and casserole dishes. Some weeks Luke sold a lot of her work, worth a few hundred pounds, and some weeks he sold none at all. Tamsin quite liked the flutter of unpredictability but was looking forward to the introduction of her harvest and cider range, and so was Luke. She was no longer a spare time potter, clay no longer a diversion, a treat set up and encouraged by Robin. It was her and Michael's living, or would be in the not too distant future, she hoped.

A scattering of drinkers, presumably on their way home from work, was sitting on the terrace of The Black Swan which overlooked the river. Striped parasols, shading white furniture and a confetti of potted blooms littered the terrace. The Harrow Arts Centre next door had been designed so that it too faced the river with its back to The High. Its three enormous arched windows shimmered with light from the water and the sky, duskily reflecting the cross currents of life on the river and its banks.

On over the bridge, along The High and left into Sydney Street at the end of which was Michael's school. On a blue board in white letters was the name of the school, Riverside, and underneath also in white letters Mrs Green, Headmistress and Mr C. Wilson, Caretaker and his phone number. It no longer said Special School: the initial positive discrimination for choosing this term, it would seem, no longer positive.

Tamsin parked under horse chestnuts heavy with leaf and young, green spiky cases. She liked the school; its red brick pre-war building with lots of acute angles, eaves and gables, nooks and crannies, small attic windows, all of which gave it a distinctiveness. Only the ground floor was used for the children. The first floor was given over to the staff-room and offices. Tamsin climbed the stone steps with a cardboard box under her arm and pushed open the double oak doors, climbed the wide staircase, deposited Mrs Green's ordered soup bowls outside her office and then retraced her steps downstairs and went into the hall. Penny Simpson, Mrs Dixon and three or four other mothers were already mingling. A circle of blue chairs had been arranged in the middle of the hall. The kitchen hatch shot up and Ginny Smart's head appeared through it. She pushed forward cups, saucers and a plate of digestives. This cued the mothers to move forward and dump their handbags and jackets on the chairs and then collect a cup of tea and biscuit from the hatch. All except Penny, who became entangled trying to unravel her jacket and long scarf from her shoulder bag.

"No Roger tonight, Pen?" Tamsin was curious.

"Couldn't get a babysitter, and he said he could trust me to get all the necessary gen anyway."

Mrs Green pounced through the hall on the way to her office; "Hello everybody." Her smile stretched alarmingly and her eyes were like chocolate buttons. "Won't keep you a minute, ladies."

"I expect she's relieved it's the end of term," one mother said.

"I am not relieved," said Mrs Dixon loudly while stirring her tea rapidly and splashing it into her saucer.

Penny put her shoulders back, visibly bracing herself. "I think Mrs Green works very hard. She's done wonders for Kylie, and Roger must be one of her greatest fans I should think. He's fed up he couldn't come tonight."

Tamsin moved away from the group to stand by the hall window which looked out on to Michael's classroom jutting out at right angles from the rest of the building at the back. She didn't want tea or a biscuit. She realised she was looking through three sheets of glass, three windows, the hall's, the classroom's and those of the open French windows on the other side of the classroom leading to the play area. And through the trebled sheets of glass she could see John tidying the outside sandpit. He was like an echo, far removed, from the past, or a vision from the future.

It came as a small shock when Tamsin became conscious of the fact that this was the only place where Michael spent time without her. This was where he breathed in an unknown day, without her.

Mrs Green came back into the hall with Susie Barmouth and a sheaf of papers which she distributed to those mothers already seated. "Would someone call John, please." There remained one vacant chair which Mrs Green stood by, puffed up like a bird until Tamsin came and occupied it. Then and only then did she give Tamsin her set of papers.

"And thank you Tamsin for the bowls. I'll settle up with you another time."

"Any time will do."

The two top sheets were charts: days and hours ruled out evenly and tasks finely broken down into steps, so finely Tamsin was intrigued. For instance, *Takes hand voluntarily and goes with you to the toilet,* and this would be rewarded with much praise and fuss. There were spaces for ticks and further individual guidelines. Susie had tackled Michael's obsession with running water in some depth. No way was he allowed to play with the flushing of the toilet, even as a reward for performing. Difficult, thought Tamsin, as she pictured her son's bare bottom, his delight and nimble feet as he tried to dance with his dropped shorts hampering his ankles while flicking the gushing water. Tamsin read on: *Being allowed to play D flat must also not be used as a reward.* Susie reasoned that it could lead him in the future to perform whenever he heard that note. Tamsin felt hysterical. *But on the other hand washing his hands under a running tap (another of Michael's obsessions) after he'd performed would be appropriate behaviour in the circumstances and could therefore be used as a reward.* Tamsin saw what Susie Barmouth was getting at and felt a thrill of joy. This behaviour consultant was going to get Tamsin's full attention and cooperation. She looked up with renewed energy all over her face, but found that Mrs Green and Susie were both looking stern. Mrs Green's nostrils flared as she tilted back her head. Tamsin realised they were listening with barely controlled patience to Mrs Dixon.

"He likes my bunch of keys to rattle… right near, in front of his eyes."

"What, no screaming?" asked Susie politely with wide eyes.

"Well, if I'm near him when he takes in that big breath, I shove the keys at him. And it works. It distracts him. He loves them."

"But you do realise," said Susie patiently, "that he is just swapping one obsessive behaviour for another."

"Wouldn't you call it an hysterical mannerism for a ritual, a ritualistic behaviour?" Mrs Green pursed her lips and concentrated keenly, like a bird, on Susie's reaction, having quite forgotten Mrs Dixon in a near moment of triumph.

Susie opened her mouth and closed it again.

"Anyway, the point is," Mrs Dixon said slowly separating the words in an attempt to recapture the attention of the professionals, "I can take Brian into a café rattling a bunch of keys whereas I can't if he's bloody screaming."

"Language," Mrs Green interjected loudly.

Tamsin felt like whooping for joy. What a woman Mrs Dixon was. So in touch with her gut instincts. Tamsin felt great admiration and envy. Where was John? Oh, there he was. And smiling into his hands.

"I think we should deal with this case singly after the meeting, Mrs Dixon, in my office."

Mrs Green then gave out the name of a website and an email address for those parents who might need support during the summer holidays. For those without a computer she suggested Linbury Library had internet access. "And they are very helpful to those of you who are not yet computer literate. And don't forget, we at school already fulfil the requirements of each programme and you are free to come into school with your child for further help before the holidays."

Tamsin noted that she did not give out a telephone number. Need would have to be a considered need, and not on the spur of a desperate moment.

Tamsin breathed a sigh of relief as she changed down into third gear to take the corner at the top of the hill by the woods. She was in the home straits. Ahead in the valley lay the cottage, its rendered cob patchy and familiar against a purple sky. Its shadow stretched towards her, reaching out to her.

She parked the mini and, feeling lucky, started to walk up the thirteen steps. Half way up she turned to look back across the valley. The slopes were lit by a low evening light leaking over the brow of the hill where some of Joe's cows chewed and climbed, silhouetted sharply against the skyline like a child's painting. Tamsin took a few deep breaths. Night stocks released their scent. A mist seeped over the lane from Brock Farm. It dipped and spread, thinning out before continuing its wispy journey upstream.

Chapter Seven

"Ninety-five, ninety-five, can I see a hundred anywhere, a hundred, a hundred. It's with you sir, at a hundred. Can I see a hundred and ten anywhere? All right I can do a hundred and five. Hundred and five. You look as though you need a good wash, sir. Can I say a hundred and ten for you sir? Are you sure? Don't be like that, sir. Are we all done then? All done at a hundred and five." Jaguar raised his gavel and looked around the room one last time before he hammered it home. The over polished mahogany Victorian washstand had not reached its guide price of a hundred and twenty to a hundred and fifty.

Although Robin was concentrating hard on Jaguar it was not the lots and the prices they were fetching that held his attention. Today it was Jaguar himself. Not yet forty, the owner of Lindon Auction Rooms sported a moustache that would have graced a second world war pilot. Auction Day was, for Jaguar Lindon, a ceremonious occasion which required particular vestments: his ginger corduroy suit, ill fitting, loose and made by his doting mother, and a yellow ochre spotted bow tie. To complete the outfit he wore exquisite, Italian designer leather sandals and no socks. His feet were clean and freckled, his nails neatly trimmed. Jaguar wasn't bumbling. He was nearly bumbling. He wasn't elegant but he was almost elegant. Having a double edge gave him a unique style, and for that he earned Robin's admiration and respect.

The ginger suit triggered a train of thought for Robin. Corduroy, Michael, Jan Mirtez, Tamsin, birthday, what to get, a camera, landscapes. That was it. He had been wondering what to get her for her thirty-fourth birthday which was today, Saturday, when he'd said he would help John lay the ground floor tiles in the granary. Last weekend they'd fixed the banisters to the staircase and afterwards gone for a couple of pints at The Black Swan together where they had talked about why John had taken up care-work.

"Except that you can't say care-workers in some places, you have to say managers and deputy managers, and in the last place I worked you couldn't say clients any more. They are service-users now, apparently. All this pc stuff does get in the way of doing a job sometimes. And think of the word *user,* that's already halfway to being a term of abuse as it is, isn't it?"

"I see what you mean," said Robin, when in fact he had no idea what John was going on about. "But what made you go into this kind of work?"

"Well, as you know, I used to help my mum look after my dad when he could no longer take care of himself. Wash him, feed him, dress him. God, he was heavy. A dead weight. Too much for my mum on her own."

"But I would have thought that would have put you off. Care-work. Not take it up for a career. Don't get me wrong, I'm glad you did, though. Your refs were excellent."

"You checked?"

"Of course." Robin held John's gaze for an extra moment.

John smiled. "No. I like being needed for simple chores. It's real. He was a nice fella, my dad. You get down to the nitty, gritty, the basics of life. After all, life first and foremost is about feeding yourself, having shelter and keeping clean and warm. Without those things in place it is difficult to have a decent life."

"Are you sure? Haven't you set your standard a bit low? Don't most of us rather aim towards taking those things for granted? And I, for one, certainly want more out of life than that." Robin didn't think John was right anyway. What about all those starving writers and painters shivering their lives away in lofts and garrets? Or maybe that was too nineteenth century. Too romantic a notion.

"I am not saying there's not more to life than that. I am just saying food, warmth etc. are the real foundation for life. You have to get those in place first and with care-work you get very close to people. Stay in touch. And helping people and their families to be comfortable is very rewarding. I'd be no good in an office or business. I don't want to sit at a desk, I want a bit of action… "

"Action? What about the building trade? You are good at that. Property development? Everybody's into that these days."

"Yeah, but I prefer people to bricks and mortar."

On his way back into Linbury Robin thought about what John had said. Did he, Robin, prefer old tables and desks and dressers to people? How strange, but he supposed he did. No, no, he didn't prefer them to people, but they were easy company, less complicated; he could relate to, touch the patina of oak and know where he was which he often didn't with people and their expectations. You couldn't go wrong with things. Especially if you were careful. He laughed quietly to himself. He supposed the men in his family were care-workers after all. Of a different kind.

Tamsin was like John. She loved people, and one human being in particular. But she was branching out. She was beginning to really love clay, her pots. They were no longer just a diversion, a hobby.

And now maybe with the present he had in mind she might love something else as well. She'd been keen on Jan Mirtez' photography since college days, his landscapes. Although to liken Michael's eye to Mirtez' was going a bit far. But that was Tamsin. Positive to the point of being sentimental. What was it she'd been going on about after that embarrassing scene in Linbury Gardens? The furrow and the corduroy? He looked over at Jaguar on his podium in his ginger jacket and imagined toy tractors running up and down the velvet furrows. Crazy woman. But the problem of the present was solved. A digital camera. Not something Mirtez would have used of course, but to be able to zoom in, transpose and extract detail would give Tamsin a challenge and some fun. And if anybody needed some fun in her life these days, it was Tamsin. And she loved the landscapes around here. And churches. They'd both loved church crawling, when they'd had time. In the dim and distant past, as it now seemed.

He wouldn't give her a card or wrap the camera. That might be misconstrued and going too far. This went against the grain, for presents were Robin's *thing*. He loved to give, and it was his way of showing how big and real his love was. Presentation was extremely important to him as well. Arranging the antiques in the shop gave him so much satisfaction that often he was loathe to sell an item in case its removal disturbed a painstakingly ordered scene. Some days revolved around selecting the right piece of porcelain to enhance a walnut feather or burr, or juxtaposing a variety of framed geometries on the walls which would please the eye with balance. A simple oval gate-leg table was Robin's favourite shape. Its moderate curves, nothing extreme, understated a slow, gentle blossoming of beauty. So in not wrapping the camera nor giving an intimately chosen card Robin was deliberately being restrained.

Once Tamsin had been a present and he'd wrapped his arms around her tenderly. "For ever. You and me." Now he was amazed at his crass naivety. He'd wanted children. A child he could relate to. So there would never be a permanent *you-and-me* situation. But the child would grow up. Leave home. And then there would be *you-and-me* again. Different but better maybe; unless the child was Michael.

Although Robin touched Michael, carried him here and there, he could not wrap his arms around him with love, let alone think of him as a present as Tamsin wanted him to. But he did love him. He wanted to do what was best for his son. He felt sad and sorry for him and was affronted by Tamsin's current password to her heart, *love-me-love-my-child,* articulated by the disappointment in her eyes and the stiffness of her flesh. Tamsin's love for her husband had drifted from joyous celebration after the birth to cool acceptance and tolerance when Michael's condition was diagnosed. She'd physically adopted an on guard position when they'd made love, her head turned towards the door, her escape route should Michael call out. More and more frequently over the last few years she would freeze at her husband's touch or try to move away when he reached out for her. Sometimes she softened, but then on these occasions he began to hold her more and more tightly until the night she thrashed out and shouted, "Leave me alone, Robin, leave me alone."

And he had. He'd driven into town at breakneck speed and slept in the car by the river. The next day he'd gone into The Black Swan where he'd stayed all day, leaving only at closing time. Outside on the pavement he'd not known which way to turn. He couldn't go home to Brock Cottage, so instead he'd slunk back into 'Coopers and Son' and crashed out in the upstairs storeroom. Since then he had not been back to Brock Cottage to sleep. But within days he'd found an anxious excuse to phone Tamsin about some bills he needed bringing into the shop. And then he found a tenant for the granary, John, a tenant he could get on with, trust and who would give Tamsin a hand with the logs. And in no time Robin and Tamsin were friends again, politely sharing many things except the bedroom and their son.

"What do you think? It's for my wife."

"Just the thing. She doesn't have to print anything she doesn't want, zoom into detail, store stuff. She can play around for hours. Have fun. Just the ticket. And when you've got one, after the initial expense, it's a cheap hobby. You won't regret your purchase, sir. Would you like insurance?" It was obvious the new, young sales' assistant in COMP GK had been on a course and was giving the same patter to all the customers. His broad, toothy smile was as standard as his flash uniform.

Walking back to the car parked outside 'Coopers And Son' Robin thought of the photographs Tamsin could take. She could photograph background scenes for the exhibition: harvests, men at work, Green Men. As a couple, they had often come across these icons in churches on bench ends and roof bosses. They fascinated Tamsin. Brilliant. Robin was pleased with himself. And she could photograph her pots. To sell as well as the pots. Studio shots. Blow them up. The harvests jugs especially. She could make a portfolio for commissions and to advertise her work more widely. She could print off postcards on the side… And it wouldn't be long before she'd need a website.

As he turned into Brock Cottage, he wanted almost immediately to turn around again and leave, for there at the top of the slope a party was going on. There was drinking, the chink of glasses and a lot of laughter. Robin wished he hadn't come. The parasols were out and sitting on the loungers were Anna and Joe and Tamsin. Muscular Sam in his black singlet was sitting on the grass and dipping his hands into an old tin bath overflowing with froth and making a large circle with two thumbs and two forefingers through which he blew enormous soapy bubbles into the air. A summery breeze whipped them and pulled a dancing string of sun-slashed baubles across the garden. But where was Michael? For that matter where was John?

"Hi-ya mate." Joe stood up and walked down the steps to meet Robin, holding out his hand as he did so.

"Hope I am not interrupting anything." Robin hesitated and looked around frowning, puzzled. "Where is Michael?"

Tamsin jumped up and went to meet him too. "Come on, Robin. Glass of wine or a mug of cider? Luke's best."

"Happy Birthday Tams, but where's Michael?" Robin continued to look around as the three of them walked back up the steps in single file, Tamsin first.

"Well, it's all a bit of a surprise really. Sam came over early to help John with the tiles. They are finished but might need a few hours for the adhesive to do its job."

"Oh good, that was quick. But I was going to… " Robin felt hurt and quietly angry. He'd been deposed, usurped, again. "Yes, but where is Michael?"

"Gone out with John. Don't ask me where. John was very mysterious." Tamsin flopped down again into the lounger.

Robin glowered over Anna's shoulder as he kissed her on the cheek and put the plastic carrier with the camera down by Tamsin's lounger. "Look at it later," he urged. He was annoyed now and wished he had bought just a card after all. He felt quite exposed, and superfluous up here on top of the slope on Tamsin's birthday with the neighbours.

"Hi Sam. Thanks for laying the tiles. All right?"

Sam nodded and blew another bubble.

"Oh, thank you Robin. Can't I have a peep?" Tamsin stiffly stretched up and kissed Robin on the cheek.

He shook his head. "No, leave it until later. When you are on your own."

"Michael was really enjoying watching Sam blow those bubbles, wasn't he Tamsin?" Anna absent-mindedly picked and pulled at the dark hairs on Joe's tanned arm as she lay back next to him and basked in the sun with her eyes closed.

"Yeah, he loved it and was very annoyed when he couldn't catch them, Robin. He kept running after them, all head-in-the-air, but then kept falling over."

"So where is he?"

"I've already told you, I don't know," Tamsin said with exasperation.

"He got pretty wild though," Sam butted in, "when they burst. Cor mate … you should have seen him. I wouldn't like to be… "

"Yeah, so John's taken him out for a bit. To calm down, I expect," Tamsin added hastily.

There was a tooting from the lane. Tamsin's red mini streaked into the drive, nearly bumping into the rear of Robin's van. John and Michael didn't get out of the mini immediately.

"What's going on? What are they doing?" Joe leaned forward and put his mug of cider down on the gravel. Anna sat up blinking, eyes wide.

John and Michael eventually got out of the mini and walked up the steps slowly, John behind Michael holding him loosely by the shoulders. In Michael's hands was a large bunch of flowers, antirrhinums. Michael gripped the foil around the stems tightly.

Robin now felt embarrassed, wrong-footed in the garden he had tended for years.

John started to sing, "Happy Birthday to you, come on Michael. Happy Birthday… "

They all watched Michael and started to sing labouringly with John, who leant forward and put both his hands around Michael's grip. He pushed him towards Tamsin until the little boy's hands were outstretched and he was looking up at his mother.

"Dear mummy… " sang Michael.

Tamsin began to quiver, but before the rising tears sprang, they all clapped and cheered. Michael jumped. Tamsin forced a smile. "Ah, that was lovely. Ah, and look, Michael. Look who's come to see us. Daddy. It's daddy… "

Michael ignored her and ran over to the bath of soapy water. Splashing it he sang, "Mummy, mummy. Tap, tap."

"This is better than the tap Michael, isn't it? You can have bubbles as well." John said.

Sam had retreated, shuffled along the bank, to watch Michael and John with a very baffled expression on his face.

Tamsin went over to Michael and guided him back to where Robin was standing. "Michael," she said with the flat of her hand on Robin's stomach, "who's this?"

Michael said nothing.

Tamsin asked again, "Michael, who's this?" Robin looked grossly uncomfortable and wished the earth would open up and swallow him.

But suddenly Michael glanced up at his father. It was a dart of glance and then he dropped his gaze to the ground again and whispered, "Michael."

"No Michael. It's daddy. You're Michael. Who is this?" Tamsin patted Robin's stomach again.

Robin wanted to disappear. He felt panic rising.

Michael looked up at Robin again. "You're Michael," he said.

Tamsin let out a loud sigh. Joe cleared his throat.

"Sometimes he gets things mixed up. Pronouns. *You* and *me* especially." John had come over and was stroking Michael's hair appeasingly.

Robin was red in the face. "I think I'd better go… " He strode off down the slope at speed, tripped and corrected himself. He turned sharply and called back over his shoulder, "Would you move your car Tamsin, please?"

Robin could not remember the journey from Brock Cottage to Mollie's arms. It seemed she opened the door and her arms in one movement. His cheeks twitched with weepy gratitude.

"God, you look rough." She asked no questions. "I've a bottle of red already opened, or maybe you'd prefer something else." There was indeed a bottle of red opened and standing on the granite worktop beneath the subdued hidden strip lighting of her kitchen. "Pity you don't smoke." She lay her long holder down across a marble ashtray.

"That'll do fine." He left her pouring wine and went and

fell on her sofa in the lounge. A long sigh slid from him.

Mollie came in with their wine and a maroon box tied with pink ribbon on a silver tray. She sat down next to him and took both his hands. She rubbed them between hers as if they were cold and she was warming them. "And I've some champagne chocolates to celebrate."

"Celebrate? Celebrating what?"

"Being at home on my own on a Saturday night." She dug him in the ribs.

"And now you are not. I feel like a prize." He took a chocolate and let his tongue play with the fragile chocolate coating before gently crushing it and letting the soft fizz of cream flow around his mouth. Robin noticed she was wearing make-up and a gold chain which slithered and swung between her breasts as she leant towards him. She looked hot, sexy. Maybe it was the vivid yellow of her dress sparking with her hair. Had she been going out? On the other hand Robin wouldn't put it past Mollie to dress up to just to stay in. He couldn't imagine her slobbing around. When he came to think of it he couldn't remember ever seeing her without her high heels. Except in bed and in the shower of course.

"Telly?"

"Okay."

"In bed?"

"Ooooh."

"Go on then. Here you take the wine and choccies." She held them out for him while he hauled himself up from the sofa and then she clattered off into the kitchen slapping the tray on her shimmering thighs as she went.

When he was huddling into a rolling landscape of cushions and pillows on her divan, she came into the bedroom and kicked off her shoes while deftly balancing the tray now bearing taramasalata, bread and olives. They ate and guzzled, loudly calling out answers to the questions on Millionaire.

At one am Robin woke with a mouth like a blanket having slept heavily. It must have been the en suite shower door closing as Mollie tiptoed through the distorted angles of streetlights dissecting the room and back to bed, wearing only her high heels and a drift of body lotion. Robin squinted at her. Her bouncy red hair looked like a hat. She reminded him of an endearing cartoon character or one of those little girls in the street where he lived as a child, who tried on her mother's too-big high heels. How she'd waved and swung her non-existent hips as she'd waddled up her garden path.

Robin badly wanted to make love to his Saturday saviour, but was too aware of his own unshowered and sweaty self. He turned over and grinned into the pillow. Soon he was breathing deeply again.

At eight, having showered but not shaved, he crept back to bed and wangled his way into Mollie's sleepy body with a little caress here and a little caress there. She woke slowly and raised her arms around his neck, pulling his head down to her lips. "Nice wake up call, Mr Cooper."

"I hope I didn't alarm you, Miss Mollie."

Chapter Eight

"It's nearly ready," John called.

Tamsin padded bare foot into the kitchen. She'd changed into a floor length denim skirt and an off-white T-shirt. Earlier she'd asked John if he wanted to come for supper, after Anna, Joe and Sam had left Brock Cottage. When the mood of the afternoon veered into confusion, time for the visitors to make tracks for home was signalled. Robin's departure was sudden. Nobody knew what to do. Anna had said, "Poor Robin," and then hastily added, "Poor Tamsin, too." She'd looked helplessly distraught. And when she and Joe came to say goodbye with young Sam in their wake she'd allowed her perplexed expression to be relieved by the certain knowledge that they were not leaving Tamsin completely on her own with only Michael for doubtful company. "I'm glad you've got John nearby."

Tamsin countered her look of sympathy with, "I did that badly, didn't I? Really buggered it up. I'll give Robin a ring."

John had tried to smooth things over. "As I said to Robin, sometimes children like Michael mix up pronouns. I've heard them do it. Or it could be echolalia."

Tamsin knew he didn't mean to be as arrogant as he sounded; he was young. Nevertheless she snapped, "Or it could be Michael just being Michael. He is not a set of symptoms."

"I was only trying to help," John snapped back.

And then there was a tussle about the flowers. Tamsin thanked John. He said they were from Michael. She said, "Oh, come on." And then they laughed and John said, "They were only from the garage. Look, it's your birthday. We should be celebrating."

"Come for supper then. It'll give the tiles a chance to really stick and settle."

With her impetuous invitation accepted, Tamsin suddenly remembered the camera and felt guilty about that too, but when she rang Robin to thank him his mobile was turned off. She felt sorry for him and had wanted to console him with a friendly hug over the mix up with Michael, but hugging her estranged husband in front of others without intimacy seemed oddly off key: more of a holding situation, a holding at bay. During the afternoon Tamsin and her visitors had experienced a range of heightened emotions ending with a whimper on a wrong note.

"What do you think?" John cupped a wooden spoonful of

bright Bolognese sauce and offered it to Tamsin.

The smell of pungent garlic and fresh oregano seeped through the cottage, and Tamsin let the dry cider she was drinking draw the juices in her mouth. "Perfect," she said, feeling heady, hungry and like a happy guest in her own kitchen. "Can I do anything? It's lovely being cooked for."

"Forks, bowls. And could you pop that crusty loaf I found in your freezer in the microwave. Oh, and pepper."

She took the brown jug of garage flowers into the sitting room, carefully positioned the jug in the hearth, stood back, admired it and then grinned as she realised the flowers were snapdragons with ferns for foliage. She returned to the kitchen for the rest of the things, her feet freely slapping the cold stone flags in the passageway as she went.

"Guess what? You bought snapdragons. Did you know? Very appropriate, eh?"

John lifted the lid on the pasta, twirled some onto a fork and blew on it before he bit it. "Yeah. That's done. Are they? Flowers are all the same to me. Snapdragons? Is that their real name?" He loaded two trays and they filed into the sitting room, one behind the other.

The spaghetti was rich and vivid with tomatoes and the green of more chopped herbs added at the last moment.

"Yummy," said Tamsin, settling into an old square armchair and balancing the tray on her lap. She wriggled back into a large cushion for support.

"Nice room." John put his tray down on the arm of the other matching chair and went to the window which overlooked the slope and her sheds.

"Haven't you been in this room before then?"

He turned round to look at her. "No?" It was a query rather than a statement. "Oh, he's nice." John came back across the room to study two drawings: one was of a man's face with leafy branches sprouting from his mouth and the other was of a labyrinth in terra cotta on turquoise.

"He is nice, isn't he? If you want to see him, he's over at Justleigh on a sixteenth century pew end. Before we had Michael, Robin and I used to love searching for Green Men, in churches mainly, and we liked wells where sometimes you would see a labyrinth design scratched on stone."

"I have heard of Green Men before but don't know much about them."

"Robin's the expert but not in a culty way. It was just that a lot of churches ignore their presence, because of their pagan connections, I suppose. And there is no written evidence explaining their origins anywhere. It was fun. A bit like an Enid Blyton adventure, seeking them out. And labyrinths and mazes look a bit like brains, don't they?"

"Do they?" John looked puzzled. "How do you work that out? Well, never mind. Tell me some other time. Eat your spag bog before it gets cold. Do you mind if I turn the telly on?"

They slurped the spaghetti and watched a game show without saying anything. Tamsin now felt a little awkward about asking John in. Had she been a bit hasty? With Michael in bed she couldn't think of anything to say and she was tired. Were Michael and pots all they had in common? When she finished eating she slid down into the chair, loving the familiar scuff of its rough pile on her arms. Her body slackened and she drew her feet up under her. A newscaster's voice began to drift in and out of her awareness.

"You are tired, aren't you?"

"Help, no. I'd better go and lift Michael."

"I'll wash up then."

"No, no, you can't do that. You are kind," she said.

"No I'm not." John rescued her empty bowl and empty cider mug from the broad arm of her chair. As she climbed the stairs she heard a gush of water and the rattle and crash of pots and pans coming from the kitchen.

Michael's bedroom was emulsioned in soft green. A variety of shapes just broke through the surface of the paint, all that was left of the cheerful, short-lived nursery rhyme characters, who had reigned to distort Michael's visions with terror rather than, as Tamsin had hoped, befriend his loneliness.

"Maybe they are too stimulating," Doris Nokes had suggested when Tamsin had mentioned the wallpaper on one of her visits to the school.

"But I thought… " Tamsin had started to challenge but had not continued.

Michael swayed half asleep as he peed. Tamsin held his shoulder firmly.

"Tap, tap?" Michael cried.

"Finish peeing first, love." Michael jumped and would have banged Tamsin's chin if she had not moved swiftly and in such a way as to suggest that for her all this was routine like one of those choreographed, jerky modern dances.

Downstairs the News was finishing as Tamsin reappeared in the sitting room. She fell back in her chair and opened her eyes wide and child-like in an effort to keep awake.

She stared at the screen. A forthcoming programme about another tragedy was being previewed. Beautiful children were wandering aimlessly in front of the camera, their dark eyes roaming beyond the television like hungry lenses. Tamsin shivered. "Michael was good. He didn't try to play with the flush. He just wanted the tap, but even then he was dropping off to sleep. The programme is really working."

"And look at his mother! She should be in bed too."

Tamsin shook herself and sat bolt upright. "No, no I am all right. I always feel sleepy after I've eaten. Especially if I haven't cooked it… Michael's face when those bubbles burst! He was amazed. It was as though he'd popped himself. And I think he has a super sense of priorities. Knows what counts in life. I love the way he sees things and gets excited. But poor Robin, I do wish I could find a way through."

"Yes, but Michael's not some wise child, Tamsin." John licked his finger and pointed to the ceiling. "Early wind on the cheek, late rain on the heel. That's not Michael. He's not some wise, wild child. He makes no perceptual links for the good of the tribe. In fact he makes no links at all. Not even for himself, his own safety… He'd see a distant wisp of chimney smoke and dash straight across the road in front of a bus, given half a chance." John was now sitting on the hearth rug, clasping his crossed legs and looking up at Tamsin. He saw her expression drop. "Oh, I'm sorry. Going off on one like that. Getting carried away. I'm really getting into these programmes. I'm working on another one for Michael to do with the piano. Ginny's said she'll look at it after the holidays. And I am not right. Michael does make links. You know when Michael spoke to his dad and called him Michael, he had made a link, hadn't he? He knows who's family and who's not, doesn't he? Like me." John chuckled. " I saw my dad in the mirror the other day when I was shaving. Michael is cleverer than we give him credit for, you're right."

A smile spread on Tamsin's face like a fire in a dry forest. "Oh yes. He did make a link didn't he, when you think about it? Do you think I should tell Robin?"

"Well if you do… choose your time, woman."

"You're wise. Are you wild too? " She laughed . "You'd make a good dad, you know. And a husband. You're kind and tolerant. What about children, do you want your own one day?"

"I don't know about that. I am good at sorting out other people's lives but I make a right mess of my own. A right mess. I have the knack of always picking the wrong type." He got up to go.

"Wrong type? What do you mean? Have you any one at the moment?"

"Well, I am going over to Paris at the beginning of the holidays to see someone. Next week, isn't it? Wednesday we break up. Must throw some pots when I get back. If that's all right with you. God, only four days to go. We've been having a rest from one another… since I came here, I suppose. Before that it was on and off, but I am going to help them with their work. Then I might bring them back to the granary for a week or so."

Them? Who?

"It's been a nice evening." Tamsin followed him through to the kitchen feeling much more positive about Michael. And even more curious about John. "And am I going to be allowed to know her name before she arrives?"

John had his hand on the back door latch. "Tamsin. Her name is Lawrence."

"Oh." Assumptions in Tamsin's head began to fall silently like a row of lined up dominoes. God, he's gay. "Oh. Oh right. I'll look forward to meeting her. Him."

"On the other hand, don't bank on it, Tamsin. We might end up not speaking and only after a few hours together and then he definitely won't be returning with me. But if he does, I'll get him to bring you some off-cuts of ecclesiastical cloths. Fabulous stuff. He restores things for churches and cathedrals. A peripatetic ecclesiastical restorer, that's what he is. Anyway, see you tomorrow some time. Sleep well."

That was the last thing she was going to do. Sleep well. Gay? Oh well. Her mind was buzzing. She stood at the back door allowing the light from the kitchen to show John to his door. The crescent moon offering no light tonight hung like a charm in the indigo sky over the granary, an orange segment concentrating purely on itself.

Chapter Nine

The Black Swan's welcome was twofold. In winter a warm glow permeated the main bar and leaping flickers from the log fire lit conversations like dramatic punctuation. But in summer, and especially on a Sunday morning, its welcome, if anything, was even more perfect. Customers were drawn through the bar to the gently stepped terrace overlooking the river on which the inn's occasional ferry, *Pen-Ultimate,* bobbed, tethered to the small jetty and swept by curtains of willow. It was winter's dream of a summery Sunday morning. The papers, a coffee followed by a couple of pints or as in Mollie's case a couple of glasses of dry white wine. Rising above red-tiled roofs, like a teenager outgrowing its best mates, appeared the steeple of St Andrew's, its churchyard yew smudging the gap between two brick end walls with a deep, livery green.

"Phone." Mollie pointed with an ivory cigarette holder, nipped tightly between two slim red nailed fingers, at Robin's jacket, hanging on the back of a chair. He'd just returned from the bar with a large cappuccino and a pint. He ducked under the striped parasol and put them down on the white metal fretwork table before reaching for the bleeping mobile in his pocket.

"Thanks." He flipped open the mobile, saw it was Tamsin but that she'd rung off. "No message. Better ring her back. It might be urgent."

"Hope not."

"Suits you." He nodded at a fringe of froth on Mollie's upper lip and wiped his mouth with a smirk.

Mollie delicately licked it off, giving the corners of her mouth an extra tweak with her tongue. If she had been Tamsin and if it had been ten years ago he might have offered to lick it off for her.

Even though the traffic noise from The High was subdued, almost as if it knew it was a Sunday morning, Robin cupped one ear and wandered off down the steps under an archway of massed pink roses weaving in and out of an old wisteria, generously in leaf but no longer in flower. He stopped and checked his balance by holding on to the white rails and rope meant to steady toddlers and the stiff jointed, as two boys pushed and raced passed him with fishing nets, on their way down the steps to the river's edge.

"Don't tease the swans Jack. Ben," called a dad, from behind the sports' page of The News Of The World, with his feet up on the chair next to him.

"Yes, yes I knew." Robin studied the blue and green glistening striated slate of the terrace beneath his feet. Of course he knew John was gay. Wasn't it obvious? "Hey? I just thought you would too… No, no I didn't know he was going to Paris. But he's a free agent… That's all right Tams. You were doing what you thought was best. You weren't to know. But I think you expect too much of Michael sometimes." He was calm now, but even if he hadn't been there was no way he would have told her that he'd broken down in Mollie's arms last night, unable to put into words the cause of his distress. How could he say what Michael had failed to say? And Mollie was better at coping with anguish rather than the causes of anguish. She offered an ear, a drink, a hand, even the wand of silence and a practical solution if there was one and she never pushed for explanations.

Mollie was Jaguar Lindon's right hand woman. Sophisticated and uncomplaining, she tripped around the auction room offices, her red curls bouncing and her high heels clicking as if she were caring for a stately home and its master. Usually she carried some item which she used to point and dish out directions: a clip board or at the very least a smouldering cigarette in an old ivory holder. She could exude a sense of *everything's under control* as though it were a perfume she deigned to waft as she passed by. And sometimes she took control of Robin by taking him to bed, to sleep, rarely to make love but when they did, like this morning, they surprised themselves with an explosion of luscious energy and a wonderful stretch of relief to follow. They had never dated. He had just ended up at her place one evening after a particularly bad day, a bit like last night. He hoped he wasn't making a habit of it. There had never been a seduction plan. Their friendship was something comfortable to slip into. And out of.

To Robin guilt seemed inappropriate, a lame luxury, an accomplice feeding off its deed like a parasite. Guilt was a sort of lie. He was very fond of Mollie and knew there'd be no complications. He was not part of her life plan, but her sophistication amused him and the cool, nonchalant way in which she comforted him when she held him and stroked his hair relaxed him, made him feel okay about himself again. And there was a certain disconnected alertness about her, an alertness somehow directed elsewhere, that made Robin feel she had her eye on someone else.

He folded his mobile and slipped it in his pocket. "Would you know a man was gay when you met him?"

"No. Well not at first, or even for some time…" She stubbed out her cigarette. Someone had put on a Will Young tape. "I do like him."

"Oh?"

"They give us girls what we want, you see…" She spoke gleefully, conspiratorially.

Robin was astounded. "Want?"

"They listen, aren't a threat, luuuv shopping. It's all a bit of a cliché. And they don't let themselves go like married men. Not you of course, Robin. Well not yet…" She grinned. "What's this about anyway?"

"John doesn't like shopping." He told her about Tamsin's reaction to John.

"Lucky Tamsin… Young, beautiful, helps out with your son. What more could she want? My round. Do you want another pint? I've had my caffeine fix now and am ready for a wine."

"If John is going to Paris then maybe I ought to go back and camp in the granary while he's away. Maybe I shouldn't have been so hasty in the first place. I mean with John away and Anna pregnant, who's she going to call on?"

"You of course. Like just now. Robin? Do you want a pint or not?"

"Sorry. Yes please." He loved Mollie's practicality. No, he couldn't ask John to let him camp in the granary. it was John's place now. What was he thinking? That would be too intrusive.

Mollie turned round and called over her shoulder, "Jessica, Luke's daughter, from The Mill is looking for a holiday job. She came into the Auction Rooms on Friday asking if we could find her something to do in the office, but we don't really need anybody. She's doing some childcare course at the college… "

Mollie disappeared into the pub's inner darkness through the French doors while Robin mumbled, "Childcare course? Ummmh," and sorted out the sections of The Observer he wanted to read and those he was going to chuck. He patted the wanted pile, smoothed the cover of the colour supplement, fingered the glossy paper lips of Kate Moss and thought what a fool he'd been, hasty. He could have moved into the granary himself instead of all the way into town if he hadn't been so impetuous. Would it have worked? But of course none of it had been planned. Both he and Tamsin fell towards decisions and then into them only to find no real decisions had been made, only muddles. They had a lot in common.

"Lovely morning." Robin looked up and saw Jaguar

Lindon standing in the middle of the terrace surveying the lunchtime throng and sipping what looked like a double gin.

"Oh hi-ya Jags. Mollie's at the bar. You must have just missed her on your way through."

"Oh… No… I've got some explaining to do then." He came over to Robin's table wearing exquisitely cut linen slacks, a fitted T-shirt and his usual sandals. Three or four ginger hairs bristled on his Adam's apple and even more on his freckled arms. Jaguar had not let himself go. Not yet anyway, as Mollie would say. But come to think of it he was rather camp. But not gay. He came across as a sort of nineteen forties ladies' man and now that Robin thought about it, Mollie herself reminded him of those early promotional shots of film stars who crossed their silk-stockinged long legs and let cigarettes dangle seductively from loose, upturned fingers.

"I thought I'd pop in for a swift drink before lunch. Just come from Mass. So much to confess."

Mollie having caught sight of Jaguar was now hesitating on the threshold of the French doors while holding a pint of bitter and a flute of white wine. Jaguar went towards her and took the drinks out of her hands. "I am sorry about last night, dear heart." He kissed her on both cheeks. "Did you get my message and chocolates? I left them on the step. You were out. I am so sorry, but Mother is so down at the moment, so low and began to fret as soon as she knew I was going out. Apparently it was her and dad's anniversary. Not something I'd remember. She tried to hide it from me, bless her… "

So Robin had hit lucky with Mollie's misfortune last night. At the time he hadn't been surprised by what he thought of as her usual vagueness. Now reviewing his arrival at her door and her instant welcome, he realised she herself had looked lost, not vague. Her distance, as though she was constantly preoccupied, was part of her elusive charm and not something he usually questioned.

Robin considered Mollie and Jaguar as a pair. Both had red hair, Jaguar's lighter than Mollie's and sprinkled with grey. There were the tailored slacks, and Mollie's black and white floaty dress which looked more like an underslip. Both had very pale skin; Mollie's shone like porcelain. As a twosome they were striking, glamorous, if a little eccentric, and together they accentuated one another's assured, dependable ostentation.

Mollie took out and lit another cigarette. The flame on the lighter gave away her slight tremor. Not so sophisticated after all then. "That's all right Jags. I had plenty to do. And the choccies were exquisite. Champagne chocolates." She gave Robin a sidelong glance and he felt a charge. She was prickly with vibes but the vibes were not directed at him.

Robin felt sorry for her. Jaguar could have been more tactful; made his apology less public.

"Can I borrow her for a minute?"

With his arm under her elbow Jaguar guided Mollie down the steps and embraced her beneath the trailing willow. He ruffled her hair and for a while they were absorbed deep in conversation.

As they slowly returned Robin heard Jaguar say, "I'd better be going. Lunch will be on the table. See you tomorrow then." He kissed her on the cheek. "I'm off now Robin. Mother's. Leave you two to sort out your collectables from your antiques." He laughed. "By the way, how are Tams and the boy?" He put his glass down on the table and left with a flourish and without waiting for an answer.

"You've got a bit of a thing about him, haven't you?"

"He's adorable, isn't he? But his poor old mother has had a bit of depression since his dad died. Not nice."

"You are a lot younger than him." Robin was experiencing twinges of unexpected jealousy and possessiveness, but mentally slapped his hand. She was not his. Had been though. Recently, too. But that was only for a little blissful while.

"I know. But he's so classy, so… I dunno, so life-affirming." She lit another cigarette and then delicately picked a tiny bit of tobacco from between her teeth before inserting the cigarette into the holder, her red nails glinting in the sun.

"You're rapidly becoming a chain smoker, you know… "

"Oh help. Do you think it will put him off… ?"

"Shouldn't think so Mollie. It hasn't yet, has it? Mind you, I didn't know you'd got it together. But I don't think his mother will be impressed by your smoking from what he's told us."

"Right, tomorrow I give up. Definitely." She flicked her ash for emphasis, "This is my last one. He's taking me out to lunch tomorrow after we've done a bit of valuing, up at Justleigh Barton. And for the record as you say, we haven't got it together. But I'm hoping." She tipped back her head and blew broken smoke rings into the air. Someone nearby coughed affectedly.

"Maybe you should take up jogging!"

Before her husband's death, Muriel Lindon, Jaguar's mother had been a regular vision around the streets of Linbury, as an early morning jogger. A fit and determined tiny seventy year old, she'd made a fine figure in her grey tracksuit and black peaked cap.

"Can't see that happening."

"Neither can I. You in trainers? Keep me in mind when you're at Justleigh Barton, will you? If you can. I am on the look out for small stuff at the moment. Sewing tables, nursing chairs, Davenports, that sort of thing. Oh, and smoking cabinets and pipe racks. Smoking accessories are going to be the next in-thing as far as collectables are concerned."

Mollie turned her nose up.

The prickly charge he had felt coming off her earlier was ebbing away. She was more vulnerable than he realised. He was very, very fond of her. After all, she had taken his mind off Tamsin and Michael for a good few hours which was some feat these days. And he did perversely feel guilty about that, but only because he wished he could go home to Brock Cottage and share his sense of renewed well-being with his wife and son.

Chapter Ten

Michael performed without fuss. First he led Tamsin to the bathroom by taking her hand. Then he chanted, "Tap, tap, tap, tap," as though it were an intricate spell and then he calmly washed his hands. Success.

To his further delight Tamsin reminded him how to blow soap bubbles. "Remember Sam, darling?" And she lifted her son onto the loo seat so he could blow bubbles out of the high window and watch them float away and then together they chased a salvo out of the bathroom and along the landing. The string of transparent bubbles elongated and curved the reflections of the white bedroom doors left ajar and snatches of windows full of sky, the framed painting of a wheat and poppy field on the landing wall and intimate glimpses of bedroom interiors. They chased and Tamsin sang, "Fly, fly, let's fly to the sky, fly in the blue, fly in the blue… " And then they danced and spun, holding hands. The centrifugal force kept them safe as they pirouetted at the top of the stairs.

On the way downstairs to get some breakfast Tamsin made a mental note to buy some balloons when they went into Linbury later for some food shopping. How would Michael react if one burst? Had she never bought balloons before? Unbelievable. But maybe he had seen them at school. Of course he had. It was just he didn't talk so she couldn't share with him what he'd loved, seen, heard when she wasn't there with him.

It was the first day of the holidays and the programme was going well. Not ideally, but then it was never going to be ideal. Becoming conscious of this major detail was a step forward Tamsin acknowledged.

During a breakfast of toast and honey Tamsin and Michael played with three fallen snapdragon heads, yellow and ruby red, lying in a dusting of pollen on the pine table. They looked more like rabbits' heads than dragons'. Tamsin picked one up and squeezed it close to Michael's face. The flower's mouth opened and two stamens flicked up like a tongue. Michael jumped. Tamsin then offered him the flower which he took and slowly crushed in his palm. Opening his fist he studied the crinkled flower as its creases darkened and bled. Then he put it in his mouth.

"Honestly, Michael." Tamsin squeezed Michael's cheeks with a finger and thumb until his mouth opened and she could hook out the petals with a crooked finger.

"I know Michael, we'll put some washing in first and then I'll glaze those delphinium ginger jars in the shed. I'll throw a couple more mugs and you can pour the water over my hands to keep them wet. Do you remember? When I am on the wheel?"

Michael's reply was to sing, "Pour on water, pour on water, fire, fire, fire, fire."

"Darling." She nuzzled his hair and kissed him. "And we could water the garden first, couldn't we? With a watering can. Those new big daisies John put in last week next to his herbs."

"Don."

"What did you say? Don? Good boy."

Michael turned away and went over to the washing machine where he growled softly as he hopped and jiggled on the spot.

Tamsin smiled and put a bundle of clothes into the wash. She let him hold the packet of soap powder with her while they filled the compartment together.

"I think I'll give Anna a ring because we could go over to Justleigh and show her the Green Man. She said she wanted to see him. And I want to photograph him again. We'll call in at Linbury on the way back. What do you think? Maybe pop in and see daddy? Take his lovely book back. Daddy?" She looked at Michael hopefully.

"Bo peep, Bo peep."

"Yes, darling we'll pass the sheep on the way."

They watered the big white daisies together using brown rain water from the rusty old corrugated butt which leant against one end of the granary in a fringe of long grass, and then they went down to the sheds.

"Oh look Michael, there's the heron." Michael did not look up at the heron as he tripped nimbly down the steps with his mother. Tamsin thought the heron was a gangly thing. No more than a feathered egg on legs. It landed in Anna's and Joe's bit of stream across the lane.

"I took some photos of Michael in the wheel-shed this morning. They are super, even if I say so myself."

They were in the mini spinning along the back lanes to Justleigh. Michael sat in front, Anna in the back. Tamsin was being careful. "He can't reach you there if he does have a hissy fit. Though I don't expect he will anyway. We've had a lovely morning."

"Now that you work on your pottery more these days aren't you going to miss it, Tams? What with the holidays and Michael being at home all the time?"

"We'll manage." Although Tamsin had to admit the thought had also occurred to her. She hadn't realised until this summer how much the emphasis of her days had gradually changed over the years since Michael had been at school, and then even more noticeably since Robin had left. These days she spent more time with clay, less time in the cottage.

"Look darling. Little Bo peep … "

Every now and then the dappled secretive lanes would burst into brightness and there would be fields of sheep or cows. The three of them sang a medley of Mary Had A Little Lamb, Baa Baa Black Sheep and Little Bo Peep.

When Michael had started school the separation from her son had been sudden and hard. Incongruously Tamsin had felt lost and unsafe without him. But as his first term wore on, the separation was passively levered into a routine by the trusted Doris Nokes. And then Tamsin's days opened out into weeks and eventually years, giving her space to choose how she should spend her time. Tamsin had relaxed and grown accustomed to her new freedom and began to go down to the sheds again and use her wheel for pleasure. So when her clay work became a serious commitment she had time during the school term. But now with the arrival of the summer holidays she realised she was going to need extra help and had naturally thought John and Anna would be there to blur and plug her absences from the cottage. But Anna was pregnant and John was in Paris. Gay Paree.

She knew Robin would like get more involved with arranging childcare for Michael but that would defeat her aim of independence; an aim that was ambivalent, for she also wanted to show off her independence to this man. The man she had hurt by her lack of desire. This lack stalked her like a shadow slip-sliding, belittling her, attached, flat and two-dimensional. Desire itself was an elusive memory.

Anna was laughing nervously. "How can you see? It's blinding."

They had just dipped from strong sunlight into a leafy tunnel. One car coming towards them had actually flicked on warning headlights.

"By keeping my eyes on the verge and the road and not looking at the sun. We're practically there." Tamsin slowed down, turned right and parked on the village triangle opposite the church, under the shade of the oak by the old, red and now gutted telephone box. "Think of all those calls to the doctor and to sweethearts in the past… "

"You old romantic… "

"No I am not." Tamsin was irritated but decided she was being over-sensitive and thought instead of a moody photo she'd taken that morning of Michael's hands on the curved body of one of her jugs, a discard. It wasn't an original idea. Once she'd seen a photo by Mirtez of hands opening a book. The thought of this image moved her still. But then Michael immediately let go of the jug and as it fell she'd pressed the button again. This time the flash caught him in a halo of light appearing like a visiting angel, hands flying upwards and back. The breakage was not important. The jug was a reject and the previews of the photos thrilled Tamsin. Her preference would be two-toned: more direct than a myriad of colours. Would Robin like them?

The three of them walked up the church path. Michael's walk was more of a skip and a jiggle. Tamsin had brought her camera with her. She wouldn't need to use flash outside. "How about a photo of a real green man, in the yew tree?" The giant yew by the south porch door, so ancient it had to be supported, was hollow and famed for its long life of a thousand years and featured in many reference books.

Michael wouldn't go and stand inside the tree as Tamsin wanted, fancying him as a leafy fellow. "No, no, come back, this way." He had tottered off towards the tower end of the church. He did not appear to be attending to anything Tamsin was saying. He could have been miles away on another planet but he came straight back. "Would you pose for me instead, Anna?"

"He seems to understand you." Anna was obeying Tamsin's pointed finger to enter the hollow.

"Yes, Doris Nokes and Ginny both say his comprehension's good, when he's in the mood. But of course it's his expressive language he has difficulty with. Put one arm up and rest it in the tree. Pose. A Mother with Child In The Green. That's right. Now rest your other hand on your tummy. No, no, too cliched. As you were. Lovely."

Inside the church there was a mixed aroma of damp and calor gas. A modern stove was chained to the screen. "As if that would be the first thing people would take. I think it's quite wonderful that some churches are still open. You know it's millions of pounds worth of stuff we're free to look at here." Tamsin took Michael's hand and brushed it over the face of a carved leafy man on a sixteenth century bench end. "Your daddy loves wood, Michael. And we've got a drawing of this one at home."

"Home," said Michael.

Tamsin smiled.

Anna was looking up at the top of a stone column. "I've found another Green Man."

"Yeah, that's only one of them though. There are more on the roof bosses. But this one here is the best, I think, on the bench end. Careful. Look where you are going." Anna had tipped back her head to look at the wagon roof and was walking nonchalantly backwards up the aisle when she bumped sharply into Michael who was hopping and clapping in the middle of the aisle unaware that he was in Anna's way. Tamsin's heart missed a beat. She walked slowly over to Michael and without rushing him guided him away from Anna. "Sorry, sorry Anna."

"Excuse me." Anna dashed from the church with her hand over her mouth. Tamsin stood helplessly in the aisle with her arm around Michael's shoulders, not knowing what to do. Stay with Michael or go to her friend. She could hear Anna retching by the north wall and she mentally shrivelled as she envisaged the anger on Joe's face.

Anna returned. She was laughing and wiping her mouth. "Talk about morning sickness. It's bloody - oh sorry - " She made a face at the altar. "But it's all-day sickness as far as I am concerned." She stared at her friend. "What's the matter?"

"I thought it was… " Tamsin drew Michael closer to her side.

"Oh don't, Tamsin. Michael didn't hurt me. It was my fault anyway. I should have been looking where I was going. No harm done, honest." She bent down and briefly brushed Michael's cheek with the back of her hand.

Not this time, thought Tamsin. Feeling a gush of relief she looked up at a Green Man on the roof. Was he smiling or was he in pain? And what about the future? Was her life always going to be full of palpitating fears, knowing that at any time her son could seriously hurt someone? Was Robin right? Wanting to plan the future before he could deal with the present?

"Oh Tamsin. Come on. Tell me the history, Tamsin, of these Green Men. They are intriguing and I've never really noticed them before."

"They are a mystery." Tamsin sniffed, smiled and hesitated to check Anna was really all right and was not feigning interest.

"Yes? And?"

"Well, they don't appear on invoices, church inventories, anything like that. Nothing had been written down about them until recently and yet they go back hundreds of years and crop up all around the world. Robin believes they are an insurance. Just in case the Christians have got it wrong. But I do think the interweaving of branches with a man's face means we are interwoven with the earth and what we do to the earth, we do to ourselves."

"My Joe would be interested then. Wouldn't he?"

"Then take him into the shop next time you're in Linbury together and show him Robin's Welsh Dresser. The drawer handles are men's heads. You tuck your hand in a mouth when you pull open a drawer. That's what got Robin interested in the first place. He knew he'd seen something similar in churches. Now he won't sell the dresser."

"You two were meant to be together, I think. It's a pity you can't sort yourselves out."

Tamsin sighed in resigned agreement as they wandered out into the sunshine again. It was quiet except for birdsong and the drone of a not too distant lawn mower. On the far side by the church wall were two women with their backs turned. They couldn't have been more different. One might have walked right out of Brideshead Revisited and the other was an older tiny neat woman with boyish short hair, in cropped trousers and sandals.

"It's Mollie and Mrs Lindon, Jaguar's mum. Hi… " Tamsin waved.

"Hello." Mrs Lindon took Mollie's arm and walked over. "We've just been into Justleigh Barton to check a few things for Jaguar. Mollie asked me if I wanted to come for the jaunt. Wasn't that sweet of her? And now I am wondering if my husband wouldn't have been happier here, in the country, rather than in St Andrew's."

Both Anna and Tamsin looked flummoxed, not knowing quite how to respond. They glanced at one another, their eyes playing with visions of digging up dead Mr Lindon.

Mrs Lindon saw their confusion and smiled. "Cecil," she said relishing the name. "Oh, don't mind me, dears. I am as mad as a hatter. Talk to him every day. How's that lad of yours, by the way?"

Tamsin noticed that, from a distance, stature and figure-wise, boyish Mrs Lindon could pass as Mollie's sister, especially as she wore no make-up. But close to, you could see the wrinkles in her soft, freckly skin which gave her age away. And style-wise the two women were poles apart.

"I mentioned to Robin the other day that Jessica was looking for a holiday job." Mollie smiled tentatively at Tamsin. "She's doing a course at the college. Childcare."

"He is doing fine, Mrs Lindon." Tamsin deliberately addressed the older woman first, then she turned to Mollie. "Oh, you mean for Michael, Mollie? Ummmh."

"Oh Muriel, please. That Jessica has done really well. It's such a young age to lose your mother. You know, your... " Mrs Lindon hesitated, looking at Michael.

"Michael... "

"He's a beautiful lad, isn't he? And maybe he's lucky, you know dear. He'll never know loss, loss of a loved one, or fear, fear of cancer... and worse... "

"That's right, Tamsin," agreed Anna quickly, giving her friend a quizzical, sidelong look. All five of them started to move towards the village green and their cars.

Tamsin looked at Michael. Of course he would know loss. And grief. He wouldn't understand it or have any skills to help him handle these acute emotions. A rush of renewed love and protection surged through her.

"And if he's always surrounded by kindness, he'll only ever know innocence. He'll be a true innocent." As she warmed to her theme, Tamsin noticed Muriel Lindon began to look and sound more and more like her son, Jaguar. "And you could trust that Jessica too. I knew her mother. A good woman. Hard worker, and her daughter from all accounts takes after her. She's been an absolute blessing to her father. I sometimes wish we'd had a daughter... Still," she looked at Mollie, "they come in many guises."

The day had been challenging. Tamsin would ponder the elderly lady's recently uttered philosophical insights. Maybe she was on to something. Michael could not fear the future: waste time fretting over stuff that might not happen. His fears were spontaneous, located in the present. At least he wouldn't experience the debilitating gnaw of indecision and uncertainties. Would this compensate for his deficiencies? No, not really. Tamsin put an arm around Michael's shoulders. It would be her shoulders that would bear the weight of his share of life's anxieties.

"What do you think about Mollie's suggestion? About

asking Jessica?" They were driving back through lanes singing along with Michael. Anna had just said as they'd passed some grazing cows that there were no nursery rhymes just for cows and to the two women's delight, Michael had chimed in, "...the little dog laughed, the little dog laughed... " and the two friends had happily chorused, "...and the cow jumped over the moon."

"You brilliant boy, Michael. Yes, it was good of her to think of me, but we will be all right, I think. John will be home soon anyway... "

"Tamsin." Anna frowned. "What do you mean, John? He's on holiday. He's got his own life to lead. He is your tenant, neighbour. Okay he's a friend as well, but you can't rely on him too much. It wouldn't be fair."

Tamsin was taken aback by Anna's implied criticism. And was Anna thinking about the way Tamsin had relied on her? Too much? But the fact was she was right. "Yeah, you're right. I am not thinking straight am I?" Nevertheless, what was she going to do?

Chapter Eleven

A solitary blackbird sang in a bush, seeing off the storm in a celebratory manner. Tamsin could see the cocky bird in the fuchsia bush directing its triumph up the valley towards the sound of a few lingering tired rumbles.

As expected Michael's reaction to the thunder and especially the lightning was to run amok, backwards and forwards from the sink to the table. As this was not directed at anybody or anything she just allowed him space in the kitchen and restrained her need to comfort him, valuing her flesh and bones, especially her chin which he had banged a few times in the past with his head.

"Anybody would think you were thanking the rain. We needed it, didn't we? Joe will be pleased."

Michael shuddered and flapped his hands. For all the response she got from her son Tamsin sometimes felt she was addressing a disdainful cat.

It was already August and she really should begin to think about getting ready for the exhibition. Pots had to be sorted and packed to take to The Harrow, but Michael was jumpy. More than usual. She couldn't risk him dropping a valuable pot or freaking out in the shed. It was still hot and humid. The thunderclouds had not finished with them yet. They would come back.

The passage where the piano stood between the kitchen and the front room was crossed with blue shadows from the small high window. Unripe elderberry sprays fanned the muted light which slipped down the inaccessible dark, rocky bank at the rear of the cottage. Tamsin took the little key and unlocked the piano's glossy mahogany lid. Should she allow him or shouldn't she? They both needed their own thing for a while. Just a little while. She felt guilty. Mrs Green and Co would not approve.

At the sound of the key turning Michael immediately ran and came to stand beside his mother. Feverishly he let his finger hover like a hawk and then let it drop onto the long, slim elegant black D flat. As he struck the note he bent forward and held his ear as close to the piano keys as possible. His mouth gaped as though he were breathing sound. The piano was a honeycomb, humming. Only when the note faded did he jab it again. This time he went and crouched at the side of the piano and rested his ear against the smooth cool wood, listening to the chamber of taut wires reverberating.

Tamsin tiptoed back into the kitchen and sat down at the table to make a list of things she needed to do: collect blown-up harvest photos from the Journal, drapes, bales of hay - see Joe, Blu-tack, labels, statement, catalogue. Today the repetition of D flat did not disturb her. It was like having a piano tuner in the cottage listening to a note resonating, and only when its echo died did he strike again, but the air was still clammy and oppressive and she was tired. She had stayed up late last night surfing the autism websites, something she often did, looking for answers but as usual finding only what felt like punishment. Many of the sites were at odds with one another: '...for the record autism has no cure...' and then '...autism can be cured...' Some parents had set up their own websites: parents who, dissatisfied with facilities and the extent of provision available, initiated their own programmes and even schools. The sponsored fund-raising runs were numerous, and one single mother who had three autistic sons was taking a degree, giving lectures around the country and had written a book about her experiences which she said 'had enriched and revitalised her life..'. Just reading her biography on her website made Tamsin feel tired, small and totally inadequate.

There were sites recommending clay baths for bodies ridden with toxic metals or how to deal with autism and yeast problems. Many sites were given over to diet and environmental circumstances.

One site that drew Tamsin's attention particularly was a site about a Hug Box . Its principle was based on deep pressure. A hug so firm, no response was possible and so one relaxed, gave oneself up to being held. Apparently it had been observed that when cattle were held in secure wooden crates for the purpose of giving injections they did not panic but became calm and remained calm for another hour or two after being released from the crate. Tamsin liked this and fancied being held in a hug box herself, let alone Michael. She saw the sense of it, although she could not see herself actually commissioning one or one having a place in her cottage.

She studied Michael in the shadows of the passageway framed by the open door as he tinkered at the piano. He could have been the figure in a modern Dutch interior: brown, the rich shine of mahogany accepting, absorbing and then reflecting the geometries of violet light. And Michael, keying one's eye to the black and white geometries of music.

Tamsin wanted no more than a normal life and Michael to be a part of it.

She looked out of the kitchen window. The sky had darkened once again and fat spots of rain were hitting the glass. No blackbird could be heard now.

Dong went D flat.

She put down her pen on top of her list of things to do and joined Michael in the passageway, standing behind him. She stroked his silky hair and kissed it gently. "Good boy."

Dong. Michael moved to the end of the piano and crouched again, putting his ear to the wood.

As he did so Tamsin moved forward into his place and held her own forefinger above the keys where she let it drift, playfully selecting, swooping and retracting as if the keys were teeth.

Her finger dropped suddenly and hit middle C. Its full, cool, round tone had such a staying quality she hit again. C natural. She closed her eyes and tipped back her head. Michael returned to stand alongside her and with two hands he took hold of the piano lid and rammed it mercilessly down, trapping his mother's hand.

Tamsin cried out and sank to the floor. Her hand throbbed as she slowly and painfully slipped it free. Her ears drummed and her mouth went dry. Michael skipped and jumped while he lifted back the lid and hit D flat. Then he whimpered and ran into the kitchen.

"Sorry Michael." Tamsin hauled herself along the floor into the kitchen. "I am a stupid woman."

Peering through the open back door at the freely moving dark green of the trees and fields with a distant sky filling the gaps like navy blue jig-saw pieces, Tamsin was tempted to see it as an escape. But an escape from what? From Michael? No, just from the slow, halting motion of occupying him during the holidays. She wanted to be in her shed throwing a heavy ball of clay onto the wheel-head, controlling it and then kicking away as she grasped the clay with the right amount of pressure so that when it centred the spinning ball of earth beneath her fingers would feel still, tamed and at peace.

Something had happened. Without fully realising it she had become used to having her own space and time and the full impact of the difference between a little help and virtually no help at all dawned on Tamsin as she sat on the chilly kitchen floor nursing her hot swollen hand. It was not a little difference, it was a huge, life-changing difference in which her inability to cope on her own was magnified. She had lost Robin to Linbury, John temporarily to Paris and Anna to pregnancy in one fell swoop.

"Tamsin! Tamsin! What's the matter?" Two dark figures at the door loomed large like shadows in the dim light, but Tamsin knew Luke's voice. In her pain she hadn't heard a van arriving. The two came in and Luke knelt down beside her and tenderly took her hand. Jessica stood behind her father with a worried expression on her face.

"It's all my fault. I was stupid." Tamsin tried to stand up.

Luke put a hand under her elbow. "Now are you all right? Robin suggested we drop by. Said you might be able to sort Jessica out with some work experience." As he leant towards her his beard brushed against Tamsin's cheek. It felt fatherly. Tamsin shivered and suffered a pang of nausea, remembering as she did from time to time, at the oddest of moments, that she did not know who her father was. Who was he? Where was he? For a second she wanted to cling to Luke.

"We must get you to the health centre in case you've broken it," Jessica said looking up at her father. "If you let me have your keys, I'll go and you stay here dad, with Michael, hey?"

"No. No," protested Tamsin. She noticed Michael was looking at her from by the sink. He appeared frightened.

"Okay, don't worry. Dad can take you then, and I'll stay behind with Michael. You'll be all right with me, won't you Michael?"

Michael growled softly and started jigging about on one leg.

"No. He doesn't really know you. Either of you."

Jessica frowned and thought for a moment and then her eyes lit up. "We'll all go. We'll take Michael with us."

"Thank you," said Tamsin meekly and closed her eyes as if she were praying.

Chapter Twelve

Through the kitchen window Tamsin could see Jessica laughing with Pete the Post over the five-barred gate at the bottom of the slope. In one gesture Jessica drew back, pursed her lips and raised her eyebrows. They were flirting and it was nice to witness. He handed Jessica a small pile of mail, and as she climbed the steps she was still smiling as she turned over a postcard and appeared to read it absentmindedly. She must have realised what she was doing, for she hastily returned the postcard to its face-up position and shuffled it to the bottom of the pile.

"I'm sorry Tamsin. I've just read your postcard. And it's private. I don't know what I think I was doing. Honestly, I am really sorry."

Tamsin laughed. "I know what you were doing, you two. And how is Pete? Asked you out yet?"

"Nooo. He's got a girlfriend over Justleigh. How's your hand?" As Jessica handed Tamsin the postcard, the rest of the letters fell onto the kitchen floor. "Butterfingers."

"Still a bit sore but it's fine. Look." Tamsin showed Jessica the shiny zigzag bruise spreading across the back of her hand. How proud of it she would have been if she had been a child. "And what did it say then? 'Weather fine. Wish you were here.'?"

Jessica looked embarrassed. "No, actually it didn't. It's from your mother." She looked up at Tamsin ruefully as she gathered up the fallen post.

"My mother?" Tamsin looked down at the postcard. It was from Brazil.

"She's coming over. Sorry. I shouldn't have read it."

"Coming over? Coming over to England? She can't be. I haven't seen her for nearly thirty years. Why? Why now? And why announce it on a postcard? Why not an email?" There was panic in Tamsin's voice.

"I didn't know you had a mother, Tamsin. Sorry… I shouldn't have said that. Everybody's got a mother. Sorry. Sorry." Still flustered, she put the other post down on the table.

"Bills. Don't worry Jess. Isn't that John calling you?"

Before Pete had arrived, John, back from Paris with a certain sulky Lawrence, had been playing chase with Jessica and Michael .Or rather John and Jessica had been playing chase while Michael looked on from a distance. Lawrence too had been an observer, peering over the top of *The Times* he was supposedly reading while seated on a chair just outside the granary.

Tamsin flexed her freed hand and then grasped the postcard again. She'd taken off the dressing this morning which had made her hand look like a large magnolia bud. The swelling gone down and the remaining tattoo-like bruise which was all it had turned out to be, not a broken bone, was now a dirty, yellowy navy. It appeared drab, crude next to the glossy exotic blue, green and orange parasols of the beach scene she was holding. She turned it over to read: *I am coming home to England for a while. At last. I will ring as soon as I arrive. Love, Mum.*

Tamsin sat down at the kitchen table, her heart racing. How could her mother re-enter her life after all these years? There were no ways back now. The ways had closed over like scars, and yet Tamsin's heart was hammering to open one up. She felt sick and frightened. Why now? Debbie Cabral had not come home for the funeral of her father or even for her mother's. *I am desperate to come but Ferdinand cannot manage without me, even for a day,* and then Tamsin had thought hard and long about inviting Debbie to her wedding. A mother should be there, but in the end Tamsin had tremulously decided not to. She wanted her mother to have an invitation but she didn't want her to accept it. Her wedding day could not be the day for a long awaited mother-daughter reunion. And sadly there had been no negative reaction to her omission, only *I hope you will be happy.*

In the seventies when Tamsin was born, her gran said the locals had labelled Debbie... easy, anybody's and worse. When talking to Tamsin about her mother Tamsin's gran had always referred to her as Debbie, never 'your mother' or even 'your mum'. And never, 'my daughter'.

"Marry him, marry him, girl," your grandfather had pleaded.

"I can't," Miss High and Mighty Debbie said.

"Why not, if he's the father?"

"I can't, I can't, I can't."

Apparently Tamsin's grandfather's heart had been broken. And then they'd rowed so much when Debbie wouldn't tell them who the father was that she'd started sleeping out and running wild. When challenged she said she might as well live up to her reputation.

Tamsin's gran blamed herself when Debbie left for Brazil. "We should have tried to understand more. But your grandfather was so ashamed and stopped keeping company, on market days in the pub, with the other farmers. And he stopped going to church where he'd been a sidesman since he was sixteen. But I should have been more forgiving. I blame myself."

Ferdinand had been an agricultural student and had met Debbie, when Tamsin was five-years old, at a dance in Linbury Assembly Rooms.

"But your grandfather wouldn't let him in the cottage. Ferdinand said another woman's child would not be accepted by his family. He looked like a film star, Tamsin, tall, dark and handsome, so different from the boys around here, and he was so romantic, with a lot of fancy talk. We didn't trust him one little bit. He did sweep Debbie off her feet. We weren't used to people like that round here. She was determined to follow him and wouldn't listen to anybody, least of all your grandfather and me."

Tamsin grew up wanting to believe her mother was a victim of a passionate love affair and had no choice but to follow wherever it led her. For if she had had a choice, she surely would have taken her little daughter with her.

When Tamsin became a teenager she and her grandmother used to read Women's Weekly and The People's Friend together, especially in winter by the fire after tea. They quietly marvelled at the illustrations showing men and women embracing, openly in love. Tamsin knew she wanted to marry for love like her mother. But she wanted her child to be born within the safe confines of a marriage. Many times she had imagined family life in the future. She and her loving husband would be playfully swinging their child between them as they walked along the sand in sunshine or through a wild flower meadow. Her child would be happy with a mum and dad on either side, and they would all adore one another. And she would never, never leave *her* child. The train window, with her mother waving goodbye, hung in Tamsin's mind like a framed dark oil painting of an ominous ancestor.

And there was also an irregular space, like a map, inside her chest which she secretly called Brazil, and in this space she carried her mother everywhere. This space was waiting next to her heart. And today the mother who'd grown dumb after so many years in her chest was clamouring to be let out again.

Tamsin went and propped the postcard on the windowsill behind the taps and next to some odd slivers of green soap and a jam jar of dandelions. Outside on the slope John and Jessica were now patting a purple balloon to one another, and every now and then one of them patted it Michael's way. So far he had let it bounce on his nose or his bent head and then let it land on the grass at his feet without retrieving it. He was standing halfway down the slope and flapping his hands while at the top still outside the granary door sat Lawrence staring and now not even pretending to read *The Times*. Every now and then Lawrence shook the paper in an exaggerated manner.

He made Tamsin feel uneasy. He was slight with long, bony fingers. She had no trouble in imagining him with a needle and thread in hand, plying the air over some ecclesiastical cloth. He appeared uncomfortable in his own skin and stared more than he talked. A bit Proustian Tamsin felt, taking everything in and giving nothing away, although she had no knowledge of Proust's actual appearance. An aesthete, dilettante, Lawrence made John look quite robust beside him.

Tamsin didn't care for this friend of John's, didn't trust him, and in her opinion John was much too good for him.

Lawrence had hired a car, and at night he and John drove off with gusto. Goodness knows where. They came back late, a little drunk if the totter of their feet on the thirteen steps was anything to go by.

Talking in the shed shortly after he'd introduced her to Lawrence, John asked Tamsin what she thought. "Do you like him? He's got style hasn't he, but he's very damaged, very vulnerable… " John had registered Tamsin's frown. "I know he's stubborn. He's his own worst enemy. He was really bullied at school."

Tamsin had felt awkward as she'd clumsily and slowly, with her still painful hand, packed her heavy exhibition pots in bubble wrap. She couldn't see that Lawrence had any style at all unless it was his lank, long black hair. Style? He looked rather grubby to her, and when introduced he had merely mumbled and avoided eye contact. So far Lawrence had not even approached Michael, and if their paths looked like crossing Lawrence stepped aside, giving the boy a wide berth.

Jessica's comment was, "Weird or what? I could sort John out with much better totty from college."

Tamsin wondered if John had seen Lawrence narrow his eyes to slits when he watched his friend playing with or attending to her son.

John and Jessica got on like a brother and sister. When Jessica had brought a water pistol to the cottage one day for Michael and he'd gone berserk as she'd squirted water at him, John had laughed. "Some children like Michael hate to be tickled. It feels more like an assault."

Tamsin was in her shed at the time and on hearing John had called out, "Yeah, I saw that programme too. On telly, where that woman said you must make sure your touch is firm. You mustn't pat or tickle, she said. She said some autistic children panic the same way as animals do… "

"What programme?" he called back, but when Tamsin went to the shed door to see Michael's reaction for herself, she saw John wasn't listening. He was more interested in the workings of the water pistol.

"Look." John gave the pistol to Michael and held the child's hand, showing him how to use it.

"Look Tamsin, he's loving it." Jessica clapped her knees in childish excitement and giggled. "Come on Michael."

John let Michael squirt the pistol on his own which he did randomly, all over the place, squinting and squeezing up his face into a half smile as he did so.

"Brilliant," said John. "We might be able to use this as one of his rewards in the future." He picked up Michael and swung him around, at which point Lawrence, who was sitting in his usual place, outside the granary, had got up and flounced inside.

"Spoil sport," jeered Jessica in a whisper.

Tamsin remembered the light hearted and happy feeling she had had as she'd returned to her work bench that day.

The difference between a little help and no help at all were words Tamsin had played like a favourite record in her head ever since last week when Jessica had come to help and the troubled lovers had returned from Paris. The difference was *a whole new world* and it was not a cliché.

"But it's not fair, Robin. You can't afford to pay for Jessica as well as maintain Michael and me."

"I don't have to pay for Jessica. You can, eventually. With all the money you're earning from your pots."

"Yes, but I was hoping to use that in the future to support Michael and me. Instead of you always having to do it."

"But don't you see? You say you don't want any help with Michael, but if *you* pay for it, pay for the childcare… you know what I mean… And in any case don't push me right out of the picture."

Tamsin did like the idea of paying for Jess herself, a few hours a day, four days a week and the outlay was only during the school holidays. And it had been absolute bliss. Jess was such fun: laughing when she got it wrong, dodging out of the way if Michael flipped, praising him willy nilly.

"A fabulous idea. Where did you find her?" was John's reaction.

For a week now, Brock Cottage had been simmering with activity, sometimes good, sometimes not so good, but always manageable and best of all, Tamsin, despite her hand, had been able to get on with some of her work. Fortunately no more throwing needed to be done, mainly glazing, and she was practically ready for her first solo exhibition.

Michael's toilet programme had gone really well, so much so that Tamsin was annoyed with herself and the system for leaving it until now to implement. Maybe the clinical approach of breaking a skill down into so many small actions had not appealed to warm, down to earth Doris Nokes. Putting an ordinary, everyday routine under the microscope and then re-introducing it in minute and graded steps matched with rewards would not have occurred to Tamsin either.

Jessica came in for mugs of water for her, John and Michael.

"Michael's said Don twice this morning. Just like that. Right out of the blue."

"Really," said Tamsin, wishing instead her son could acknowledge his father in some small way. "Sit down a minute. Michael will be all right with John."

Tamsin wanted to tell Jessica the meagre story of her impoverished relationship with her mother.

It didn't take long. There wasn't much to tell. After Debbie's departure there had been letters. Exotic postcards. Emails. Two or three a year in the early days of their separation, but it had been a long time since Debbie had written *I am going to come home to England and see you.* Or later *I am going to come and see you very soon.* Or later still *I will come one day.* Before her marriage to Robin Tamsin had decided to visit Brazil herself, but then nerves got the better of her. So the marriage went ahead without Tamsin either seeing or sending a wedding invitation to her mother. And then Michael was born.

"That's terrible. I can't believe it. That a mother should leave her child like that... Oh, I am sorry, I didn't mean to criticise... What do I know...?"

"That's all right Jessica. It is hard to understand, isn't it? Since Michael was born, I have never been able to understand it."

"Why do you think she wants to come back now?"

"Something must have happened. Something major. Or maybe she's having a mid-life crisis."

"She wouldn't know a crisis if it broke her nose. A woman like that causes crises, she doesn't have them. Sorry again Tamsin, but honestly... I lost my mum two years ago and I don't know, but I feel luckier than you. I have good memories and bad ones... " Her voice trailed away and she stayed silent for a moment. Tamsin wondered if she was remembering her mother's illness. It must have been unbearable for an only child, and a teenager at that, to witness.

Jessica continued, "But I know she loved me. And being wanted I took for granted. You do, don't you? Want your children? It's nature."

"Yes," said Tamsin and stretched across the table to hold Jessica's hand whose eyes had darkened with tears.

"I still miss her every day." Jessica smiled and touched her tears with her finger tips. "And I know it sounds silly but I quite like crying. It's sort of comforting. The wetness."

Tamsin thought how reassuring it was to have someone share your shadowy corners.

Jessica rubbed her eyes more firmly and sniffed with determination. "But you will see your mother now? That's got to be good."

"Oh yes. I'll see her. And you never know, do you, what will happen." Something like unrequited desire twitched and tightened inside Tamsin's chest.

"Yeah………. it could be brilliant." Jessica didn't sound convincing. "I'd better get back out to Michael and John. Dad will be here soon to pick me up. I am sorry I looked at your postcard but I am glad you told me, Tamsin. When do you think she'll come?"

"I've no idea Jessica. I've packed some pots for The Poundhouse and some for the exhibition. Your dad said he'd drop those off for me at The Arts Centre."

Chapter Thirteen

Robin served drinks from an improvised bar as the invited guests for the preview filed by and then mingled in The Harrow's upstairs gallery, sipping, pointing and clutching their catalogues. Some catalogues were being used as fans, for it had been another hot August day and there was a rich steamy heat rising from The Harrow's restaurant along with the aromas of spicy meat sauces. Some people were leaning out of the open sash windows which allowed the background noise from young revellers on the river and the chatter and music of the more serious drinkers on the terrace at The Black Swan to vie with the canter of a Chopin piano etude spilling from The Harrow's internal sound system.

Robin was glad he had persuaded Tamsin not to have sheaves and bales of straw or apples, however appropriate to her theme. The stark white plinths supporting single pots or small arrangements were much better and took no attention away from their exhibits. Spotlighting allowed the flat shadows of vessels to slide, stretch and bend across the white surfaces. Pinned to the wall, sepia enlarged mounted photographs of local farm life from the Journal's archive modestly directed and focused the perusals of viewers. Next year Tamsin might be able to display her own photographs by using the digital camera he'd given her.

As self appointed barman for the evening, he had said a tentative no to the sweet or dry cider Tamsin had suggested be on offer. Robin smiled to himself. Tamsin had really got into the spirit of her exhibition theme. He wouldn't have put it past her to turn up in dungarees and pink gingham chewing a piece of straw.

"Keep it simple Tams. Let your work do the talking. Don't detract from it."

"No, no," Robin mouthed and wagged his head as Tamsin, posing in profile and with one leg in the air for a photographer, held up the harvest jug and proceeded to pretend to pour from it.

"You were right" her smile now said from the other side of the room as she put the harvest jug back on the plinth and stood stock still with her arms by her side. She was wearing a plain brown dress. Her shining blond hair swung loose on her shoulders. Lovely, thought Robin, a study in brown.

She said thanks to the photographer and came over to join Robin. "I have had three orders so far for harvest jugs. Two from wives as anniversary presents, and they want them to be inscribed with harvest sayings."

Robin felt a twinge of discomfort at the word 'anniversary' but he let her chatter on, trying out rhymes.

"*Our harvest is blessed.* What do you think? Double entendre?" She did a quick twirl. Her eyes were sparkling. Robin noticed how her eye make-up emphasised the sparkle.

"I know this might sound odd, but today is a bit like the day Michael was born."

Robin was gob-smacked. But whatever she meant, his wife was as high as a kite and happy.

"Creation, and all that?" Tamsin waited for a response, but seeing Robin was still nonplussed she added, "Oh, never mind." Suddenly caught by another thought Tamsin frowned. She anxiously looked around and flicked her fingers. "I'll just give Jessica a ring. See if Michael's all right. If I can find my phone, that is." She continued to scout about for her bag, lifted the black and white check cloth on the drinks table and found it underneath on the floor.

Tamsin was shaking her mobile. "I'm sure I charged it up."

"Here, use mine. Why don't you text Jessica instead? In case she's busy with him."

"Yeah, I must make sure I keep it charged up, in case I have to get in touch with Jessica again, like now. Luke's popping into Brock Cottage this evening to see that everything's okay. She's excellent. I am ever so grateful to you for setting it up. Life's been so much better at last." She proceeded to tap out a message on Robin's phone, then gave it back to him.

"Good," he snapped.

"What? Oh, I'm sorry, I didn't mean that… "

"I didn't mean anything Tamsin. I just meant, good."

"Did you see my one photograph? I've been using the camera quite a bit." She pointed to a black and white, blown up to A2 size. It was of a pair of hands holding a jug. "They're Michael's hands. Not my idea. I've copied the idea from Mirtez. He did the same thing with a book."

"What an exquisite image, Tamsin. I want a copy. Actually you should make some copies to sell. It really is a good image. Resonates." He loved it. He'd scanned the photos as a whole, not really taking in their content until Tamsin pointed out hers. It made him catch his breath. Michael's disembodied hands. Calm, gentle, lying on the curved body of the jug. His son's hands. Unused, innocent, still and looking so sensitive.

"Come on. Come on." From across the gallery Jaguar was beckoning them to the window. He was leaning out of the old sash window and trying to tuck his white shirt, which had come loose, back into his trousers. Mollie was with him, and Muriel Lindon. Robin noticed Mollie wasn't smoking. Had she and Jaguar got it together yet? There was a sudden hooting from the river.

"What? Oh look," said Tamsin, rushing over. Cruising by in The Black Swan's ferry *Pen-Ultimate* were John and Lawrence. They were standing up, staggering slightly while holding up a banner saying Congratulations Tamsin Cooper.

"Ahh, isn't that lovely?" Tamsin waved and blew them a kiss.

Lawrence looked a bit of a startled beauty in a long brocade coat, not his usual dissipated camp self, and wasn't he wearing make-up? What a metamorphosis, from grub to butterfly.

Robin's attention was caught by a scattering of guests below on the paving, among them Anna and Joe by the potted palms and just about to enter the foyer. Anna saw them and called up to the window, "Robin. Can I see you for a moment? Down in the foyer."

"Sure." He turned to Tamsin, "What does she want with me?"

"Nothing's happened to Michael has it?" Tamsin called down to Anna.

"No, no, nothing like that."

"Phew." Tamsin came away from the window and shrugged, "Dunno then, but you better go."

And then Robin spied Mrs Green heading in Tamsin's direction. Mrs Green had a woman friend with her.

"Tamsin is one of my mothers. Very talented." The woman friend nodded at Tamsin with weak curiosity.

Why did teachers have such loud penetrating voices, Robin wondered.

He passed Joe on the stairs. "What's it all about?"

Joe rolled his eyes. "Prepare yourself."

Anna drew Robin outside away from the entrance, past tubs of geraniums and anonymous stone busts and to the riverbank. The purple evening water lapped the stone steps.

"She turned up in a taxi about an hour ago. Jessica wouldn't let her into Brock Cottage without Tamsin being there."

"Who turned up? Who are you talking about? Anna?"

"Tamsin's mother."

"Tamsin's what?" Robin inhaled deeply. "That blasted

woman. Where is she?"

"In the car. Our car. She wants to come in. She looks very tired. Very frail."

"Certainly not. Not a good idea at all." Robin shook his head slowly. The exhibition was an important confidence building day for Tamsin. Her comment, likening it to the day Michael was born, was still fresh in Robin's memory. Even if he couldn't quite believe or relate to the comparison, what he did know was that this day was bloody important to his wife and after nearly thirty odd years, her errant mother could wait a little longer.

Anna waited for Robin to say more but continued when he didn't. "Tams did tell me a bit about her mother when we went for a walk in the woods one day. But she didn't say anything about her coming over. From Peru? Brazil nowadays? Isn't she?"

"Her mother, God. I don't know if I can even be civil to her." He felt bloody angry. "Brazil. Yeah. Tamsin did say something about a postcard and the woman coming over but I don't think Tamsin believed it would happen. And you say her mother's here? Now? In your car?"

"Yeah, and wanting to come in to the exhibition."

"Nooo way. Look, I think it's better coming from you, Anna. Go back in and take Tamsin into the cloakroom or somewhere and tell her calmly. God, it was all going so well."

"You never know, it could get even better. Tamsin's been waiting for this moment for a long time."

"Maybe. But not like this. Never like this. Anna, she's been absent for the whole of Tamsin's adult life and most of her childhood. Right, I'll tell you what I am going to do."

A pink moon striated with thin lines of navy clouds was rising behind St Andrew's, and moths seduced by the retro street lamp on the terrace were competing for position. It was still warm enough for the lightest of clothing. Robin, suddenly aware of Anna's bare arms, guided her into the foyer, followed by John and Lawrence running skittishly from The Black Swan's jetty still holding their banner. Robin drew Anna aside to let the revellers pass. He lowered his voice. "I'll take her next door into The Black Swan and only when the crowd upstairs begins to thin and you think the best is over, tell Tamsin that's where we are."

"I think she's hoping to stay at Brock Cottage, your mother-in-law."

"You're joking? I'll see if the Black Swan have a room. Later will be up to Tamsin. But don't tell her her mother's here, while the fun's still going on."

"Where shall I say *you've* gone meanwhile?"

"Anywhere. Make something up. As you asked to see me and not her she'll expect it's something to do with me anyway."

"Catch." They both looked up. Joe had come to look for them and was chucking car keys down the stairs. They twizzled like silver ash keys and plopped heavily into Robin's hands.

"I'll collect the keys from The Black Swan later, or Joe will. We won't be too long I hope. I get ridiculously tired these days." Anna turned and climbed the wide, royal blue carpeted stairs.

Recognising Tamsin's mother was not difficult.

"I've booked you into a room overlooking the river. It has a lovely view." Which of course she would not be able to see tonight as it was already getting dark. "I'm Robin, Tamsin's husband." Robin slid in to sit by Tamsin's mother on the dark oak settle in the inglenook.

"Tamsin? Where's Tamsin? "

"She'll be over soon. This is a big night for her. You've chosen an important day to turn up. Out of the blue."

Robin felt assaulted by the sight of this woman who looked, he was sickened to see, like a sun-dried, older, smaller version of his wife. He didn't want to engage with her any more than superficially. "Can I get you a drink?"

An arrangement of larger than life dirty yellow and rust coloured silk flowers spilled smugly from the inglenook's log basket. Tamsin's mother looked tired in her travel creased clothes: pale green linen slacks and cream jacket.

"How's the exhibition going? Anna told me. I recognise you, by the way, from the wedding photograph."

He hadn't known that Tamsin had sent one. In fact he didn't know they had been in touch about their wedding. He knew there had been, over the years, the occasional email. Very occasional, he thought. Tamsin had rarely spoken about her mother; just enough to fill him in with the stark facts. And he'd added a few imaginative details of his own. "Oh really? What was it you wanted to drink?"

"Uhmm, just water, I think. Still water." She looked defeated. The skin around her mouth was wrinkled and her lips lay thinly set, firmly together.

"Right." He realised he didn't remember her name, neither her married name nor her Christian name and he certainly wasn't going to ask her. Had he ever known it? Usually at this time of night he had a pub sandwich or a take-away. He turned back to her. "I'm going to have a sandwich. Would you like one? I can recommend their pork and stuffing sandwiches."

"No thank you. I couldn't."

There was a medley of musicians in tonight, seated at the long unpopular trestle table at the far end of the bar on the way to the loos. The fellow with the Uillean pipes caressed its apple green velvet bag as he good naturedly argued with the Bodran drummer. Robin heard the Uillean pipe player say, as he joined the long queue to the bar, "You, you're just prejudiced against counterpoint."

Mickey, a tiny but compact lively old man and a Black Swan regular, was sitting sideways at the table next to the musicians and started to swing his feet and knock his heavy gold wedding ring on the table in time to the music as the band began to play again. His hands were mapped with thick, knotted veins. The toecaps of his brown lace up shoes and his wedding ring glistened in the candlelight. Robin guessed he had either a contented, understanding wife or memories, good memories waiting for him at home. On returning to the table by the inglenook without a sandwich or a drink for himself, Robin looked at his watch. He'd lost any appetite he had. It was a quarter to nine. He put down a glass of water and a packet of crisps in front of his wife's mother.

"Look, I am going to take back Joe's car keys and see if Tamsin's nearly ready to come across. Okay?"

Tamsin's mother was stroking the back of her small, tanned left hand as it lay on the table top's shiny dark varnish. He noticed the gold band. No engagement ring. In other circumstances Robin might have felt sorry for this frayed, jet-lagged woman, had he not lived for a long time with the damage she had caused.

Walking back to The Harrow across the terrace Robin saw the dark shapes of Jaguar, Mollie and Muriel Lindon heading for the car park. Jaguar had his hand under Mollie's elbow. Had they got it together yet? And what was Jaguar like in bed, the old bastard?

Chapter Fourteen

The ladies cloakroom with its warm womanly
Arts Centre at the preview of her first ex
background to a scene etched and encapsula
for the rest of her life.

A chain flushed and a loo door opened to reveal Sarah .
shyly smiling in the flat stare of the strip lighting. Tamsin and Anna
had retreated to the loos and were mumbling about the guests and
how successful the evening was, as though they were marking time.
They were awkwardly but unintentionally standing in Sarah's way
as she edged around them to a line of small white low-hung wash
basins.

"Sorry," she said as she splashed her hands and looked at
them in the mirror.

"It's so nice of you to come Sarah. I do appreciate it,
especially… " Tamsin wanted to ask how Sarah was, how she was
coping since the death of her husband, but didn't know how to.
What if Sarah had forgotten her grief for a few brief minutes and
Tamsin's question cruelly reminded her? Even so, Tamsin felt a
coward for her easy avoidance.

"Your pots are lovely Tamsin. Sam brought me… " The
metal casing holding the royal blue roller towel clanked as Sarah
pulled down a clean portion on which to dry her hands.

"Oh," said Tamsin with surprise and immediately
envisaged Sam's muscular physique among her pots. As the heavy
door swung to after Sarah's exit, Tamsin raised her eyebrows at
Anna and queried, "Ohhh?"

"Tamsin, listen." Anna firmly clasped her friend's arm. "I
have something to tell you. It's a bit difficult, uh uhmm … "

"It's Michael."

"No, no." Anna hurried on, "Your mother arrived a little
while ago at Brock Cottage. In a taxi. We brought her to The Black
Swan. Robin has been talking to her. Trying to give you a bit of
space until you were ready… he told me to tell you… "

Tamsin breathed out and froze with attention and thankful
relief that it was not Michael. Her mother, here though. In England.
In Linbury. Postcards, old infrequent letters, the curling, small faded
snap saved by her grandmother tumbled and tangled in her head,
behind her eyes. The odd email, the odd phone call. But this was too
immediate. Too intimate. Face to face. Somewhere nearby was flesh

od and bones and the face of a woman who once had, but no longer, belonged to Tamsin, as her own flesh and blood ld not belong to her when she herself was dead.

The physical intimacy she could not remember sharing with her mother had dispersed into air and oceans a lifetime ago. So who was this, beating in her chest, longing to be let out?

Two women, one sitting on her own slowly breaking and nibbling broken pieces of crisps, the other standing in the entrance of the river door at the rear of The Black Swan, recognised one another, each in her own solitariness. Kin. They looked like kin.

Tamsin subconsciously knew she could not fill this moment with all that she felt. She had to vacate the moment somehow. Dilute it . Weaken its power. Pretend she was not fully Tamsin, not fully here. Deny the intensity. It was not a conscious defence. It had something to do with survival. She hesitated on the threshold of the darkly lit room and blocked the rush of sensations battling to take hold of her.

Thus fortified with denial, Tamsin moved towards her mother, vaguely scanning the flesh that was on view: the face, soft rather than firm, hands, tanned, shiny and elegantly bony with some age spots and two hilly ranges of white knuckles. Her hair, once maybe the same shade as Tamsin's, was now coloured with streaks of light brown and blonde. And it had been blow dried, unlike Tamsin's which flowed freely to her shoulders. Her mother's face looked pleasantly forgettable. Like the many middle aged women Tamsin saw on the pavements of Linbury every week. Except that Tamsin would never forget this moment or the face at the centre of it. But incongruously Tamsin remained untouched in The Black Swan by what she saw, more immediately aware of the darkening blue light from the slot machines swirling sociably beneath the low, yellow, beamed ceiling of the River Bar and the brush of blue shadows across the scene swaying like animate matter, flicking and playing with hairstyles as the band tripped and soared delicately, cradling custom without intruding. And yet, later, every detail of this meeting would invade Tamsin's senses and she would lay them out as if for sacrifice, vulnerable beneath a microscope, ready for her scrutiny.

"Hello. Have you been waiting long?"

"Hello Tamsin."

"Pity you can't smoke. Not inside anyway. Which is a shame." Tamsin pressed her fingers together.

"Do you want to smoke? Don't mind me."

"You can't. Inside. And I gave up when I was pregnant." Tamsin stood awkwardly bending over the table her mother was seated at.

Her mother scrunched a crisp packet. It crackled loudly like static. "You look nice."

Tamsin smoothed down her brown dress. "I rarely wear a dress these days."

"I used not to wear trousers very often. Better for the plane though and … I can't wait for a bath. Robin has booked me in. It was nice of him."

"Do you want to go up now?" Tamsin hoped that she would. She was floundering already.

"Tamsin." Debbie Cabral wiped away a tear with her fingers and smiled feebly but she did not get up. "Don't worry. It's the plane. I am a bit tired."

Tamsin saw her mother as cowering, withdrawing, and distrusted the display of tears. She wanted to get away but was riveted to the spot, towering and growing larger and clumsier by the second. *Mother, mummy, Debbie.* All inappropriate terms of address.

Her mother patted the seat beside her on the settle and said with her head on one side, "You can sit down, Tamsin."

"Okay then." Tamsin pulled out a chair on the opposite side of the settle's table and sat down facing her mother, wondering what had brought her back to England. Could it be she finally wanted to see her daughter? That she had actually come back for her, Tamsin? "Why? Why now?" Something more realistic struck her. Had Ferdinand died? "Is Ferdinand all right?"

Mrs Debbie Cabral started to cry again but the only noise she made was to sniff gently.

Tamsin waited. Something she had done for years.

"He has left me, yes. Is it that obvious?" Debbie Cabral's attempt at a laugh turned into a snuffling noise.

Tamsin felt cold. "After twenty eight years?" The rattle of conversation, odd words, the background noises of the pub circled around before filling Tamsin's outer ear and then skidded and slid across her eardrums.

"For Paula… "

"Don't you think you should rest? And I'll come and see you tomorrow."

Debbie Cabral shook and sighed with a single sob.

"You have come back to England because a man has left

you? It's not that unusual these days. Why? What about your life in Brazil?"

"A man? He was the reason I went to Brazil. Have stayed in Brazil. She is younger, a lot younger. Only a girl, really."

"That's what men do… " Tamsin wanted to say 'mother' to emphasise her niggardly remonstrance but couldn't get her tongue around the word. Her tongue felt heavy and swollen. "It happens all the time…"

"You don't understand…"

"Oh I do… Robin has left me… But I wouldn't leave home or Michael because of it. Surely you have a life in Brazil. Friends?"

"What? But he was here only a minute ago. What, for another woman?"

"No, no. It's complicated." Tamsin went silent. She wished she hadn't mentioned hers and Robin's separation.

"Yes, I did have a best and dear friend but Ferdinand's family, and the Firm, the family business, couldn't be happier now. It proves what they said all those years ago is right. That I am no good for him and threatened their precious business. Not his kind. They were always worried about the money side of things. Robin has left you? I can't believe that. I am sorry. What I meant was, he seemed very fond of you. Earlier. When I saw him. Are you not together then?"

"He *is* fond of me. What about your friend? Wasn't she able to…?" Tamsin recalled Anna's support. She'd even arranged this meeting, thinking how she could make it easier for all concerned.

"Isabelle. Isabelle is Paula's mother. Ferdinand has gone off with Paula, my best friend's daughter. It's hard for her. My friend."

Tamsin blew out a breath, "So that is why you have come back to England? Even so… "

"I wanted to run. Run away."

Tamsin, with the inattentiveness of someone just listening to words and not their meaning, looked under the table and saw her mother's feet neatly clad in fawn suede trainers. She also was surprised to see a beautiful slim walking cane, with a maroon bone handle, trimmed with a brass ring, and shaped like a dandy's quiff, lying on the floor beside her mother's tiny feet.

"When the surgeon said I would need an operation within the next year or so, I took to wearing trousers and trainers and began to have dreams of running… Filling a field with my running. Run and run… "

"You have lost me now. Would you like another drink? Was that gin or vodka?" Tamsin pointed to her mother's empty glass. "Something to eat? A sandwich?" The ice in her mother's glass had nearly melted and by it a slice of lemon curled like a fallen feather.

"No thank you. Some more water would be good though."

Tamsin took deep breaths and steeled herself as she went to the bar for another glass of water and a lemonade for herself.

"Mr Cooper was in here earlier." Tiny Mickey skipped and pirouetted in the queue with his empty glass and made way for Tamsin with a bow and a flourish. The band was having a break, heads down and chatting while concentrating on producing roll-ups for later.

Here she was in a pub she knew well, surrounded by a blurred backdrop of local people, many of whom were familiar to her, and by a river she loved, next door to an art centre holding her earthenware creations. She turned round and there, no more than ten feet away, was a miserable, middle aged woman. A stranger to the pub, to the town of her birth and to Tamsin. Her mother was a stranger, and Tamsin shivered and shrugged as if she were sloughing off a skin.

She returned with the drinks and sat down again, gently pushing a glass across the table to her mother who looked, she knew, like an older, shorter, smaller version of her mirrored self, and quietly said, "I thought you were saying you had come back to Linbury because Ferdinand had left you for your best friend's daughter. What's this about an operation?"

For the first time in ages Tamsin fancied a roll-up. She stared sympathetically at the black sweatband on the wrist of the Bodran drummer twisting and turning, as he bit his fingernails.

"It's the dreams. I kept dreaming of running home. And then I didn't know where home was."

"Home?"

"England?" It was a whispered plea, barely audible. "I need a hip operation… But it's not that… I just want to run. I know it sounds silly… Debbie Cabral put her head in her hands and Tamsin saw her shoulders shake.

"Come on," Tamsin said, "Let's get you to your room. Here." Tamsin picked up the stick and gave it to her mother.

"I don't need it all the time. Just on bad days."

"Have you got some painkillers? For tonight?"

"Plenty." For the first time her mother smiled. "Will you

come and see me tomorrow, Tamsin? After you, he was all I ever wanted."

Tamsin grimaced.

"Nobody liked me here. You were the apple of their eye. They adored you. After you were born they had no time for me. I had brought disgrace on the family and you became their new little girl. I think they were glad when I left. My mother wouldn't let me near you. Wouldn't let me bath you, feed you. Said I didn't know how to be a mother. Wouldn't let me have you when I pleaded. I'd brought Ferdinand around to the idea and… " Debbie was standing now and clinging on to the table. She sniffed and her mouth twisted, trembling in an effort not to cry again. "I suppose it would be different nowadays. Back then the village… "

"You pleaded? No one told me. You wanted to take me to Brazil?" This abortive effort was not what Tamsin wanted to hear about. She could feel the ugliness of a struggle in her heart. Her mother had pleaded but not fought tooth and nail. But she'd pleaded. Why hadn't Tamsin been told? Tamsin imagined her mother running across a field while pleading for her daughter. She looked down at Debbie as she stood up. Standing still Debbie looked sprightly enough, early fifties, still quite young, but when she took her stick she leant heavily on it.

"Look, I have to go." When Tamsin saw the panic in her mother's eyes she responded by saying, "I'll come and see you tomorrow."

"How is the boy? Has he got over his problems yet?"

"No, no he hasn't and that is why I have to go. Come on," Tamsin said gently and put out an arm for her mother and guided her to the reception area and the wide stairs with its sweeping, glistening mahogany banisters.

Overly cheerful and fervent paintings of local scenes looked down on a familiar pairing as, out of step, they climbed the stairs.

It was really dark now. The road home was empty. No warning headlights burst intermittently through the hedges, so as Tamsin drove, she swung her mini gracefully, swerving from side to side along the lane in time to an old waltz playing on Classic FM. She held the steering wheel loosely and sang, "I've got a mother, I've got a mother, I've got a mother I can call *mine. Mine.*"

When she came to the five barred gate at the top of the hill she drew in and stopped. She got out and leant on the gate. A cow grew out of the gloaming followed by four more who gathered behind their leader like ladies-in-waiting. Tamsin stroked a black wet nose. "I have a mother. She might not love me very much but *my* mother does this and *my* mother does that... And my father," she paused for a moment and inhaled the night, "whoever he was," she paused again, "was a wanker. Whoever he was."

Chapter Fifteen

" Peppermint?"

"Tch! No thanks. So how's it going then? With Jaguar? And without fags?"

"Very well indeed."

"So you two have got it together?"

"Nooo. But he loves me. Says he's loved me for years."

"So *you* don't have sex with someone you love?"

"Oh shut up. Anyway *we* don't have much sex do we? It's sort of by the by: accidental, incidental? But you're lovely." She stroked his cheek.

"True. Well, what do you mean? He loves you?" Robin was nervous. To him, Mollie was a lifeline.

"Come over here." Mollie tripped between the aisles of mainly dark wood dressing tables, sideboards and desks with Robin tailing her. A line of their own mirrored images multiplied and acknowledged their progress until they arrived at the far side of the auction room. On the wall beneath a high arched Victorian window were a collection of framed paintings each numbered boldly in black with a stuck on ticket.

"He actually said that when he gets married he wants to do things properly. He waxed lyrical about this old painting when it came in." Mollie pointed to a painting of a man on his knees before a girl. "It's called The Betrothal and Jags has made rather disparaging remarks about his old dad being a bit of a ladies' man. Wants to do things differently, he says. I think it's a bit dull really. What do you think?" She ran her fingers over the lower edge of The Betrothal's gilt frame.

"Yeah, Cecil was a bit of a lech."

"Robin!"

"And Jags is nothing like him. Looks like him but that's as far as it goes. After all, Jags likes this painting."

"Robin!"

"The pose is stiff. It needs a good clean but worst of all the subject matter is whimsical. Very questionable." So had things, as he suspected, moved onto a new and more committed level with Mollie and Jaguar?

"The subject is about a question…" Mollie pouted. "Joke."

"Uh?"

They were in the sale room checking out a collection of

thirteen oil lamps with a reserve of six hundred. Robin thought he could get a good profit from them and they would look perfect in 'Coopers and Son' without taking up much space. One here, one there. Some had brass stems, some had bronze and the shades and bowls were a mixture of plain and floral porcelain and cranberry glass.

"So where does that leave you and me ?"

"Well." Mollie struck a flighty pose beneath the four sombre eyes of the betrothed pair. "Still good friends?"

"But if things are progressing with Jaguar…"

"Very slowly and very nicely. He's deliberating."

"Deliberating? I don't like the sound of that. So what if you are not a good match? In that way?"

"We'll work on it."

"I don't like the sound of that either."

"He's a good man, Robin. And technically I am still a free woman."

"Well, I am not going to quarrel with that."

"I need some chewing gum, I think. Or patches. Peppermints are no good."

"You're a mess without fags aren't you? And… Is that a Ma Lindon effect?" He put his hand on her shoulder.

Mollie shrugged it off. "Careful, Jaguar's about… "

Things could get messy. Very messy on a personal and work level, Robin mused. He removed his hand and put it firmly on her bottom instead. "I love it when you smoke. I like watching you light up, insert it in your holder and that first drag on your lips. Oooh… but sadly, very sadly, I think we should call it a day. Very sadly, Miss Mollie." He kissed her on the cheek and leapt back as though he'd kissed hot coal.

"Helloo… oo." On the other side of the room, visible between the wardrobes and mirrors, were the heads of Tamsin and her mother beneath a chandelier. Tamsin's head was tipped to one side, her eyes were cold and her lips stretched tightly as she smiled a resigned, taut smile.

How much had she and her mother heard? Seen? Had they glimpsed the kiss? No, they couldn't have witnessed anything. They were four cluttered aisles away.

"I was just thanking Mollie for drawing my attention to these… those, over there, oil lamps." He pointed to them, arranged over several pieces of furniture in the centre aisle.

"And to this painting called The Betrothal, would you

know, which Jaguar is all over at the moment. I am just off to have lunch with him. What do you reckon my chances are?" Mollie laughed and Tamsin said nothing, just kept her eyes on Robin's face as he and Mollie weaved their way towards mother and daughter.

"Jaguar?" Debbie frowned. "Hello, Robin." She smiled shyly.

"Do you know him then?" Mollie was surprised.

"Of him. I know *of* him."

"Of Jaguar?" Tamsin looked bemused. "I am sorry. This is my mother Mollie. She's lived abroad for many years."

Mollie offered Debbie her hand. "Well mustn't keep dear Jags waiting. Don't forget to check over the lamps, Robin. I saw a couple of chips on the porcelain bowls but nothing to worry about, I don't think."

Tamsin addressed Robin as Mollie left the sale room. "I am just taking Debbie to look at a holiday cottage to rent for a few weeks. Their booking's been cancelled."

"So you're thinking of sticking around?" Robin's tone was caustic. Some mothers stuck around. Followed their child's every move, welded, attached from birth. Cutting the cord was merely a ritual. Look at Tamsin. But Tamsin was reacting instinctively to need. He knew that, deep down. But coming to terms with it was a different matter. Robin's own mother had left Linbury for a part time job in Yorkshire to be near his high-flying unmarried sister, Christine, after their father had died. His mother's departure had affected him like a desertion. She had not only deserted him, but she also had deserted the family's roots and business; the love of his father's life.

"For a little while. I am not sure yet." The end of Debbie's nose twitched. Just like Tamsin's, Robin was appalled to see. That was Tamsin's mannerism. And then with the tip of two fingers Debbie rubbed the twitching nose, squashing it. Just like he'd often seen Tamsin do. For fuck's sake, they hadn't seen one another for nearly thirty years. The underhandedness and imperiousness of genes.

"But what I came in to ask was... " Tamsin was talking again. "Luke wonders if I would like to join him when he delivers next, on one of his coast runs. We'd start early and arrive back very late. And John is going off with Lawrence to Canterbury, for a few days before Lawrence returns to Paris. Jessica says she'll be fine with Michael but I don't like to leave her all those hours on her own with no one to call on." With reliable help for Michael, Tamsin's proud independence had mellowed.

"Back home they have places for children like Michael …"

"I thought England was your home… " Tamsin turned quickly on her mother.

"Yes yes," Robin quickly butted in. "You go Tamsin. Give my numbers to Jessica. And I'll ring her in the day anyway. She's with him now isn't she?"

"Of course," Tamsin snapped and glared at Robin, her cool mellowness bridling for a moment.

Debbie casually stroked an antique table. "It's lovely. We had all ultra modern at… in… "

"Look." Tamsin got out a pamphlet from her string shoulder bag. "I've made a sales brochure, Robin. Would you like one? And these are for you." She gave him a wrapped packet together with a brochure and price list. "Photographs. Including a copy of the one you wanted. I'll take some brochures with me when I go with Luke."

"Thanks. I'll look at them properly later. Glad you're beginning to get some use out of the camera." He put the packet in his pocket but flicked open the brochure and proceeded to study it. "Umm. Very good. You're going to need a website, you know. You can't run a business without one nowadays. Then they can download price lists and brochures, order, use Paypal. Would you two like some lunch by the way?"

"We haven't really got time. We're a bit late as it is. But thanks all the same." Tamsin turned to her mother. "Sorry. Is that all right with you?"

"Yes that's fine, Tamsin."

As they turned to leave Robin thought they did look like mother and daughter but somehow in reverse, despite Debbie's stick, because it tended to diminish her presence as Tamsin hovered over her.

Left standing in the sale room Robin experienced a sensation of being split in half. Tamsin and Mollie were leaving him on his own, anchorless and going off in different directions absorbed in their own preoccupations. Had Tamsin seen the kiss?

Not wanting company he decided against The Black Swan and bought a pasty and cream slice to take back to his room.

Settled in an old low wooden arm chair, with a can and baker's bags as plates, he opened the hard packet Tamsin had given him. Inside were three photographs. One of Michael's hands, just his hands, lying on his mother's jug, a print of the one in The Harrow. As Robin looked at it, he felt such a loss clutch at his heart. His son's hands evoked such an absence. Robin put it down on the table, gulped a mouthful of beer. The next photograph was in a small silver oval frame. So Tamsin wanted him to put this one up somewhere in his room. He didn't like this one. He drew back from it. She had caught just the head and shoulders of Michael who was looking straight up and into the camera. It gave the impression that Michael was engaging in long eye contact with whoever was looking at the photograph. It was a contrived deceit. Occasionally his teachers and Tamsin had successfully held questionable eye contact with Michael for a few seconds, but it was rare and something he, Robin, had never experienced. Now in his room it unsettled him. Tamsin had caught their son looking up from under his long eyelashes and he seemed to be scouring deep into Robin's soul. The last thing he wanted in his retreat above the shop were Michael's accusing eyes. But he would give the photograph a place for Tamsin's sake. And he would train his own eyes to blank the silver frame.

The last photograph was a surprise. It was almost like a Victorian family pose. Seated ageing father dangling his child on his knee, his young wife standing beside him with her arm on his shoulder. It was of course bearded Luke with his daughter, Jessica, and Michael. Michael was relaxed and lolling on Luke's knee. Jessica was smiling down at Michael and Luke was looking proudly at the camera. Robin didn't like this photograph either. Where were the landscapes? The studio pots? He looked back at the photo. This was the ideal, the so called ideal family Tamsin yearned for.

His room was no longer a retreat and he needed a drink in a public bar.

Chapter Sixteen

"Debbie?" Tamsin's tone was sharp.

They had just left Robin and were in the red mini on their way to look at the holiday cottage in Justleigh.

Debbie turned to look at her daughter.

"Debbie, who is my father?" Seeing what she had just seen in the Auction Rooms had given her a provocative, aggressive courage. Only since her mother's return from Brazil had Tamsin begun to wonder seriously about her father. Who was he? Now, she thought her previous airy fairy curiosity weak, inappropriate. For if she'd known his identity she could have pursued him. After all, she presumed, he surely lived in England and very probably in the Linbury area. Why had she given him only an occasional thought? Why had all her identity angst amassed and then dived, like a cloaked being, a dark mist, around her mother? Until recently, in her imagination, her father, a passionate stranger, had made a brief appearance on the night she was conceived and then vanished into the ether of the universe. But now with the physical reality of her mother: a voice, a face, beside her in the car, he had quietly returned, big time, an incomer. His indistinct face slipped around the edge of her vision and she wanted to know his name, the name of this prodigal father. "Debbie?"

Debbie dragged her gaze from the outside, the fields of corn stubble and into the mini's interior. She pulled down the sun-shield and looked at herself in the mirror. "I've never told anybody." She sat with her knees together, her stick resting against her cream trousers. She snapped back the sun-shield to its original position.

"I am not ….. anybody." Tamsin waited.

"Even he doesn't know. I never told him."

"He doesn't know? For God's sake. Didn't he guess?" So I am as anonymous to my father as he is to me, Tamsin reflected. "He needs to know as much as I do, surely?"

"He wasn't a boyfriend. Nothing like that… "

So he was a stranger then.

"And in any case he wouldn't have believed me. He would have said I was lying. I was a nobody then and he thought he was somebody. Young Conservatives, him and his wife … "

"Wife?"

"Yes, wife. Young Farmers, tennis club, and me a farm labourer's daughter living in a tied cottage. It only happened once after The Bonfire Dance, November 5th, in the park. I didn't like the rockets... he said he'd look after me, in the club house. The next time we met he didn't even know my name."

Tamsin waited.

"Cecil Lindon." Debbie clicked opened her handbag, ferreted inside and closed it again, without taking anything out or looking at Tamsin to see her reaction.

"Cecil Lindon?" Tamsin slowed down a little and then braked carefully and pulled over onto the grass verge by a field gate as she absorbed this information.

Debbie was agitated and glanced behind her out of the rear window.

Tamsin stared at her mother, affronted; not only did she not like Cecil Lindon but he wasn't her type of person at all. And yet, and yet that was exactly what he was, wasn't he? He was her kin. Her skin prickled. She wanted to rub, no, wash him off. "But not only was he married he... Debbie, Jaguar is older than me."

"And now that Mollie is going out with him."

"When she isn't sleeping with Robin... "

Debbie gave Tamsin a look of gloom. "I thought there was something. You can always tell."

"Rubbish."

Debbie slumped in her seat, "What a mess we're both in..."

Tamsin disliked her mother's comparison almost as much as she disliked her innocent attachment to the arrogant Cecil Lindon. She started up the car again, slid away from the field entrance and drove on in silence. Tamsin liked Jaguar. You just couldn't help but like him: harmless, bumptious and kindly, but how unlike herself who was tense, uptight. He was so laid back, and she knew herself well enough to know that that was possibly the last thing people would say about her. Especially at the moment.

"They married young in those days. You were on the shelf if you weren't engaged by the time you were twenty."

"God... He died this year." They were passing Justleigh churchyard where, only recently, Muriel Lindon had wished she'd buried her husband instead of in St Andrew's yard.

Debbie showed no sign that she was surprised. "Dead, huh. As far as I am concerned he died a long time ago. Dead, buried, gone." She brushed her trousers vigorously with the flat of her hand and took a deep breath as though resurrecting herself. She turned again to Tamsin. "You didn't miss anything, Tamsin. Sorry. I can be so stupid. What I meant was… "

"I know what you meant." Unhappily Tamsin was inclined to agree about Cecil Lindon. But say if he had been nice. Everyone wanted a nice dad. Grandfather had been a sturdy, distant and puzzled substitute. Not unkind, but hardly available in the dad-sense. You could see him looking sometimes, trying to make out what made her and gran tick. A nice dad would have unfolded a new life-map of routes and crossroads for her. Even now.

"What about grandfather?"

"I brought shame on him in front of the people he had known all his life. Said I wasn't worth a cow in calf. That was when he was mad. Later after you were born he would look at you and say, 'We don't want you going the same way as your dozy mother.' And he didn't like Ferdinand."

Just as children live with a surprise or two their parents know nothing about, so do adults, it would seem, pondered Tamsin. Now it was obvious, but as a child she had not thought about it. She was not greatly distressed, more insulted, shocked, annoyed by her relationship to Cecil Lindon. Nor was she particularly upset by the new slant on her grandfather. It was just that the news could have been better, less fickle, and could have made more of a life-changing difference to her future, along with the reappearance of Debbie.

Tamsin swerved onto The Green and switched the engine off. "Look, there it is. What do you think?" The cottage was pretty, white terraced, with a picket gate and a honeysuckle arch over the brick path. The door was dark green and its brass number and door knocker gleamed. Attached to the white rendering was a black and gold metal box saying, superfluously, Post.

"The picture of English bliss for you, Debbie," Tamsin flamboyantly announced and wondered who it was who had said, Nostalgia is the whore of memory.

Something about Cecil Lindon used to gleam. Oh yes, he had a cane too, silver tipped, and he used to swing it as he walked the pavements of Linbury, the stick taking on more of a military role than a medical one. When Tamsin got together with Robin she became an acquaintance of sorts, someone Cecil nodded at in The High but not someone whose name he felt a need to remember. Tamsin envisaged the cold, stiff, buried DNA she now shared with her warm half brother.

"Come on," she said gently to her mother as she reached across to open the passenger door. "Your stick?"

"I don't need it today." Debbie smiled, leaving it by her seat.

Suddenly and for some almost unfathomable reason this lack of need in her mother made Tamsin want to weep. A long-held burden had been passed on. Debbie, glowing with relief, stood shrugging and bracing her shoulders by the car.

Once inside the cottage they saw it was furnished with all the necessities, but there was also a certain bareness about it. It had a sort of second-best feel. It was clean, dusted but not polished. The air smelled of recycled dust, moved from here to there and back again.

"A bit musty?" said Tamsin, waving a hand in front of her nose.

"Just needs the windows opening."

"Michael was christened at the church over there." Justleigh's church tower and yew trees were picturesquely visible through the cottage's front sitting room window. "Cecil Lindon is buried in Linbury Church, St Andrew's. Would you like to visit his grave?"

"No. What on earth for? He's irrelevant, Tamsin. It's sad. I know he is your father but Cecil Lindon means, meant nothing to me. What about you? Do you want to visit it some time? I would come with you."

"I was at the funeral, Debbie. With Robin." Tamsin felt weird as that memory encroached and reassembled. But maybe, just maybe, one day she might revisit the club house. And that would be on her own. And Bonfire Night and rockets she would now see in a different light altogether.

Debbie stared at Tamsin. "Sorry."

The garden at the back was cottagey too, like the one at the front: a small crazed terrace with steps up to a lawn bordered with beds of huge white garden daisies and pink hollyhocks. Blue aubrietia crept and scurried along the edges of the lawn.

"What do you think?" How long was her mother going to stay? Did she really mean to see a consultant about her hip? Had she enough money? What about her citizenship?

The love between them had gone missing, somewhere over the Atlantic and the years. But Tamsin knew she wanted her mother not to go back to Brazil. She wanted her here in England. She wanted her physical presence nearby.

"I like it."

"Good." Tamsin blushed.

"I would have to get a job."

"A job? Why? Do you need money?"

"Not desperately, but I would need a job. I have always worked."

"What about your hip?"

"What about it? It depends what sort of job I look for. And anyway, I'm going to have the op, aren't I? I might look for some bar work."

"Bar work? In Linbury?"

"Why, would you object?"

"No, I don't think so, but I am only just getting used to the idea of having a mother around, let alone anything else."

"It would be okay then? I would be welcome here?"

Tamsin, unable to put into words what she was feeling, nodded.

"Oh, I would have to go back to Brazil first, I think. Settle things. Money needs sorting out. Talk to Isabelle. And Paula. I was very fond of them both. Poor Isabelle… My friend, going to be a grandmother to my husband's child. Maybe I won't make a decision about a cottage just yet."

"Oh no, the cottage might not stay available for long… " Tamsin became agitated. Her mother might not come back. She might change her mind. Ferdinand might change it for her. Or was this excursion just to test the water?

"There'll be others." Debbie smiled.

Chapter Seventeen

Jessica waved them off, looking, Tamsin thought, secretly thrilled. She was biting her lip and grinning at the same time.

"Your daughter is lovely, isn't she? Warm and giving, but won't she get bored?"

"Yes. She is lovely. No, she has plenty of college work to do when Michael goes to bed. So don't worry. That's the whole point: to give you a long day out without worry. And we don't have to rush back, once the business is done." Luke wound down the window, checked his rear view mirror, and called, "See you later, Jess." He reversed a little, straightened up and then they sped off up the lane in his white and battered van, sending up small puffs of dust from the gravel in the verge as he did so. "Heaven. I like to be out on the road." He chuckled and unselfconsciously checked his smile in the rear-view mirror. "We are lucky. Wonderful countryside. Roads not busy. Think of all those trudging mindlessly in the city. And how are you Tamsin? Jessica says you've been having a tough time lately. I loved the exhibition. It will have done you a lot of good. Hand completely better?"

"Absolutely." Tamsin flapped her hand for his inspection. "I'm okay. Up and down really, if the truth be known. As always." She wished she could say more positive things about her life, instead of stating rueful truths. But maybe Luke was a bit too positive.

Luke waited for her to say more but she had already turned to look out of the window and stayed silent, listing items she'd brought: brochures, price lists, samples, postcards of her huge harvest jug, with the epigraph *Once a pip and now so fissy* . Had she enough samples?

"How about a bit of music? The Beach Boys suit you? Or The Rolling Stones?"

Tamsin hadn't heard of The Beach Boys and wondered if they were as old as The Rolling Stones.

"You choose."

Music she didn't recognise punctuated their journey and wove the surrounding countryside into a score for drums and guitar. Luke's accompanying, lively slaps on the steering wheel though, did nothing to enhance the performance.

Before they reached the coast road they stopped on the moor at Overbridge and Tamsin got rid of a few postcards and one of her modest sales' brochures and a price list.

Luke unloaded plastic crates full of plastic flagons of cider. "Well done," he said, patting Tamsin on the shoulder. "Did you leave Vi-with-the-big-boobs any samples? Why don't you offer her a couple of cider mugs, on a sale or return basis? Go on."

"Okay." Luke let her go back into the shop with its multi-coloured clutter, on her own. Every bit of space had been used for displays of holiday trophies, even the floor. Tamsin stepped gingerly between the propped umbrellas and parasols, and waited as Vi-with-the-big-boobs scooped ice-cream and served a young boy with a cornet and a box of cream toffees. Tamsin came back out of the little stone gift shop looking very pleased with herself. "Good idea. Vi, is it? She said if she sells them she'll put in an actual order."

"See? There you go. We'll sort you out a good customer base before the day is finished. Coffee? Cappuccino? Special Hot Chocolate, I can highly recommend." Luke pointed to the tearooms on the other side of the green. "We could sit outside. But be warned, their *small* is regular and their *regular* is huge."

There was a slight, pleasant breeze, and Tamsin enjoyed the sensation on her face and in her flyaway freshly washed hair as she waited on a wooden bench under a conker laden tree outside the tearooms, with its predictable but comforting bay window and bubble blown panes.

"How is your mother? It must be lovely to have her home at last, in her rightful place." He stroked his upper lip and pointed at Tamsin's moustache of cappuccino froth while digging deep into his pocket for a clean white handkerchief which he offered to her.

"It's all right, thank you." Remembering what Robin used to do, she wiped her mouth with a finger and licked off the froth. Lovely wasn't a word Tamsin would associate with her recent reunion with her mother. "Gone back. A few days ago. To Brazil, to sort things out. She didn't stay long in the end. It is very unreal." Then she saw Luke's frown and added, "But was better than I thought it would be." She gave an embarrassed sniff when she saw her remark had not served to remove Luke's slightly disapproving frown. She felt awkward. "It is difficult and, I don't know, all so clumsy. But I can't expect anything else really, after all these years, can I?" Tamsin decided not to explain her feelings any further to this seemingly uncomplicated and straight-talking man, who probably saw family ties as laces drawing together and restraining the shoes of generations.

For the last few nights she had lain awake thinking about

Debbie and herself, and had come to realise that if their reunion had been a weepy affair, a breathtaking success, she would now be grieving for the terrible waste of twenty eight years. As it was, a space had been given to her in which she might, at the very least, take time to juggle and readjust her feelings for her mother and grandmother. And, in readiness, outside this space, was a tentative ripple, eager for a new present and future.

If, that is, her mother came back. Lately Tamsin often admitted, to her bedroom ceiling, that she did want her mother to come back. She wanted what had started at The Black Swan on the night of her exhibition preview to continue. And when she'd snuggled into her pillow remembering her gran as all sweetness and light, she had felt guilty and puzzled. She tried to remember her gran being angry, judgemental, but she couldn't. So she'd conjured an ugly mock-up of her gran with a network of wrinkles criss-crossing her face. Debbie's version of events differed from Tamsin's gran's. Whose version was the right one? Poor Debbie. Had she really been too frightened and powerless to stay around Linbury? Had she really wanted to come back from Brazil and fight, in the courts if necessary, for her child? One thing Tamsin knew: she truly hoped her mother would return to England, to Linbury.

Tamsin hadn't emotionally been able to go to the airport with her mother. So she'd used Michael as an excuse. After all, this thing between Debbie and Ferdinand might just be a blip, an expensive mid-life itch. Still there was a child, Ferdinand's child, waiting to be born, and his family. It was selfish, Tamsin knew, to hope, but that is what she did. Hoped.

Their oak timbered hut high in the cliffs was olive smooth, oiled by the hands of the curious over the last century. Tamsin leaned across Luke to peer at some graffiti above his head. Her heart was tired. The graffiti had been neatly incised with a narrow gouge; obviously a premeditated act. The gouge had been brought purposefully to chisel TINA KING WAS HERE. Here with the lingering spirit of the Victorian vicar whose hut it had been. There had been some strange allies in this cell, on the edge of the land by the sea.

"It's so nice to be alone with you at last, Tamsin. I've been looking forward to it all day."

"I am really grateful to you for pushing me to spread my business wings, and it is nice of you to bring me today. It'll make me get on. Especially when Michael's back at school." They had made three more successful stops, where her work had been welcome on a sale or return basis. Luke was obviously liked, had a good and relaxed rapport with his customers, and was well respected. The link between her cider ware and Luke's cider was a good business marriage. It would help her enormously to get repeat orders, commissions and widen her reputation in the craft world, and Luke was obviously enjoying helping her. He had a spring in his step, a bounce in his pony tail. She was aware he was making an extra effort for her.

On their way to the vicar's hut they had passed a church Tamsin was dying to look over. She missed her church crawling days with Robin. Blinking in the sunshine, she'd turned to Luke. "Shall we have a look in the church on our way back to the van?"

"Okay. You're a fan of churches, are you?" He gave her an indulgent hug.

They left the heather covered hut and, with Luke giving her an unnecessary but friendly helping hand, climbed back up the cliff. Pimpernels scarlet and proud sparked the stubble. They stood breathing hard on the top of the cliff. "Straight across to Labrador," said Luke, shading his eyes as he gazed out over the ocean. "The old vicar used to spend hours in his cliff hut. Bring a caddy of tea, tobacco and lots of pipes. He used to write his sermons here, high on laudanum, and thought he saw mermaids lazing on the rocks below."

Tamsin was impressed. "How did you know all that?"

"The pub's got a leaflet. I used to bring Jess here in the school holidays, when I was on a delivery."

"And you've never been in the church?"

"No." He shook his head vigorously. "Should I have done? I used to tell her stories about the wrecks. That was fun. Churches are a bit depressing, don't you think? Anyway, no laudanum for us, just good old health food. What about here?" They flopped down into a patch of grass encircled by heather and emptied a plastic carrier into the space between them. Seagulls squawked and dipped, but succumbed to the swirl of thermals and did not land.

The couple lay back on cushions of heather, sharing meat and apple pasties, and cans. Tamsin started to doze.

"Come on then, young lady." Luke leapt to his feet and stretched out a hand to Tamsin, hauling her up from the grass. "Take me to the church."

What a lovely, lovely father you must be, thought Tamsin

as they turned inland and climbed over a stile, at the far side of the field, where the clink of their footsteps on worn-smooth granite drowned the sound of surf and emphasised the silence of the preoccupied couple.

They tripped down the cobbled path to the Norman church with its eroded zig zags, like petrified stone waves, on the archway into the porch. It was dark in the church after the sunlight outside and they were disoriented.

Luke put an arm around Tamsin. "Steady," he said.

Tamsin gently pulled away although she longed to linger in the warmth of his non-threatening closeness.

As their eyes adjusted, Tamsin saw the light switches by the ancient, hunky, black oak door and went and flicked them on. "It must be Saxon." Tamsin had drifted towards the font. It was pitted granite, roughly hewn, an asymmetrical oval; a little of the earth's swing frozen for centuries in its near roundness. As she stroked the stone she remembered Michael's baptism at Justleigh. It had been a beautiful afternoon, and how pleased they had been that their son hadn't cried. Tamsin remembered her confident pleasure as she'd witnessed Michael's fixation on the dribble of sacred water as it twisted like barley sugar, catching the amber light from the stained glass windows. They were already becoming a family with their exclusively personal ways. Little did she know that this fixation was a sad sign of things to come. But she was in awe that day. When she'd changed Michael's nappy she'd been spellbound by his tiny, red heels, their roundness, and she'd circled them dotingly in the palms of her hands, round and round. She'd wondered where his feet would go in the future. She imagined, at first, over grass, wet grass to the stream and the stone bridge and then further afield, beyond the hedge into what was now Anna's and Joseph's paddock. He'd look around, twist on his little feet and marvel at the height of the trees in the fir wood, tremble at the dark resiny spaces between the slim trunks. A sound might lift him on to his toes, a sound from the sky, a wing, a song. And then, one day, something small and bright would cause him to run forward, further and further, until he was lost and came home crying into her arms. Of course he would trace and retrace the lane. His feet would grow too big for the lane, too big for Linbury, this county even. Maybe he would travel far, his feet sink into distant sand and snow.

But no. It hadn't been like that. Michael's feet never left home alone. Their life was four footprints joined by a fearful cord, which could not be cut. Tamsin rubbed the granite font until it scratched her palms and she felt soothed. But the memory of Michael's heels had been oddly comforting.

Luke was over by the organ studying a small book.

"Look, have you seen this?" she called, pointing to the capitals on the column by the font.

Luke came over. "The mice chew the leather straps on the organ pedals apparently. Yes? What? Oh yes. And it says over there that this was the first church to bring the harvest festival in from the fields."

"Really? I am not surprised. Look, a Green Man. Isn't he gorgeous?" The face was carved in stone, the mouth open, disgorging vines which wrapped themselves around, hugging the column. Robin would love this church. Where was he today? With Mollie?

Luke nodded at a pew end; "There's another. He looks rather grotesque, don't you think?"

"And that one there, looks rather benign." Like you Luke, she thought, with your beard, folksy pony tail and kind face.

"What are they doing in here? In a church? A Christian church? Pagan, aren't they? And rather gloomy."

Tamsin laughed. "Well, so were harvest festival rituals at first. Pagan. I am going to use the motif of a Green Man on one of my jugs one day. One day soon. I like the way they depict us as being part of the earth, its growth and decay. You are coming, by the way, to our Harvest Festival tea in Joe's and Anna's field?"

"Of course. I wouldn't miss it for the world. I was a child the last time I went to one. Harvest Home, they called it. And then it wasn't in the fields, it was in the parish hall on unsteady, as I remember it, trestle tables. And beetroot everywhere. Beetroot stains."

"Just checking, cos I want to order some cider. It is going to be fabulous. It was Robin's idea. There's going to be a band. And I am going to christen my harvest jug. Pour out libations of cider. And Michael is going to help me."

"No problem. You can have as much cider as you want. Libations, eh? And that harvest jug is a precious work of art." Luke stroked his beard while studying her face.

"I think they, the Green Men, are guardians, reminding us of our origins. And yes, some do look as though they are in agony but others… " Her voice with its enthusiasm trailed away as she registered Luke's wandering lack of interest.

"How is Michael getting on with John? Where are the lights?" He scanned around. "It seems odd to me."

"Fine, as you know, you've seen them together often enough. What do you mean? Odd? There, look… "

"Well, you know… " He switched the lights off and they were in shadowed darkness again.

"His being gay, you mean?"

"Well, yes. Doesn't it cause problems?" The door clunked behind them. "Oh, the sun's gone in."

"I don't see why. It has been marvellous over the holidays with Jess and with John. The toilet programme has worked … "

Luke gave her a long meaningful stare.

"He is gay Luke, not a paedophile, for god's sake."

"Sorry. Sorry, I know Jess thinks the world of him like you, but… " As they walked up the path, by the grave of the wreckers with its cream and maroon figurehead, one breast naked and the other covered, a cloud stalked the sun. Tamsin shivered. "Is it going to rain?"

"Three more stops, then how about a drink and dinner somewhere? Jess said we needn't hurry back. I am sorry. I like John too. Where is he at the moment? Gone off with that friend of his? I am just a bit old fashioned, I suppose."

Silently Tamsin agreed with him.

Luke put his arm around her shoulders. It felt nice. Safe. She leant into his ample chest and could hear the thump thump of his old fashioned heart.

Chapter Eighteen

It was late September and in Joe's and Anna's field a picnic waited, fresh from local fields and gardens and kitchens. Old recipe books with dusty, doughy thumb-prints had been taken down from shelves and consulted. Emails had been sent, letters written, phone calls made. Grandmothers and great aunts had been closely questioned. Notes had been taken. And now the field, stretching and gently sloping down to the stream, was flamboyant and busy with colour and chatter.

April was the summer coming and September saw it on its way. Would September be as cruel as Eliot's April, Robin wondered. He used to love the first signs of autumn, but this year the signs filled him with a sense of unease. It was too opulent. Next stop, decay. The trees across the stream leading the way to the Chantry Chapel, where Michael had been conceived in a flurry of carefree love, already shone with hints of saffron and rubies which could only mean slow death after slow death, as flighty leaves fell without a care in the world. The lamb now turning on the spit had, only months ago, gambolled in this very grass. Robin shifted his feet and watched Sam, also lost in thought, brush the carcass with mint and oil and wine vinegar. Sarah came up and put a hand on Sam's shoulder and whispered something in his ear. Nice one Sam, thought Robin. Run with it. With her. He had no time for the predictability of some people, gossiping about the speed at which Sarah had sought consolation, so soon after her husband's suicide. Predictability bored Robin. What did anybody know about what Sarah was feeling? A laugh, a smile, a calm demeanour meant nothing. They could be masks: how you presented yourself to the world. And yet…

People were still coming through the gate with baskets and plastic carriers and emptying them on to Joe's sheet-covered, bunting-decked trailers. Everyone seemed happy, yes, waving and catching up with friends. The band was warming up by softly playing a syncopated version of All Things Bright And Beautiful. This was a special day for Tamsin. The climax to her harvest jug project. Tamsin looked fevered as she fussed, arranging and rearranging the large bellied jug on old style bales covered with red cloths embroidered with galaxies of white daisies. The amber glaze of the jug shimmered and sparkled in the low sun. Beneath the coiled handle and apple tree motif, Tamsin's inscription *Once a pip and now so fissy* was drawing attention and comments. There were pint-sized slipware mugs with man-sized handles and stoneware goblets decorated with minimal brush strokes, depicting pink fuchsias and blue delphiniums. Luke hovered at her elbow. Robin wished he wouldn't. Although she was politely accepting his help, Robin knew she needed her space. Or did she? Was she unpredictable too? She had just joined hands with Michael and Luke, to make a circle with Jessica and John in order to sing Ring A Ring A Roses. When they all fell down, Jessica and John pulled Michael backwards into the grass with abandon, while Luke and Tamsin did not fall but crouched awkwardly in the grass. Robin heard Michael say, "Gen fall down, fall down. Jack and Jill … Pour on water, pour on water. Fire, fire… " and was a little embarrassed. Michael in the usual way of things would have been much too old for this sweet hilarity. At his age Michael should have linked forces with the couple of lads buzzing around like flies, trying half-heartedly to sabotage the event by nicking the odd cake and sandwich from the trailers loaded with pink, thick hams, beetroot jellies and all kinds of seeded bread. They were teasing the dogs too, egging them on to bark madly. They just couldn't keep still and were now racing around the field, grabbing adults as they changed direction and swung around to go and jump in front of the trailer accommodating the band, and mimic the gingham kerchiefed guitarists now soaring into their stride.

"Anna, don't lift that! For God's sake, woman… "

Robin turned round to see Joe on his tractor, shouting and pointing at a plastic barrel of cider Anna was trying to shift, by bending her knees and grabbing it around its middle.

"No, no I'll do that… " Robin called out but he was too late. Luke had got there first.

"Honestly. She will forget she's pregnant." Joe jumped down from the tractor he had just driven into the field for the children to ride on later. He joined Robin and they sat down on the grass to survey the scene. Joe leaned back, resting on his elbows.

"She looks well though, Joe… " Robin couldn't seem to find a position he was at ease with on the grass. In the end he followed Joe's example, but then sat up again, crossed his ankles neatly and brushed some wisps of hay off his trousers with a flat palm.

"You don't mind about the babysitting, do you? Well, Michael-sitting… "

"Sorry?" Robin frowned at Joe. "I don't know what you

mean. You've lost me… "

"I just can't risk Anna getting a head butt from Michael or a shove… "

"No, no I see what you mean now." Robin sighed and rubbed his weekend stubble. "Jessica has been helping out all summer, so Tamsin has had some help. John too, when he's around, but she is beginning to get tired again, now that Jessica is back at college. The school day's so short. Anna's always been great too, but we don't expect it now. I don't know what to do, really. Hey, look at Sam and Sarah… "

Sam in a white singlet, revealing a glistening sun-tanned range of sweet toned muscles, was shunting Sarah back and forth, as they danced and cavorted to the rhythms of the band now in full swing. She giggled, looking not at her partner but at her feet, and submitted as he spun her around and under his arm. Although Robin was sensitive about gossip, he had to admit, he himself was fascinated by this unusual liaison. The age difference for a start. "But Joe, her husband only committed suicide a few months ago… " The protest was mild but then realisation rippled across his face. "Or was this why? Was this already going on? Surely not?"

Joe sat up and moved nearer to Robin. He spoke quietly. "No. Sam's older brother committed suicide. Bullying at school, I believe." He nodded over at Sam. "Reason for his constant working-out I suspect… And his fellow feeling for Sarah. I wish you and Tamsin would get back together. All this doesn't seem right." He looked over in Luke's direction.

"Yeah." Robin looked across to the patch in front of the trailer where more dancers were gathering. An enthusiastic Mollie and Jaguar were among the group. Mollie looked happy, extrovert that she was: bright red lipstick as usual, red checked skirt, and Jaguar reminded Robin of Toad of Toad Hall: a ripe recruit for checks and bow ties, and a hoe-down.

Tamsin had wanted to talk about Jaguar the other day, when she came into the shop, asking all sorts of questions. She even broached the subject of old Cecil. Had he been a good father to Jaguar? What kind of a question was that? Was she getting at his own paternal instinct, or lack of it again? Had Cecil been an honest business man? What were his good points? Was this oblique approach her way of introducing the subject of him and Mollie? But she hadn't mentioned Mollie, and he was sure she knew. He was glad he and Mollie were over, for their intimacy only signalled more diversionary complications for the future. Nevertheless, there was a twinge of regret that he'd brought their light-hearted dalliance to an end.

"Luke selling Tamsin's pots at his other outlets now then? So Anna said. They went off for the day together, delivering, didn't they?"

Robin stiffened when he saw what Joe had seen: Luke taking Tamsin to the already worn dancers' patch. But before they could even get started, a photographer and a reporter interrupted Tamsin and Luke, and was obviously asking for a photo. Tamsin went over and nudged Mollie and Jaguar, and organised a pose for the four of them on the edge of the boppers. Then she ran over to the bales, remembering the harvest jug it seemed, and gathered it in her arms, as if it were a baby. Then she dashed back yet again, this time for a mug which she handed to Jaguar and dragged him to stand next to her, so that she and Jaguar were the central figures of the foursome pose. Why Jaguar? Why not Luke? Or had she got designs on both? The recent gift from Tamsin, the rather Victorian photograph of Luke, Jessica and Michael, flashed before Robin's eyes as irritating as grit.

"Eh? Robin?"

Robin was watching Tamsin smile for the camera as she pretended to fill Jaguar's mug with cider. "Sorry, Joe. Yes they did. Went to the coast. And the moor." He had felt pleased at the time, for it meant it would save him surreptitiously buying enough of her pots from Luke's Pound House to make her sales look reasonable, only to secrete them away in a linen press at the back of the shop. He had asked Luke to swear he wouldn't let on to Tamsin, and Robin believed he wouldn't, but observing them now, dancing together, he was discomforted. Tamsin's style was sprightly, Luke's sedately out of time, always a step behind. How old was he? With his old-rocker pony tail? Quite a lot older than Tamsin. Robin did a bit of mental arithmetic and came up with a useless, anything between thirty eight and fifty eight, but his guess was that Luke was about forty sevenish although his manner made him seem older. Robin was embarrassed. What would people think, seeing his wife and Luke dance together like that?

Tamsin ran to the edge of the dance-patch and kicked off her flip-flops and then skipped back, barefoot, into Luke's open arms, while Robin's own arms were urging him to scoop her up and away, like a beloved child in danger.

"Time to make a move I think." He got up, left Joe lounging on the grass and headed down the slope, in the direction of the dancers.

Chapter Nineteen

The night before the harvest tea, Tamsin made a hundred scones and rolled dozens of dates in marzipan, and dusted them with icing sugar for sweets. During the night the taste of marzipan returned, sickly and cloying. It gave her a dry mouth and she screeched, trying to find her voice. The cottage became a cage of flavourings: the bars were barley sugar and rock, inscribed 'Deborah'; everything was too sweet, too salty, too spicy. She looked around for a main meal and there was none: no bread, no coffee percolating. Everything in the marzipan cottage was over-seasoned, unpalatable. She couldn't swallow. She couldn't lick her lips. Someone told her to set the table and eat every speck. Only then could she get down and leave the table. Tamsin woke with her feet already over the edge of the bed, and, feeling sick, she went to check on Michael. He was sleeping soundly. Was he dreaming too? She stroked his cheek with the back of her hand. If so, what about? Did she figure in his dreams?

She returned to her bed and tossed and turned until the sheet was wrinkly and hard. After the day out with Luke, orders started to come in. Orders she could comfortably deal with if only she didn't feel so unsettled. Now that John was back at school with Michael, Debbie back in Brazil and Jess back at college, she had time but less moral support during the quiet hours of the school day. She had got used to company, and alone again her emotional energy took a dive and sagged. The holidays, with so many comings and goings, good times and bad, had been a rich but shared meal. And everybody accepting the situation had made life seem almost normal.

Tamsin sat up and punched the pillow. Eventually she dozed and this time found herself, yet again, waving to her mother who, as usual, was waving too as her train slid slowly away from the platform. Tamsin had wanted to cry, "No, no," but the muzzle of sleep suffocated her, leaving her gasping for breath. And then the train stopped. It had not, after all, been drawing away from the platform, but had been petering out to a halt as it arrived at its destination. Tamsin's joy though was short-lived, for before her mother could step down from the train, Tamsin woke hearing Michael scream, "Water, water!" He needed the loo. The toilet programme had been a success.

Later in the morning, when she checked her emails, she found there was a short one from her mother: the sentence *I am getting everything sorted* stood out from the comments about the weather and other generalisations. Did her mother mean she was sorting things out with Ferdinand or that she was sorting things out ready to come back to England? Tamsin felt selfish for wanting her mother to leave her husband and come home to England.

"Excuse me!"

"I didn't know this was an excuse me, Robin!"

"It isn't but I will, Luke... excuse you. She is looking gorgeous, my wife, isn't she?"

A perplexed Luke backed off.

Robin took Tamsin gently in his arms and spun her around expertly, haughtily, his elbows and heels flicking nimbly in time to the music.

Tamsin's skirt flared and so did her nostrils. "What's going on Robin?" What was he doing, trying to embarrass her like this?

"Exactly. Indeed I might ask you the same. I think Luke fancies you."

"I think he might well... but what gives you the right to be so rude? So arrogant?"

"You're my wife... "

"Hardly. It still doesn't give you the right. We were dancing, not fucking in the grass."

Luke, now diffidently heading for Jessica, John and Michael who were sharing a blanket, turned around, his eyebrows sky-high.

"Ssshhh." Robin shook Tamsin.

"No I won't ssshhh. Mollie," Tamsin yelled, "do you want to dance with my husband?"

"What?" called back Mollie, looking upside down at the dancers as Jaguar bent her backwards from the waist into a beautiful lithesome arc.

"Obviously not. She is enjoying herself far too much with... " Tamsin hesitated before she added, " with Jaguar."

Robin gripped his wife tightly around the waist and yanked her to him. "And I suppose you'd like to be dancing with Jaguar too. But he's taken, Tamsin. Just remember that."

"Me remember that? It isn't me who needs to remember." She spat out the words.

Robin felt her breath and spit on his cheeks and mouth. He loosened his grip and pushed her away, but immediately stretched out his arms to catch her, as she twisted and nearly fell.

"Get away from me," she hissed. "Just leave me alone." She recovered her balance and threw back her head. "Have you spoken to Michael today? No you haven't, have you? Call yourself a father? Uh."

Everything in Robin, his breath, his stomach, his blood, seemed to drop and drain towards the ground: his arms, his face, his shoulders. "I… I… I think I'll go and get myself something to drink. Can I get you anything?" He scanned around to see if anybody was looking at them and was surprised to see that nobody was. Except Luke, who was sitting on the blanket and staring vacuously through the now skipping limbs of Jessica, John and Michael.

"No thanks. Lu… uke, can you take the bung out of a barrel so I can start pouring cider? Michael, come here. Come with Mummy." Tamsin and Robin turned their backs on one another to go in different directions: Robin to the picnic trailer and Tamsin to her jug's display. "Anna, we're ready."

Anna started to sing, "My work is done, my throat is dry, so slake my thirst with apples won…and cider high…" Her soprano voice floated lightly over the gathering and this spurred on the band to join in.

Tamsin took Michael's hand, kissed it and with it wiped away a tear trembling on her cheek before she drew his fingers to hold, with her, the gritty glaze of the harvest jug's coiled handle. While she took the real weight, they poured cider together into a medley of mugs and goblets. Tamsin's hands shook, for the jug was heavy, and she bit her lip. Luke frowned at Robin, who was leaning against the picnic trailer while nibbling on ham and half-heartedly holding a large hunk of bread.

John, deep in conversation with Sam, seemed unaware that the proceedings had moved onto its climax. Michael grew excited and began to hop as the cider corkscrewed and cascaded from jug to mug. Tamsin, using two hands, lifted the jug higher and higher until Michael was on tiptoe. They were pouring, offering refreshment, and Tamsin loved the delicate hanging quality of the amber cider as it fell, glinting and splashing into the mugs. She felt they were in the middle of some old ritual. Michael jumped and jogged her arm, snapping her in and out of her reverie. The sun shone on his blond hair and she bent and kissed it.

And then most, but not all, of the assembled company got down to serious eating and conversation. Jaguar and Mollie continued to dance while Robin looked on with a crushed expression. Luke, still looking slightly befuddled, got up to join Joe for what appeared to be a good old grumble. Soon their voices rose, vying with the music, and their heads shook, as they grappled with the rights of EU and MAFF regulations concerning the sugar content of cider, the price of calves, feed and milk prices and quotas.

Some of the children started to throw food at one another, and John instigated a game of catch the apple, while Anna lay her head in her husband's lap as he continued to grumble with Luke.

Robin wove his way between the picnickers to Tamsin. "You okay?" Robin put a hand on his wife's shoulder. "You look tired. Sorry about earlier, Tams. But I do think Luke thinks he's got a chance and I don't think… "

"Shouldn't you be more worried about what I think of Luke? Not whether he fancies me or not?"

"Well, you went out with him… "

"On business… "

"Oh, Tamsin. What do you take me for?"

"I like him. He's very kind. Very thoughtful. Very warm… Oh, for God's sake Robin… " Tamsin turned around; someone was trying to get her attention.

It was Anna. "Tamsin," Anna whispered. "Tamsin!" she urged again, more loudly.

Tamsin looked at her, and then at where Anna was indicating with an exaggerated nod.

Michael was holding the huge, but now empty, harvest jug with difficulty and staring straight at his mother. "Pour water mummy. Pour water. Fell down, fell down." The jug looked enormous in his little hands, and it was listing to one side.

"Oh my darling."

"Pour water. Pour water mummy."

Tamsin looked around and then back at Michael. The distance between her and Michael seemed immeasurable. Some people nearby had frozen like statues. The band with a clear view of what was happening wavered to a stop. How could she narrow the gap? Get to her son? Get to her jug, the pinnacle of the afternoon. How could Michael get to her?

"Yes darling, mummy will pour water. Like *Jack and Jill went up the hill to …* " Tamsin sang.

"Fell down, fell down … "

The jug must have fallen on a flint in the grass, for Tamsin saw it float down in slow motion and then rise, again in slow motion, as a multitude of flying, amber fragments before they fell again and lay finally, scattered and still, glistening in the trodden grass.

Now Michael ran towards Tamsin. "Fell down, fell down."

She by-passed him, ran around him to kneel over the pieces: twenty to thirty shimmering shards darkening in the late sun. She picked up a fragment inscribed *Once a pip* and scrabbled around for *and now so fissy*. She matched the two pieces, feeling their subtle, fitful interlocking and then she squeezed them as though she were squeezing life into them. The edges of the broken glaze and fired clay dug deep into her flesh until the blood welled and pooled; her palms opened like dark red flowers.

Michael was on her back, pummelling. "Pour water, pour water mummy."

Tamsin could feel such a strange, dissociated power wringing her hands. She wanted to wring this life, her life out of her son. Slap him all over. "Go away, Michael, go away. Please." She slumped into the grass.

Two men ran towards her, Luke and Robin, but another had already reached her and was taking off his shirt to bind her hands. "You poor girl. Car!" Jaguar yelled. "She's going to need some stitches for these hands."

Chapter Twenty

Linbury and its surrounds were hilly whereas, just beyond Justleigh, the terrain levelled into a massive expanse of flatland and one could see fields, low humpbacked hedges and sky drifting for miles.

Years ago, Sticklepath Respite Centre had been a school for maladjusted boys who were often in the habit of absconding, but they rarely progressed very far because of the flatness and visibility; possibly the reason for the choice of its location. Before that it had been a centre for evacuees and before that an asylum for the insane.

Robin drove into the pebbled, circular turn-around and parked at the bottom of fanned stone steps leading up to a pair of large double doors. He still felt ashamed and humiliated by his over-reaction in the harvest field. Was it his fault Michael had dropped the jug? Was it his fault Tamsin had cut her hands and had to have stitches in both of them? And was it his fault Michael was now in Respite? Had Tamsin caught his fierce tension, conveyed and fed it to Michael? Robin shook his head in puzzlement and disbelief at his own stupidity as he parked, for the second time in a week, in front of Sticklepath House. So far, Tamsin had been unable to visit. Even on Michael's admission day. Robin understood this.

Lawns with wooden seats and flower beds stretched widely in front of the sash windows and to the sides of the grand double doors. A sycamore tree claimed centre place in the grass on the right and straddled the blue, early October sky above. A scattering of fallen leaves lay like lost souls, and a whiff of rust reached Robin from clutches of damp chrysanthemums. There were blue and red chunky plastic swings and idly swinging on one was Michael. Robin was surprised. He had expected his son to be inside the building and under some sort of supervision at least. Robin looked more closely at his son and saw that he was fiddling with his penis through his shorts, with a faraway expression in his eyes. A void, replacing a buried but long remembered sadness, opened up a deep pit in Robin's stomach. At the same time an aeroplane ambling, softly grumbling across the sky, comforted him.

Robin crushed a few sycamore leaves underfoot as he walked over the lawn. "Hello son." Desperately wanting to make some sort of contact he put his hand on Michael's hair and Michael stared up at his father's chin.

"Water?"

A girl nimbly ran out of the front door. "Oh, there you are

Michael. I was wondering where you had got to." She turned to Robin, "Hello. You are?"

"Michael's father."

"Of course. I am Poppy. On duty today, for my sins. Sorry, I shouldn't have said that. He just ran off. I expect he's finding it a little hard to settle in." Poppy waved her arms around her in a random fashion. "But he wouldn't get very far, would he?" she offered with a smile and shrug as explanation.

Poppy was short with dark hair and very dark, flashing eye-linered eyes. Young. But then what was young? Robin was finding it harder and harder to guess the ages of those younger than himself these days. She could be married with children of her own, in her twenties, although to Robin, from her clothes, she appeared to be from another generation, mini skirt with leggings and girly pink pumps.

"I'll take Michael in for his tea. You could join us if you wished, but I expect you would like to see Max first?"

Inside the great house everything and everybody seemed dwarfed by the huge dimensions of the building: himself, Poppy and Michael. The furnishings too which seemed to have been selected primarily for their function: clean, melamine and totally without any consideration for style or originality. Robin wanted there to be deeply polished, courtly oak dressers reaching up to the ceiling, a linen press or two, great mahogany tables, to reflect the moulded ceilings, which could accommodate at least twenty or thirty people. The inappropriateness of it all made Robin feel disgruntled.

The hall was wide and the floor covered in vinyl with a mock pebble pattern. The walls were blue, shiny and washable. Poppy, Robin and Michael stood to one side to let a buxom teenage chatterbox and a patient long-eared black and white spaniel pass. Their wrangling needed a lot of room, and the spaniel skittered helplessly on the glossy floor as the girl pulled his lead with military authority but to little effect and nagged at him. "Come on Feeny. Now don't get in the nice people's way. Has new boy got into trouble Poppy? Tch, tch… "

"A word from Honeymoon and Feeny does as he wants," Poppy whispered to Robin.

"Honeymoon?" Robin raised his eyes in amazement.

Feeny pulled Honeymoon, who continued to shout, out through the door and into the garden. "Now just stop that Feeny. There's no need to be frightened of the big people."

"Yes, that's our Honeymoon. Given half a chance she

would run the place. That's why we've put her in so-called charge of Feeny, who doesn't mind one bit. He's used to it. He's Max's and Linda's - Max's wife - and has been here since he was a pup. Doesn't know anything else. A good thing really. This is normal to him. Whoops, sorry. Again."

"Honeymoon?"

"Yep. She's gorgeous isn't she? Actually," Poppy lowered her voice again to a conspiratorial whisper, "born on... their... honeymoon. Her mum and dad are a bit older than most. Whoops, shouldn't have said that either. Confidentiality etc."

Robin was liking Poppy more and more as each minute passed and she was getting older with each word she uttered. He wouldn't have been surprised if she had reached wise-old-bird status by the time they'd made Max's office. "You can be too p.c. these days. Honeymoon, though... I like that." Robin made a mental note to tell Tamsin.

"We go in here for tea."

"I know. The manager, Max? Showed me around when Michael was admitted last week."

Wafting from the dining room on a breezy aroma of cleaning fluids and warm possets of food came a muffled mixture of sounds - indistinguishable words, the odd high pitched interjection, soft cajoling. Many of the children seemed to be very busy in their own jerky little worlds. If the furnishings had little originality, the children certainly made up for it.

"Sorry. Off you go." Poppy gave Michael a gentle shove and he ran over to the trolley where there were plastic beakers and a plastic jug of milk. An obviously middle-aged woman, because she appeared much older than Robin in her saggy jeans with an elasticised waist, put her arm around Michael in a very proprietorial manner which Robin immediately found offensive on Tamsin's behalf. Her cringe-worthy smile compounded the offence.

Poppy must have noticed Robin stiffen for she quickly said, "That's God's Gift. Has Max told you about her yet?"

Michael was pouring milk into beakers with the help of God's Gift. He kept his eyes not on his father, but in the direction of his father, scanning his clothes, the aura of space surrounding him, and as he did so, he splashed some of the milk onto the floor, missing a clutch of beakers with his aim. Nevertheless, he seemed to be at ease. Robin made another note to pass this positive observation on to Tamsin.

The door to Max's office was opposite the dining room and

slightly ajar. Honeymoon came slip-sliding back down the hall with Feeny, talking nineteen to the dozen.

Poppy tried without success to slow down the pair's progress. "Honestly Honeymoon." Poppy turned to address Robin. "She's obsessed with animals. Well, obsessed with talking to them. Can't stop. Hardly says a word to us, direct. We thought she'd miss her pets, big time. But she doesn't. As long as she's got an animal in tow. Any animal. Talk To The Animals, that's a song isn't it? It's no surprise her parents need a little break… "

"Poppy. Confidentiality!" boomed Max from behind his door.

"Whoops. Sorry," called back Poppy and grimaced at Robin.

Robin knocked on Max's door and went in. Max was grinning. "Confidentiality would kick in if it occurred to her that what she was about to say would hurt someone. So don't worry. We run a loose ship here, and our staff is a mixed bunch. It's the way I like it. But Poppy's a great kid. Laid back as they come. So how are you doing? Nice to see you again. How's your wife?"

"I've come to see how Michael is, really."

"All right. Missing his mum a bit, I should say."

"Oh dear." He would need to play that down with Tamsin.

"But that's all right. Missing people is a normal part of everyday life… "

"Tell me about it… " said Robin. He blinked as a painful image of Tamsin flashed before his eyes, hesitatingly followed by an apologetic one of Mollie.

"But Michael has many threads of his normality here. He still goes to school. Sees John and his teacher. And there are a couple of children from his school on respite at the moment."

"Oh?"

"Yes, a little girl from his class. With Down's Syndrome?"

Robin shook his head and said nothing.

"So it's not all strange for him. Tell Tamsin to go away for a few days while she can. It will do her good. I mean, she can't do much until her hands are better, can she?"

"She's already agreed. Although it took a bit of persuading. Well, a lot actually. She's going to Port Rival. It'll be the first time she's been away for years. Not since her birthday when she was pregnant with Michael. And she's never left Michael since. She's feeling really guilty. And uptight. All the time. So am I."

Guilt, no longer inappropriate and a lame luxury, had

begun to invade Robin's senses since the incident at the Harvest Tea.

"Well, that's progress."

"What, feeling guilty? She always feels guilty."

"No, leaving Michael. Uptight. Yeah, I can understand that."

"You can?"

"Of course; I'd be the same. Life's dealt you a raw deal and it's difficult, and if his parents were not uptight that would be very odd in the circumstances. Uptight is an appropriate reaction. Some of the time at least. Are you going too?"

"Odd? No, I might drive her down though. Driving is still a bit uncomfortable for her. Not a good idea."

"Yeah. Odd. Not to feel tense and uptight a lot of the time. But, guilty? Think about it, Robin. Guilt is a waste of time."

"Coffee or tea?" The grey head of God's Gift appeared around the door.

"I think we'll say tea, Helen. Robin?"

"Fine."

"Thanks Helen, then." When God's Gift's head had retreated around the door like a tortoise's inside its carapace, Max continued, "Sorry about that. But the coffee here tastes like blankets. All milky and skin. I think it's meant to comfort, whereas what we need is caffeine to keep us awake and ready to kick ass,'" he said switching to an American accent.

"Really? Tea's fine with me, and then I should be going."

"Well think about the guilt, Robin. Look at me. Two kids and a wife. All normal, whatever normal is. Luck. Pure luck. And a job I like. Paid. Don't forget that. Now it's me who should feel guilty. But I just look at the kids here through no haze of guilt and some days I could knock the hell out of them. They drive me crazy. Don't quote me on that. And other days I love them. And do you know what? They amaze me. Annie brought tears to my eyes the other day - no speech, paralysed from the waist down and the effort she was going to, to sign "Hello". And her smile when she succeeded. Unbelievable. And your Michael. The joy rippling through his body when he sees something that for some reason means something to him big time. Never mind that we don't understand. Tired, yes. Uptight, yes. You should be. But guilt. Try looking at your son without guilt. Sorry, Rob. What do I know, in the final analysis?"

Robin, now feeling very safe and soothed, had a sudden

urge to confide further in Max about what had happened just before the accident with the jug: tell him about his inner chagrin, but the thought that he didn't know Max well enough to trust him unconditionally caught up with and curbed his desire. But he knew Tamsin would like Max. They had something in common. Something appealing and subversive.

God's Gift came back in with two mugs of tea and a homemade cream sponge. It had been a while since Robin had tasted homemade cake.

"This is Michael's daddy."

"Oh," said God's Gift. "He's a lovely boy. Just needs a little understanding. That's all." She stared at Robin. Her mouth smiled. Her eyes accused.

"All right, Helen."

How could a back and baggy bottom be so self righteous, wondered Robin as she left the room, slapping the vinyl precisely with her neat, small shoes.

"And especially don't let Helen smell guilt. She thrives on it."

"Meaning?" Robin slurped his tea and felt completely out of his depth, but somehow reassured again.

"Well, the trouble you are having with Michael is all your fault for starters. And Tamsin's. All your fault."

Robin looked up sharply only to see Max grinning from ear to ear. "She just thinks *she* knows best. Children are *her* precious speciality and only *she* has the answers. Or so *she* thinks. It takes all sorts to run a little world like this and what would we do with perfection? Eh? God help us. Or do as I do here. I let one of his little helpers rule with a short rein. As long as she doesn't break any of my big rules. But don't feel guilty, Robin. It's a wasted emotion. And try and encourage Tamsin not to, as well."

"I'll just go and say good-bye to Michael."

"He'll be in the conservatory pool. Through the door on the left at the end of the corridor."

Michael, in yellow and orange striped trunks, waist high in the pool, was beside himself with excitement as he flicked the surface of the blue water into sparkling jets. Sound had expanded, was fuller and floated in this languid chlorine filled air. Wonders will never cease, thought Robin. When some water went into Michael's eyes he scowled and spluttered so much that he lost his balance, and Poppy had to come to his rescue. Robin put his hand over his mouth to stop himself from laughing out loud. "Bye

Michael."

Michael recovering his frenetic balance, exploded from the water and smacked the water hard. "Water, water!"

"You can say that again son." Robin waved.

Outside the front door on top of the steps again, Robin breathed in the early evening air and looked around at the flat surrounding countryside. He felt consoled by Max's echoing words and the plain normality of the land cradling and upholding a building which had a catchment of care.

In the car he sent a text to Tamsin to say everything was fine and that he'd ring later about picking her up tomorrow, and one to Mollie thanking her for her message of concern for Tamsin and Michael.

Driving back to Linbury he decided to try and visualise Michael without feeling too guilty. Guilt for him was, anyway, a new experience. And to his amazement the image that popped up in his mind was of a beautiful boy in a swimming pool with a beautiful, black haired young woman in a red bikini. Guilt comes in many guises, he told himself, but undeterred and somewhat pleased with his experiment he wondered what might arise if he tried the same thing with Tamsin. She popped up all right, but was accompanied by a reticent Mollie and a pushy, censorious Luke.

"Bugger," said Robin aloud, and switched on the radio.

Chapter Twenty One

"God's Gift? Honeymoon? Is it a crazy house?" Tamsin fixed her gaze on the cottage wall by the piano and waggled the silky, apparently brand new teddy bear she was loosely clutching in one itchy hand. "Good. No, no. Luke is picking me up to go and have my stitches out. And then he's taking me down to Port Rival after he's dropped me off at Sticklepath House, to say good-bye to Michael. I was going to ring and tell you." Tamsin listened and then clumsily removed the phone, which she was holding in her other damaged hand, away from her ear, and held it out at arm's length for a few seconds. When she returned it, she shouted into the mouthpiece, "No, of course he's not coming into The Centre with me. He'll wait outside or drive around." She paused and dropped her voice. "I could drive myself down to Rival but it wouldn't be a good idea, what with my hands and that. It's very kind and thoughtful of him, Robin." Again she listened and then sighed wearily. "Don't be like that, Robin; I didn't know you were planning to ask me, and Luke said he can always make some belated deliveries on the drive down, so he won't be going out of his way especially for me." She sat down on the bottom stair and each word of Robin's reply seemed to deepen the furrows forming on her brow. She glowered at the teddy bear, crossed her legs and then uncrossed them again with a stamp. "He has. Anyway it's arranged now. I can't muck him about." This time when she took the phone away from her ear she glared at it accusingly. "Oh please yourself," she said with an air of exasperation and slammed it down, while clasping the bear to her chest. "Ow."

Before Robin's phone call, Tamsin had told herself firmly to go upstairs and sort out Michael's long-abandoned toys. Toys which had been lovingly bought, collected, saved, and eventually, with impatience and desperation, given to him, and with which he had never played.

Taking herself to task for procrastination enabled Tamsin to approach the brown boxes on top of the massive mahogany wardrobe, despite her apprehension. As she did so she had surprised herself with a growing curiosity stirred by distance. The accumulation of the toys had taken place so long ago it seemed, and in a world so different from her present one.

Michael being absent helped.

But now, after the phone call, a wave of exhaustion hit

Tamsin and she went into the kitchen. She couldn't face going back upstairs yet, to a bed covered with appealing, impotent toys. Feeling utterly bewildered, she went to the glass-fronted dresser and shook a couple of custard creams from the tin and offered one to the teddy. "No? You don't want it? Oh dear. You won't grow up big and strong." She dumped the teddy on the table.

There was a tap at the window, followed by a knock at the back door. Anna put her head around the door before Tamsin could call, "Come in."

"Hi Tamsin. Have you eaten yet?" Anna was offering two red and green square flat boxes. "Take-aways? Pizzas? Ham and mushroom? Comfort food?"

"Come in, friend." Tamsin chuckled with relief. "I'm suddenly hungry. Oh, you have cheered me up no end." Tamsin leant forward and gave Anna a kiss on the cheek. "Joe not with you?" She peered over Anna's shoulder into the gloom of the night, then pushed the door shut and pulled Anna into the kitchen.

"Gone to a meeting, thank God. He's really annoying me big time. 'Isn't that too salty, too fatty, too sugary? Watch how you lift that.' God, he's getting on my tits."

Tamsin looked pointedly at Anna's breasts and laughed. Everything about Anna was more Rubenesque these days. "Expectant dads, eh. Oh, this is nice." She went and turned on the oven, awkwardly tipped the pizzas from their packets and dropped them onto a baking tray. "I'll warm them up a bit, shall I?"

"Do you want me to do anything while you are away? Water the plants… " Tamsin caught sight of Anna knitting her brows as she eyed the teddy and custard creams on the table without a comment.

"No, it's fine. Thank you though. John is happy to see to things. He's going to be working on some pots so he'll keep an eye on the condition of the opened clay, one of my worries: that it doesn't get too dry. And he has a key for the cottage."

"I haven't seen that Lawrence around here recently." Anna idly fingered the teddy's hands.

"To tell you the truth, I don't think it is going that well. He's in Europe at the moment. John says he can never get hold of him. He's wondering if there's someone else. We don't need knives and forks, do we? Just plates? Actually, he's out with Jessica tonight."

"They're not getting it on are they?"

"No." Tamsin laughed. "I don't think so. What, bi-sexual

you mean? No. I don't think so. No, they're just mates and have gone to The Black Swan. There's a band from Jess's college there tonight. Jessica confessed she doesn't like Lawrence either, and I think she actually wants to match John up with some college totty, as she puts it. But I wouldn't put it passed her to try and fix him up with someone who's as camp as pantomime, she's so thoughtful and young."

"Gosh, she's grown up quickly. Maybe that's why Luke's looking more lost than ever this year. I don't think he can quite believe his little girl's a young woman already. He said as much to Joe at the harvest picnic. I think having a child to think about has tided him over, stopped him from thinking about himself too much, since his wife died. How's your Michael getting on? You managed to see him yet? And the hands?" Anna nodded in their direction.

"Tomorrow. Well both actually: seeing Michael and having my stitches out before I go to Rival. Robin says he's doing fine. I couldn't face going in before. I felt so guilty. Anyway, he's settled in without too much angst, so that's something for me to think about, isn't it ? He can manage without me. And Robin likes the set up. He's pleased. Says Max, the manager, is quite intense in a good way but pretends not to be. Interesting... your theory about Luke. I forgot, Anna, do you want some cider with your pizza? It's Luke's." For some reason she herself was not quite sure about, Tamsin decided not to mention that Luke was accompanying her to Rival.

"Ummm, as Joe's not here. Alcohol's supposed to be banned as far as I am concerned at the moment."

"The odd mug won't hurt. Look at me." Tamsin flung her arms wide. "I didn't drink every day or anything like when I was pregnant, but we did enjoy a drink every now and then and it didn't hurt me... Well... "

A moment of confusion ensued for both women.

"And Michael was not the result of alcohol... "

"No, of course he wasn't. Did you ever worry though, when you were pregnant?"

"Not after the scan." Tamsin smacked her lips with approval and sat back with a satisfied grunt. "That was lovely. I was hungrier than I thought." Again, too late, she realised, when Anna did not reply immediately, what she had just said. Scans were not guaranteed to highlight everything. Sharing the common experience of pregnancy with her friend was, for Tamsin, like catching her step as she slipped on melting ice. "Tch." She made a face.

Anna edged her chair around the table until it was

alongside Tamsin's. "Stop fretting, Tamsin. I remember my mum said that, when she was having me, she used to love going to the ante-natal clinic. Swapping stories of heartburn and painful tits until the day she lined up a large, bumpkin sized salad cream bottle, containing her wee sample, next to a dozen or so ladylike samples in little brown pill bottles."

Using two hands, Tamsin awkwardly poured the cider, grateful for her friend's digression.

"Thanks." Anna slurped a mouthful. "Good old Luke. What the eye can't see... as my mother also used to say. What's with the teddy Tamsin? Is it Michael's?"

"No. Well, yes, but... "

"It looks new. Did he never play with it? That's sad."

"Before you came tonight, I had been bracing myself to sort out Michael's toys. I didn't get very far. It's something I should have done a long time ago. Would you, there's so many Anna, like to come up and see them?" Tamsin scooped up the teddy from the table. "I've tipped them all out onto his bed."

Anna hesitated. "O...kay."

A collection of brightly coloured playthings: soft toys, building blocks in startling primary shades, puzzles, lorries, some still in their boxes, lay as if waiting for something, or someone. The horizontal array made the toys look so exposed, suddenly astonished. Tamsin tossed the teddy down next to a paunchy black and white panda and a pale blue, furry rabbit. The incongruous threesome ogled Anna and Tamsin with dark, unblinking, vulnerable eyes, almost saying, "What's going on?"

Tamsin could see Anna was moved.

"Anna, would you like them? Michael's toys? They haven't been used."

Anna flashed Tamsin a sideways toothy smile but not before Tamsin had seen her friend's eyes splinter with horror.

"Of course not. I'm sorry, Anna. Not thinking again." But Tamsin's insides wanted to cry out, It's not catching. What Michael's got. And yet deep down, Tamsin knew, with an ambivalence, a mother's second nature to be suspicious and fear the contagion of bad luck.

"Tamsin, actually, I would like to take one of Michael's toys. It would be an honour. It really would." Anna moved closer to Michael's bed and began to study the assortment.

"You don't have to."

"No I know, but I want to. How about him?" She picked up

a little black Scottie dog, no more than a handful, and made a display of nuzzling his embroidered red nose on her cheek. "Has he got a name?"

"No," Tamsin lied. "Oh, I am so thrilled you're taking something. Are you sure? You name him. When the baby's born."

"Definitely. We will treasure him."

"Don't tell Joe! Where he came from, I mean."

"What do you mean? Oh yeah, I suppose he is a bit chary where Michael is concerned. Sorry, you know what I mean. No, okay then. Not yet." Anna giggled conspiratorially.

"I know."

There was a trilling from downstairs. The two women cocked their heads on one side. "There's the phone."

"I bet it's Joe," Anna said.

When Anna had gone there was a lull in the cottage, a different, empty lull. The rucksack Tamsin needed for tomorrow was where? When had she last used it? She could not remember, so returned to Michael's bedroom to have a search in the wardrobe, where some items, not in constant use in Brock Cottage, were stored.

As expected, she found the rucksack in the dark confines of the wardrobe on the floor, beneath her wedding dress, and in front of what? Oh, The Dolls' House or as Robin referred to it, The Baby House, giving it its sixteenth century name. It had been so long since Tamsin had seen it that she had completely forgotten about it.

When Tamsin and Robin had been engaged, The Baby House had stood on a bachelor chest at the back of 'Coopers and Son'; a pride and joy, a family heirloom to which an intended new member needed to be introduced. Robin had taken out of the The Baby House a miniature brass bedstead and put it into Tamsin's extended palm, and then swapped it for a spoon-backed chair, and then a marble washstand with painted tiny tiles. Tamsin had been enchanted, especially by the family tales. It had belonged to many generations of Coopers.

"My sister and I could only play with it if our dad was present. He loved it. Used to tell us Once-Upon-A-Time stories about Mr George Hepplewhite and Mr Thomas Sheraton, but the pieces which fascinated me and Christine the most were the dumbwaiter and the whatnot. Christine used to jiggle the dumbwaiter and make it talk, 'And what would you like Lady Jam Tart? A custard doughnut or a turnover?'"

After Tamsin and Robin's marriage, as Christine had not, so far, settled with a permanent partner, The Baby House came to Brock Cottage with the bachelor chest, and had taken up residence in the sitting room: an heirloom in waiting, for its claimant or claimants.

And when Michael was a baby, Tamsin would occasionally come into the sitting room and catch Robin unaware in front of the little house and in the middle of a running, once-upon-a-time commentary, while holding a palm-sized chair or table. Embarrassed, he'd restore the pieces to their positions. Tamsin knew he was impatiently anticipating the day when Michael would be old enough to understand and join in with the Cooper family rituals. But impatience overtook him and when he tried to involve Michael one day, his son's response had been to blank his father, flick his fingers at eye-level, leap into the air with irritation and crack Robin on the chin with his head.

Now, Tamsin removed The Baby House from the wardrobe and determined to reinstate it to its former home in the sitting room. Her, and consequently Robin's, occupation of the cottage had become so narrow in the last few years. Things put away, things not done, a life not led. Tamsin went to bed chiding herself.

Chapter Twenty Two

"What is it with me and hands? And Michael? First the piano. Then my jug." Tamsin studied the light dressings which had been applied after the stitches had been removed that morning. How alien one felt, without the full use of one's hands. Ham-fisted. That was the word. It wasn't only Michael she could not cope with properly. It was the cottage, driving, even dressing was difficult. Was independence ever a realistic long-term goal? Or were the compromises needed during those times of dependence what impelled one towards achieving self-reliance? Having to be grateful to the wrong people? The ambivalence of gratitude when it isn't kindness that is given, but control that is taken. But one day there might be no choice but to lean on someone, anyone. She, let alone Michael, might need personal care. Please God let it be given by the right person, or people.

Tamsin shrugged, as if shrugging off a heavy coat, and went to collect a pair of scissors from the dresser's rickety drawer. She placed them on top of a photograph on the front page of the local newspaper which lay on the kitchen table. She sat down and huffed with good humoured frustration. There was no way she could use the scissors neatly, to cut away Mollie and Luke, and leave herself, pouring a mug of cider for her brother Jaguar, which was what she wanted to do. "Hi Bro," she said to Jaguar. She touched his photographed face. The tingling frisson inside her chest was exquisite. "Mum rang this morning, Jags. She wanted to hear my voice. An email wouldn't do. Imagine that, Jags. An email wouldn't do."

She picked up the newspaper, went back to the dresser, opened the second drawer down and placed the newspaper inside together with the scissors. The cutting-out could be a pleasure saved. She would have to exercise her hands like mad. Use that plastic ball. Maybe swim a bit. The sea should still be warm, and she wanted to be ready to use her wheel again when she came home as well. Tamsin wasn't sure what she would do with the cut-out photograph of her and her brother. All that mattered was that she get the pair of them on their own. To keep as an acknowledged, tangible reality.

Her lack of bustle, her lazy-hazy, dreamy considerations, her limitations, Tamsin relished and indulged. She felt like an old woman whose range of movements had been restricted to a smaller world with fewer choices. And she didn't care. There was something strangely luxurious and liberating about having fewer choices.

She shut the drawer. Luke was due again any minute, to take her to Sticklepath House, the Respite Centre. It was scary, but she could not go to Port Rival without first seeing Michael and where he was living. Sleeping. Sleeping without her.

Robin, bless him, had told her in great detail that Michael was fine in Sticklepath House; not missing her too much, but fine. Max on the other hand, (a bit of a loose canon, but good, said Robin) in an email, had suggested differently: that Michael was missing her, but then that this was normal. Normal? Blissful word. He had sent her detailed emails of Michael's emotional, physical, social and linguistic behaviour. God, but how she was missing Michael. Who needed who most? More to think about.

It had been Robin who had encouraged her go to Port Rival for a few days. She'd argued, but eventually she couldn't come up with any good reasons that would hold water. "All right. Why not?" In fact it was dawning slowly on her, like a threatening cloud, that it was Michael's absence she needed to get away from.

Michael had been with her in a different form these last few days, his absence in the cottage enormous. So enormous did it become, that it mutated into a presence which stood on the threshold of every room, around every door and in whose eyes she saw no past, no future, only now, now. And he demanded it so thoroughly. She saw him looming from all the dark corners. She could hear the rushing of a tap, D flat. And then silence streamed, to be replaced by an expectant hush, her head cocked to one side, listening. The kitchen became a stage waiting for Michael's entrance. Yes, he would come back. Now was an interval or those breathless minutes before curtain-up.

She began to think more and more about their future, hers and Michael's. Soon he would be bigger than her, stronger. He would need to shave. Would she have to do that? Would he still be beautiful? No, she knew that he wouldn't. Not when his bizarrely articulated life began to show in his face, distort his features. As an adult, expressions rising and surfacing in his eyes from goodness knows where might frighten people.

She was going to Port Rival because she had to do something while Michael was away. And there she could visit the gallery again and the sculpture garden: feast her eyes and mind. And then she would come home for Michael. The last time she had been there she'd been pregnant with Michael. Robin had taken her for her birthday.

When Robin rang again, this morning, asking her to change her mind about going with Luke she'd wavered, but then he mentioned he'd seen Jessica and John at The Black Swan last night.

"And who were you with?"

"Mollie… "

"Mollie?" Tamsin yelled down the phone, furious with jealousy.

"And Jaguar. You didn't let me finish."

"Mollie and Jaguar? Uh." The injustice of it all. For the second time in two days, she slammed down the phone only to retrieve it, ring Robin back and say, "I am going to let Luke give me a lift. First to the surgery and then to Rival. Get over it, Robin."

Max was on duty until three and she wanted to see this God's Gift in action. It would only take about two hours for the drive down to Rival. The plan, if she felt reassured by what she saw at Sticklepath House, was to leave for Rival straight after she had seen Michael, spoken to Max and checked out God's Gift.

Did Luke fancy her, as Robin suggested? No. He was a friend who thought she needed a bit of back-up. And a sort of business partner.

"Jess might want to work in a place like this. When she's finished her course, that is. I'll go for a little drive and you give me a ring when you're ready or a text if the signal's bad. Or… " Luke looked at her hands as she held them up to show him.

"Texting might be a bit of challenge, Luke."

"Sorry. Of course. I forgot. I'll come back in about an hour anyway. A lot of cars; do they all belong to staff here?"

"Dunno, but I see you've got your rucksack." As she was getting out of his car she saw Luke's rucksack on the back seat next to where he had thrown hers. She'd expected his battered, white van. And cider barrels and crates, of which there was no sign. "I thought it was just a lift you were offering me. Are you planning to stop over on the way back?"

"Yeah. Thought I might join you in Rival, if that's all right with you? Treat you. Book in somewhere, maybe, and take you out for Sunday lunch tomorrow?"

"Really? I better go in now, seeing as I said about one. See you in a bit."

Luke spun the car around, carefully skirting the rears of a

line of maybe twenty cars or so, and waved through the window as he headed off.

What on earth would she do with Luke in Rival?

Suddenly Tamsin missed Robin. Standing here, like she was now, he would have felt the powerful draw of this house. An ancestral home, red warm brick, flanked by a walled vegetable garden on the left and a lawn on the right, primly presided over by a sycamore tree. There were no children about. They must be at lunch. Good.

Inside she was as surprised and as affronted as Robin had been by all the washable, incongruously low furnishings. The pastel coloured melamine looked odd, and she was strongly aware of the superior high ceiling, looking down on her, causing her to feel small.

"Hi. It's Tamsin isn't it? I'm Max. Saw Robin yesterday. I won't be a minute. They are just in there, having lunch." Max, with a file under his arm and purposefully on his way somewhere, indicated a dauntingly large dining room to the right of the corridor. "Introduce yourself to Helen, and my office, when you're ready, is opposite. Here. Oh, and Feeny's under the desk pining for Honeymoon, who's home for the weekend."

"Thanks. Oh." She had been looking forward to meeting Honeymoon.

The dining room was flooded with watery sunshine entering via floor to ceiling French windows which had been refitted with double glazing. Hadn't this beautiful building got a conservation order on it? Obviously not.

At yellow squat tables in the dining room sat children eating, and talking erratically, not necessarily to one another. Some laughed intermittently. One of the children Tamsin recognised from Michael's school. And in the centre of the room at a trolley stacked with blue, red and green plastic beakers was Michael. A woman stood behind him, close, her cardigan touching him, her hands hovering over his shoulders. In Michael's hands was a white plastic jug.

"Hello Michael." Tamsin's voice was just a whisper. She did not move from the threshold of the door.

When the woman saw Tamsin, she immediately put one hand on Michael's shoulder, as though he were a prize, and then she risked a smile. It was hard to tell if it was a smile of welcome or if it was a smile to seal the status and position she held in the room.

"I think it's your mummy, Michael."

Michael glanced up, saw Tamsin and dropped the jug. He ran to his mother while milk spread slowly across the vinyl like an army digitally moving across a map. He ran straight into Tamsin's arms and whispered into her ear, "Pour water, mummy."

Tamsin crouched to cuddle him while smiling sweetly over his shoulder at God's Gift who was glowering at her. "Sorry," Tamsin said, remembering what Robin had told her about this woman's easy solution for Michael's troubles. "He is lovely, really. Just needs a little understanding. Where is he sitting? I will stay with him while he settles again." There was a bite in Tamsin's tone. She felt crappy. She wanted to take her son home with her. Not abandon him.

"How are your poor hands?" God's Gift retaliated.

In Max's office, Tamsin cried.

"On the house." Max handed her paper tissues and waited patiently as he fidgeted with the mouse on his desk.

"My son shouldn't be here. I should take him home instead of going off to Rival." Tamsin was cross. "How will he know I won't be gone forever?"

"One day you will be, so maybe he needs to practise a little now."

Tamsin took a minute to understand what Max meant, and then was appalled. From Robin's description she hadn't imagined Max to be like this at all. "I think I should report you, for being unprofessional."

"For telling the truth? It was tactless and thoughtless but not unprofessional, and I am sorry. I shouldn't have been so blunt, but sometimes we need to face certain situations." He paused, emanating an assured composure. "Michael's doing okay, isn't he? Helen's a good sort. At heart. She won't let him down. She is very fond of him already. Okay, she tends to get a bit possessive which can be a little annoying, I know. Nor will the others let your son down: Poppy, Jason, Mary, the rest of my staff. And that's what we want, isn't it? That's the main thing."

Meaning I have, Tamsin thought, but didn't say.

"What do you think about the pool? It was his first time in the pool yesterday and his dad was here to see him. Did Robin tell you? Michael loves it. Being in the water. They'll be on a surfboard together next."

"Yes, yes, he did," she lied, realising she had cut Robin short when he had tried to elaborate about his visit to Sticklepath.

Outside it had begun to rain but through sunshine. Rain spots glistened on the window, which overlooked the walled vegetable garden, where long bean sticks rose like a camp of wigwams.

"I think I saw... briefly... from Michael's class... in the dining room, Kylie Simpson, Penny and Roger Simpson's daughter? I thought Respite was for those who could not cope, and..."

"No one can cope all the time, Tamsin. If my wife can't cope with the kids tomorrow morning, then I won't be able to go gliding, and if I go more than three weeks without gliding, being up there... " He pointed to the skidding clouds and the wind chart on the computer screen. "Then I won't be able to cope. You know, being up there Tamsin, everything down here falls into perspective." He looked back at Tamsin as if to monitor her reaction. "I am not being as flippant as I sound." He leant forward and said gently, "You know Tamsin, Mrs Green says you are a devoted, dedicated mum and kept your feet on the ground with Michael's recent toilet programme. Successful toilet programme."

"She did?" Obviously Mrs Green had sent a report. "Really?" Tamsin's eyes were open wide in amazement. "But I did have a lot of support."

"Shows you are coping then, doesn't it, when you can ask for support?"

"I suppose." Tamsin was doubtful, but beginning to feel tremulously optimistic. "But it was Robin who asked for this Respite. It wasn't me."

"So, shows you work as a team then: one pushing and one restraining can help keep a sense of balance. And what's more, Mrs Green likes your pots. Is a real fan. Says you have a feel, particularly for earthenware. That your glazes never lose sight of the earth."

"Eh? No? Wonders will never... And I thought she was being... " She had been going to say 'patronising', but resisted.

"Patronising? I think buying your pots is the nicest form of patronage. Now, you have a good break and we will look after Michael for you."

"I know you will. I feel so much better. I do love origins, like the earth showing through on my pots, and Michael has this piano which I used to love to polish and polish, and wonder where the forest was, where its wood came from. Does mahogany come from Brazil? Is mahogany a tree? Sorry, I am wittering on... " She really did feel so much better.

Max guffawed and held up his hands. "I can't cope."

The sound of fresh laughter erupted from the floor above. "That's the weekend Counselling Course. A few rare mahogany pieces up there. We only occupy the ground floor and the Council, they store archive material on the second floor. Nowadays it's the children who are the beautiful pieces down here, the rich texture of the house."

"One more thing." She felt she could ask Max anything. "And thank you for your time. I worry about Michael in the future. What will happen? Robin, I know for a fact, worries about it too. Should we be making plans now, do you think?"

Max took a deep breath and considered Tamsin. "Well, and this is only my opinion, remember that Michael's future depends on you, his parents, of course and on the government and finances, but more importantly and significantly on the research and developments now going on. And Tamsin, what they are finding and planning is so exciting and changes from year to year, month to month, that any plans you make today will be out of date by the time you need to implement them. So, my advice is, plan as you go. And all the research is for the better. Things are not going to get worse, Tamsin, they are going to get better. Now, off you go."

Tamsin left Max's office re-energised and blew a kiss through the dining room door to the back of Michael's head and then left the building. Would she have accepted screening for autism, if it had been available when she had been pregnant? She guessed that living with the dichotomy, choice and its lifelong fallout might be harder than living with fate. She stood for a moment on the fanning front steps of Sticklepath House and sighed with rare acceptance. She rang Luke without dexterity, and decided to walk down the drive and along the lane to meet him instead of waiting. She had something she needed to explain.

Chapter Twenty Three

In the elegant gallery, embedded in the rocky outcrop of a steep seaside town, were the pots Tamsin had come to see, but it was before an old, fluted glass jug that she stood.

"It's still here then. You were just as transfixed on your birthday when you were pregnant with Michael. Remember?"

Tamsin turned to Robin. "Thank you for bringing me." She touched his cheek.

"Well, I am glad you didn't let Luke drive you down in the end."

"It wasn't right. Fair. I was leading him on to nowhere."

"No, that isn't fair," said Robin. His tone held an echo of faint resignation.

The jug stood high, in a shallow Georgian alcove, to the left of the chimney breast. Tamsin had to tip back her head to gaze at it. It was the light that drew her as it had all those years ago, but it was not the room's light. The huge pots, some of which were displayed on plinths shoulder high, were not diminished and distorted in the curves of the jug, nor was it the clear blue light above the sea which lit the watery sand far below with a pale, thin fragility. The jug in the gallery overlooking the bay held an older light, grey with age, years of it like limp, worn muslin. Its fluted edges were dark, etched with lines of dirt which curved around the body and twisted around the handle; a sweeping handle rising in a loop, lifting the jug's profile even higher, ashen and ghostly.

"He did fancy you though?"

"Maybe. He was a bit fatherly."

"Or like a brother?"

"No, definitely not like a brother," Tamsin said with emphasis.

There was something safe about discussing such intimate stuff in public. The boundaries did not have to be self-imposed.

"And Mollie was definitely not like a sister, was she?"

"Mollie?"

"I like Mollie. Surprisingly."

"It was just a spilling over from friendship. Over now. Though it never, really, even started."

"Apt image…"

"Sorry…"

"But I believe you." Physically separated from Michael,

Tamsin felt a surge of compassion for Robin. "You don't have to go back tonight," she said, meaning it, but then did not know how she would cope if he agreed. There was a sofa bed in the sail loft, but…

"No, I won't stay. I'll go back. It won't take me long. Two hours at the most."

Tamsin was both relieved and disappointed. The car journey down had been wonderful: bold, hard landscapes, flashes of blue shimmering sea, rocky moors, mine shafts, the sudden mellowness of meadows, and snatches of people's lives seen in yards and gardens: children's toys and washing lines. And since BSE and the re-emergence of foot and mouth, cows and sheep in the fields she no longer took for granted. These were precarious times. And then she thought of Joe and Anna. And the new baby. And the offering of a toy, and the acceptance of a black Scottie dog, once named Jet.

"Are you sure?"

"Uh huh." Robin standing behind her rested his chin on her shoulder.

"Do you think Mollie and Jaguar are really suited? *Really* suited? "

"Um." Robin was grudging. He removed his chin from her shoulder and straightened up to his usual height.

"Do you like Jaguar? I mean you've worked with him for years, haven't you?"

"He's a funny old bugger. There's something about him. An indefinable quality."

Tamsin wrapped his answer around her secret and continued to look at the jug while Robin wandered off into the garden. Her harvest jug was so different. This one conceived in sand and fire. Hers? Earth spun on a wheel and destined to be set down on the earth again and again, with a return of refreshment. If it hadn't been for Michael. She grinned at her seriousness, and rubbed together the plasters on her hands. She would take them off tomorrow. Let the sea air get to them, and complete their healing.

The garden had been carefully designed. It ran up a slope with unusual trees, some compact, others spiky, all cleverly chosen to contrast and dramatise, and from which clusters of leaves sheltered, spread, or struck out in stylised poses, like the fronds of the palm near the house. Dark shadows of these fronds deepened the texture of the glass in the massive garden door like an engraving. The blue sky through the trees was as dazzling and jagged as the smithereens of a kaleidoscope.

Robin was sitting on the grass with his arms around his knees, leaning against an oval granite sculpture. Inside the oval were more scooped shapes and triangles, which met and crossed and met again, taking the eye on a complex journey. Great urns overflowed with lush greenery, and exotic autumn roses and trails of intense blue clematis strayed from trellises. Some topiaries were so positioned as to enhance and architecturalise the garden. Tamsin went and sat next to Robin, and for a moment it looked as though she was going to lean against him, a familiar habit she had not completely erased from her repertoire of intimate responses. As she stretched instead, to rub her ankle, her light breasts swung a little, loose inside her puce T-shirt.

"Do you like these pots?" Robin pointed to a series of large shallow saucers fixed, rack-like, into the earth at ever decreasing angles. This arrangement gave the appearance of movement, like flick art.

"They are all right, but I prefer functional pots. Studio pots are okay but there is something a bit sterile about them. More art than craft, I suppose. But the thing you are leaning against. Well... It's just beautiful."

"Is it?" Robin twisted round to look at it. "Oh I know, it's the one you were telling me about on the way down: Mother and Child."

"No. Motherchild." Her eyes were wide open, full of life. "Motherchild," she repeated slowly. She wanted to say more, explain, but Robin had turned away and was peering down the hill, through the gaps in the leaves and between grey stone cottages and their ochre lichened roofs, at a tall, framed oblong of turquoise sea. There were faint reflections in the sky of the peachy sand. A lighthouse regally claimed today's soft waves, and the fishing boats aiming for the harbour were crowned by flotillas of gulls.

"You do need to let go." Robin put a hand over Tamsin's. "A bit."

"Yes, I know. Max was implying the same thing. But Michael is never going to be an independent being." It was the first time she had fully acknowledged this to herself and voiced it. She withdrew her hand and covered her face. "But you. You've never even bonded with him." She wiped her lips and tasted salt from the nearby sea. She sniffed and felt her nostrils incongruously assaulted by the aroma of fish and chips and pesto sauce.

"Bonded, Tamsin. Words. All right. I know. I do love him Tamsin, but I just don't know how to... I dunno... I just don't know what… " Robin stroked the sculpture. It was smooth, metallic on the outside, and had a gritty texture inside.

Tangles of fuchsias grew in the leaf filtered light. The sexy purple and blue flowers matched the colour of Tamsin's T-shirt, and the way the flower heads hung and dangled, pendulously curving in the breeze, appealed to Tamsin like weeping willows and catkins and snowdrops. Why was the pendulous curve so appealing? Like an oval picture frame. Mother and child, the crook of an arm, the protective, the submissive, the wing. A sphere of clay squeezed to an oval before it is rolled like pastry, an egg down the birth canal - an intrinsic time lapse visualised. An offering not yet accepted. And yet to centre the clay on her wheel was to execute the perfect circle. Her mind was whirling like the gulls in the harbour. Then Tamsin remembered someone saying to her as a child that only the mad can draw perfect circles freehand.

"I must go, Tams."

Tamsin let her swarming, chaotic thoughts fade, disperse into the garden, until she could hear the long shush of the sea. A lone gull mewed as it flew up the hill away from harbour.

"Okay."

"Here you are, my loves. Here you are."

"Eh?" said Robin looking at Tamsin quizzically. "Who the hell is that?" He peered at the gate in the garden wall from where the voice had come.

Tamsin jumped up and made her way from the centre of the garden, distinctly feeling an uncoiling sensation loosening her body. And then a white haired woman appeared to float by, outside the wrought iron gate, pushing a pram full of skittering seagulls. Tamsin leaned over the gate as far as she could stretch, and saw shoppers continuing on their way, totally unconcerned about the oddity threading her way down the cobbled, narrow street. No one was staring. Some passers-by were chatting but, obviously from their gestures, not about the birdwoman, who was now disappearing around the corner. "Blimey," said Tamsin.

When Tamsin explained, Robin smiled. "It takes all sorts and it's been one of those days, hasn't it? But I really must go. My time's nearly up in the car park."

"Okay." Tamsin felt a pang of regret.

"It's been nice." Robin gave his wife a kiss on the cheek. "Oh, and by the way. What's with the no-bra? I like it!"

Tamsin quickly crossed her arms across her chest. "It's the hooks, Robin. And my hands are still a bit stiff."

"So you are not a hooker then."

"Go on. Go, if you're going."

Tamsin's laugh accompanied Robin all the way back to Linbury.

Chapter Twenty Four

Tamsin had to admit she felt all right. Perfectly all right. Without Michael. And Robin. She stroked her stomach and looked at the vast, unreliable ocean. There was a big world out there, and all she could see was water as far as the horizon, on which an oil tanker idled. There was a scimitar of sand to her left, appeased by a ruffle of surf, and to her right, the embrace of the harbour wall .

She was standing on the balcony deck of the sail loft in her pyjamas. All signs of sails had gone from the loft, which had been updated in a white and beech minimalist style, very peaceful. Tamsin had slept well and woken thankful. There was drizzle in the air and a shy, overcast sky above. She would go in the water today. She was determined. She squeezed and flexed her hands. The salt would do them good. What would a palm-reader make of the new lines on her hands?

Even though it was early October it was warm, and the water would still be warm after the long summer, but first she would go down to the harbour for some breakfast. Now she felt discord, a strange pang in her chest, a worm of guilt. Because she was enjoying herself? Maybe that was the reason, but also because she had not ever considered taking Michael on holiday, or spending a weekend alone away with Robin. Why not? Michael had never seen the sea. She felt ashamed. Going away with Michael would not be easy, but it was difficult at home. It was difficult anywhere, dealing with Michael. Very difficult. A change of scene, somewhere different for their struggles, might have been good for all of them, as a family.

The air wafting up to the balcony was split by a piercing whistle. A black and white dog was racing to the sea's edge, obviously after a flock of gulls squabbling over something, probably fish guts. Tamsin watched and was amused when she saw the dog give up, having lost all perspective of the distance. The dog turned around and loitered back up the beach, leaving the gulls in safety a long way off.

Having rounded Chough's Point, she lay down in her wet suit on the cliff edge. She looked up at the grey clouds and thought of harvest jugs, not yet thrown but destined for a medieval display, in the window of 'Coopers and Son'. The wet suit was another present from Robin, bought yesterday when she said she might go swimming. He had asked for it to be wrapped in their best paper. They had no ribbon.

"We are a sports' shop, sir."

When Michael had dropped the jug, and it lay in fragments, Tamsin's belief in her son's extra powers was shattered too. His lack of awareness came home to Tamsin so strongly, and awoke a new tenderness in her. Michael was naïve, an innocent like Muriel Lindon said, and this could be a saintly quality in today's society. But innocent also meant ignorant, blameless, a babe in arms. Michael would never be street-wise. On the streets he could fall victim to name-calling, and worse. Michael needed protection, to be surrounded by wise people. People. One person would never be enough. It would be impossible for one person always to be there for him.

Tamsin scrambled along a ridge of rocks. She stood for a moment, poised on the edge of the world, her world, before diving into the sea. She'd chosen a small bay like a basin, a deep pool. She drifted down, down, sinking into green, and looked around her at a silent swirl of dense colour. People talked about a sea change. She could believe this, for here in the marine hush there was the wash of another life, a parallel world, with its own boundaries which needed to be crossed and re-crossed. Choice was involved. Tamsin tingled as she surfaced and scanned the cliff-face. There was a gap at the base of the cliff, like a tunnel. She decided to swim towards it. It was a cave, and about ten metres in, her feet touched sand. The dripping roof was high enough for her to stand up. The tide was going out. The cave was returning the ocean to its bed and, eventually, to another shore. She became aware of how solitary, how small a creature she must appear, and now she was frightened and wanted Michael. The sea could be an enormous, merciless enemy. Tamsin steadied her breathing, saying, "Calm," on each out-breath as she re-entered the water and rose with the element.

Back on the cliff top she towelled her hair. Her phone warbled in its turf nest with a text: "Michael's fine."

She called him back immediately. Dialling a few numbers was easier. She wanted to talk to Robin, hear his voice. "Just wanted to say, Hello, and thanks for the message."

Robin sounded surprised, "I've only just sent it. Yes, he's absolutely fine. Max is great, I think."

"I really did ring to say 'Hello' as well."

"Oh."

A silence followed.

"What was Mollie like in bed, Robin?" Idiot. Fool. She hadn't meant to ask this. She could hear Robin take a deep breath.

"Scintillating. Ten times better than you… except for one thing."

"Bastard. And what might that be?" Was she a glutton for punishment! It was drizzling again, and the sea breeze was like little slaps. She hugged herself with the phone in one hand to her ear. She shivered.

"She isn't you. And to tell you the truth I think she thought she was giving me therapy… Are you all right? You sound cold."

"That's all right then. Therapy. Uh. I have been in the water and actually I am hungry, starving, and I am going to the café on the harbour … "

Another silence.

"And can I ask you Tamsin, are we together, or apart?"

"You left. Remember?"

"No Tamsin, you left. You turned your back on me."

"Because you turned your back on Michael."

"No, Tamsin. I have never done that. I just don't know what to do. How to connect with him. And I am there for you… when you want me."

"I don't really know what to do either, Robin." Her tone was quiet.

"But you do. You are wide open for him. You try every damn day of your life… "

"And look where it has got me."

"On holiday, having left Michael in safe hands and talking to me at the moment. That can't be so bad, can it?" Was he beginning to sound a bit like Max?

"We're struggling. That's where we are Robin, in answer to your question."

"Struggling? Struggling together?"

"Together," she said.

Tamsin was glowing after her cold dip and hot shower back at the loft. The couple in front of her in Alfie's chip shop were studying the menu. There were a few holiday makers dawdling around the harbour: middle aged couples and those with children under school age. The one or two single people walking more purposefully were probably locals. The sun had broken through at last, lending the late afternoon a dozy, contented vibe. The tide was well out, and boats rested untidily on the flesh coloured sand.

"You go first. We might be some time," the man said. A grizzling toddler lay, slumped on the man's back in a sling.

The woman touched the child's nose. "What would you like? Chips?" The child cried more loudly. She stroked his hair. "He's whacked. Needs his bed." She smiled apologetically.

Tamsin was shaken out of her reverie.

Alfie, brisk in his white apron and hat, brandished a chip holder and fish slice at her. "You were miles away too, weren't you?" His thin black moustache twitched as he smiled.

"I was thinking about my son."

"Snap," said Alfie. "Tell me about it. Keen as mustard last year to help. This year… You don't want a job, do you? Teenagers! Where the hell is he? He is supposed to join me after school in the evenings, during the week, and at weekends until the damn season's over at half term. And it was his idea. Said his allowance was crap."

"Fish, chips and mushy peas, please? If that is all right." She didn't want to be a nuisance.

"Course it is darling. Don't mind me. He'll be along as soon as he remembers he needs some money for fags. Small, medium or large. Cod? Your son difficult then? Or does he still behave himself?"

"You could say he's a bit difficult. Small, please."

"Never mind. They grow out of it. Most of them, anyway. Me? I was a right blankety blank blank blank. Look there's our Bertha, which means you can go and sit outside if you want. She comes down twice a day with her pram. Feeds the gulls, which means they don't pester my customers. She might be eccentric but she's a gull-magnet, the saving grace for a lot of fast food and ice cream businesses around here."

Tamsin ducked to look through the shop window, and saw the birdwoman she had first heard when she had been in the garden, yesterday, with Robin. Bertha pushed her pram down the lifeboat's slipway, stood on the harbour bed and immediately became a perch for a mass of screeching gulls.

"Don't they peck her?"

"No. She brings them what they want, you see. Plenty of bread in tins with lids, so they can't go too mad. She likes to ration it, string it out. Sit outside. I'll bring it out to you. You might as well enjoy the only bit of sun we've had today."

"But what about the - Do Not Feed The Gulls! - signs all over the place?'

"The gulls can't read. And Bertha's tolerated by the

council. The locals would be up in arms if she wasn't, you bet. I don't think it makes them any worse. And she keeps them out of our hair for a bit, anyway."

Tamsin went and sat under the red and white striped awning and wished she hadn't left her camera in the sail loft. Bertha looked like a white sculpture, saint-like. Accepted and loved by her own community in which she had her place, a role.

"Oh, for God's sake!" Alfie came dashing out of the shop, leaving the gawping couple behind, who had now made up their minds and were in the middle of ordering. Their child had stopped crying, and was staring in amazement at Alfie's flying white apron. "Lucy, phone the police."

Lucy popped her head out of the next door kiosk, put down her ice-cream scoop and picked her phone out from under the counter.

"Wanker, fucking cunt. Birdshit… " Two lads were yelling at Bertha, as they pranced and ran along the harbour wall. Bertha turned around. One of the lads picked up a stone and threw it. His aim was good. It landed at Bertha's feet. She did not move an inch. Gulls awkwardly took to the air. Bertha fixed her eyes on the lads, still as a statue, her stare as cold and as grey as the sea on a dark day.

The lads stopped abruptly, stuck and shook their middle fingers in the air, and called again, "Wanker, wanker," before disappearing up a shadowy alley, which would bring them back into Fore Street, the one main street in the town.

"Ignorant bastards. They don't come from around here. Typical. Cocky buggers. Think they know it all."

The sound of a siren whipped the air. Then stopped.

"Yep. They've got them. They can't have been far away. Not many places they can run to, in Rival. Thanks Luce," Alfie called out of the front of the shop. "Now I'll just phone my wife. See where my lad's got to." Alfie went into the back of the shop, chunnering, "Look, I am losing business."

The couple with the child had given up and left.

Bertha was making small sounds now, and the gulls were coming back. The fish and chips looked good, but Tamsin was no longer hungry.

"Come on. Tuck in." Alfie came and sat at Tamsin's table. "My lad's in bed. Well, on the bed. What do you do with them? For once I am glad he's indoors though. It's touch and go keeping them on track these days. Lin thought he was out, but when she went up to his room, there he was, three empty cans on the floor and him asleep. I think I am going to ground him after school comes out, this week."

"Looks as though he has grounded himself."

"Uh?"

Tamsin was feeling a little steadier and started tucking into her supper. As she ate, her appetite returned. "This is good. What time does Bertha come down in the morning, and would she mind if I took a photo?"

"Many do, and anyway Bertha's quite unaware when she's feeding her flock. She's out there," Alfie pointed to the sea, "with her husband."

Tamsin pierced three chips, dipped them in some ketchup. "Out there?" She stuck the chips in her mouth.

"She, Bertha, lost her man to the sea. A fisherman. The lifeboat went out, but came back without him. She wailed, over there at the end of the harbour wall, for days, and now she feeds the birds. She belongs here. And woe betide anybody who takes the mick. Or worse. This is her place."

Tamsin chewed more thoughtfully. Alfie's eyes grew watery. His black moustache was wet with sweat.

"Well, another day's play's over. And that's what you call a sunset, eh? You packing up Luce?"

Lucy leaned over her counter. "Yep. I think they got them, don't you? Gave'em a warning, I expect."

The sun was bleeding along the horizon and Bertha was trudging back up the slipway.

"Night Bertha. You all right?"

Bertha's reply was a sad smile and a slight lift of one hand.

"That was lovely. Thank you." Tamsin pushed her plate to one side, and Alfie picked it up.

"You're welcome. And you've got yours to go back to, I suppose?"

"Sorry?"

"Your son?

"Oh yes." Tamsin smiled. And his dad, she thought.

Chapter Twenty Five

In Tamsin's and Michael's absence, Robin could not resist visiting his still warm, newly vacant former home. As he climbed the steps, the cottage struck Robin as unfamiliar; simple. A roses-round-the-door simple. Inhabited as in a child's story book with only one story to tell. And this was odd, for only months ago, life here had been multifaceted, too complicated to take. Fibrous tensions had become deformed as they were pulled in many directions, until they came apart and had split.

Instead of roses there were Michaelmas daisies and late dahlias near the cottage and bordering the steps. Black and red berries trickled through the hedge and, overseeing John's herb patch, heavily seeded heads of sunflowers swayed and acted as rich perches for sparrows. The rest of the garden was steep paddock. He must pay John, for it had only recently been mowed.

It was five-ish. The mini-bus was parked but there had been no answer when Robin had knocked at the granary door.

Once inside the cottage, having used his own key, Robin found himself, unintentionally, upstairs and on the landing viewing Michael's room from its doorway. The abrupt bareness, the basic nature, hit Robin. Its lack of character, identity, seemed to accuse him. There were no embellishments, no furniture other than the bed and huge, gruff wardrobe. No pictures or childish ornaments, no posters of pop stars or footballers on the walls, to take away the dumbness. When his son awoke in the mornings, he awoke to a barren cell.

On the bed lay a scattering of ruthlessly coloured toys. Why? Not amongst them, but on the window sill, Robin saw the blue and red plastic water-shooter Michael had loved this summer, as he'd played with Jessica and John. Resolving to attempt to entice his son into playing with him, Robin rescued the water-shooter. Instantly he recalled the bubble blowing antics, and the laughter, and Michael's dancing eyes as he'd followed flights of rainbow bubbles through flickering eyelashes.

Robin's own father had spent hours with him and his sister, Christine, as children, but more especially with him, his son. What had they played? They hadn't played childish games for sure, but what they had done was to talk, talk, talk. In his father's office, in the shop, by the fire, warm and cosy in the evenings. And then his father had taken him to auction sales to buy pieces for the shop, where they'd competed by guessing final bids. Robin often won by pure luck and was triumphant, but, as the years passed, he grew more discerning and then he was allowed to make selections and bid on behalf of 'Coopers and Son'. He grinned to himself as instinct kicked in and told Robin Michael would surely love the sudden fall and slam of the auctioneer's gavel.

Tomorrow he was taking him out, after school.

"Good idea. What do you think you will do with him?" Max had asked on the phone.

"Not take him home to the cottage. It might give him the wrong idea, as I shall have to bring him back to you."

"I agree."

But what was he going to do tomorrow? He couldn't remember the last time he had looked after Michael on his own, his sixth sense telling him Tamsin didn't trust him, and then the thought of failing her was too overwhelming. So diffidence had overcome him. Or was it idleness? Certainly it suited him not to enter the dodgy world of Michael where pitfalls abounded. Now Robin felt a little foolish. And anyway, what was he thinking? Miss Tamsin Perfect failed their son often enough, and big time, didn't she?

Robin almost sleepwalked along the landing until he was standing on another threshold, looking into what had been his and Tamsin's bedroom. It was light and cluttered: a litter of clothes on the floor by the faded pink velvet chaise-longue, paintings hanging askew on the walls. He went over and straightened one or two, and then was drawn to the collection, above Tamsin's dressing table, of small round and oval frames, some silver, some black ebony, containing miniature portraits and silhouettes; one of his mother, another of his grandfather. None of Tamsin's relatives. On the kidney shaped dressing table, its chintz curtain yanked back to reveal a jumble of knickers and bras in a half-opened drawer, strands of blond hair frizzed between the teeth of a tortoiseshell and mother of pearl comb. More strands were caught in coloured rubber bands and vivid satin scrunchies.

He looked up and saw himself in the dressing table mirror, and coming into view behind him, their bed. His stomach lurched as if he had just peered into an abyss.

The bed had been roughly made, the cream quilt creased and dragged slightly to one side. Robin turned around and slowly went to stand alongside it. He stooped to pull and smooth the quilt gently. He had to lie down. Should he take off some of his clothes? No, of course not. Instead he just slipped off his loafers, leaving them neatly paired by the foot of the bed. He turned back the quilt and pondered. No. He replaced the quilt but took out Tamsin's pillow, and without hurrying, lay down, bunching the pillow beneath his head, and tucking it around his ears, before contemplating the ceiling as if it were a witness with answers. He closed his eyes, inhaling deeply. Home. Home, at last. He spread his arms wide and clasped both sides of the bed, before shrinking back to draw his knees up to his chin and lie on his side. The white painted door, which was Tamsin's main focus when she listened for the cry in the night which might at any time bounce along the corridor, now stood benignly and irrelevantly ajar. He shut his eyes again, blanking out the door, and turned over to face the window.

The pillow smelled of Tamsin: mushroomy, earthy, of night-time scuttling, of damp undergrowth and woods. Robin buried his nose into the plump white pillow and held it there. "Tamsin?" he whispered, his face wet.

A rolling voice, a tenor, singing "Yesterday..." broke Robin's trance, startling him into action. He swung his legs over the side of the bed, ankle-wrestled his feet into his loafers, swept fingers through his hair and knuckle-massaged his cheeks, before niftily sidling over to the window where he immediately ducked down beneath the sill, for there climbing the thirteen steps, with what looked like a brown head balancing on two upturned hands, was John.

Making for the top of the stairs, Robin blinked fiercely, endeavouring to readjust a few perceptions, and come back to the brightness of the present.

"Robin." A shout from the kitchen. "Saw your car."

John was totally unfazed by Robin's shifty appearance from the bottom of the stairs.

"What do you think?" He placed the clay head in the centre of the table and stood back to admire his creation. "Do you think she will like it?"

"Oh. It's a head. For Tamsin?" Understanding dawned. "Oh, it's Michael?"

"It's recognisable then?"

Not to Robin, it wasn't. But it wasn't hard to guess whose head it might be. "The features are good but you haven't quite caught his expression yet." Robin capped the chilly, leathery clay, as yet unfired head with a cupped palm and spent a few seconds meditating with John on what might be the nature Michael's expression. "Tricky," he finally concluded.

"I'll work on it a bit more. Maybe the eyes should be looking down, so you could see more of his long eyelashes?"

"Good idea." Robin allowed the head a few more seconds of his attention, before he changed the subject. "How's Lawrence? Tamsin was telling me… "

"Don't ask," John exploded and then proceeded with another burst, "Consoling a married vicar with three children, in the middle of a divorce and *coming out*, would you believe."

"Good God."

"Well you might say that, him being a man of the cloth, this Dermot, and having to square it with his bishop. *Come out* to his church as well as his family and friends. So Lawrence is on hand, and needed to stay on hand. Apparently. Poor Dermot this. Poor Dermot that."

"Men." Robin stuck his hand up for a questionably empathetic, high five, but John was already studying the clay head again.

"I'll leave it here for the moment. It'll be safe without Michael around."

The two men caught one another's eye and snuffled self-consciously.

Robin cleared his throat. "Actually, tomorrow, after school, I've arranged to take Michael out. Any suggestions?"

"What did you used to do when you had him on your own?" John didn't wait for an answer. "He's no trouble in the car or the mini-bus. Do you want to borrow our CD?"

Robin felt childishly peeved and noticed bristles rise, and the back of his neck cool, at the word *our*. "Good idea, but I could get one myself, for us. A CD." More softly he added, "You are a Godsend, you know. You have made such a difference to things around here."

"Thanks. I love it here. So much going on… "

"What about Lawrence though?"

"It's not been good for a while… It's been petering."

Robin bit his tongue on an obvious Dermotting crack.

"What about you and Tamsin? And Luke? You know… when was it… oh Saturday night… Luke asked Sarah for a date. In The Black Swan, when Sam was having a pee. She was actually out with Sam."

"Bastard." Robin felt an inner gloat at Luke's fickleness.

"And do you know what Sam said, when he came out of

the bog? 'She's grieving, not dating.'"

"Good for Sam. I like the way Sam's keeping a brotherly eye on her. Joe said his younger brother committed suicide. Bullying. The reason for Sam's body building. He used to be slight, like his brother." Robin seethed some more over Luke. "Can't stand the bloke."

"Who? Not Sam?"

"No, of course not. Luke. Asking Sarah out."

"I think he's just lonely."

"Uh."

"Now Sam, if he asked me for a date, I wouldn't be late."

Robin smiled and edged towards the door. It was getting dim in the kitchen, and soon they would need to turn on the light. "Can I buy you a drink? At The Dragon or The Swan? I should be on my way now."

"I'd like to, but I've got some work to do for a Programme Meeting we are having soon."

They both stood by the door, looking back and around the kitchen.

"We have been talking about replacing the school's ancient piano with a portable keyboard, so that we will have the option of removing either Michael or the keyboard when we have to prize him apart from D flat. Jaguar came in today to value it. We're expecting to do well out of the exchange. What do you think? I know Mrs Green has been trying to contact you for yours and Tamsin's input. And also for you to give a second opinion on Jaguar's valuation. Oh, you've got your key."

Robin bent to lock the door.

At the mention of programmes, something clicked. Robin realised he had not caught a whiff of pee when he had been in Michael's room earlier.

They were now standing at the top of the paddock, breathing in the night air.

"I don't do musical instruments. I leave them to the experts. You do seem to be going to a lot of trouble, just for Michael."

"He's worth it. And a keyboard will be much more convenient. So Michael's problem has just made us think about a solution. That's all. No, we are looking at lots of the children and their needs. Not just Michael. For the obsessives, we are trying to nurture socially acceptable obsessions, and starve the unacceptable ones. Like Mrs Dixon, Brian's mother, said at one of our meetings… Were you there? No you weren't… She can take Brian into a café rattling a bunch of keys but not screaming like a police siren every few minutes."

"Do you think we should get rid of our piano then?"

"What do you think? Why not talk it over with Tamsin?"

On the way to The Black Swan on his own, Robin thought, looking at the water pistol he had put on the dashboard, maybe I'll get Michael a mobile of many tiny mirrors to hang in his window for light, more bubble stuff, a body board, water wings, story and rhyme CDs for the car. But not a gavel. Tch, he'd been looking forward to buying his son a gavel. He could see him. A mini Jaguar. "Ninety-five, ninety-five, a hundred, going for a hundred then, first and last time, sold for one hundred pounds." Pity. Then he had a brainwave. Maybe a drum. Maybe two drums. One for him and one for Michael. And maybe, one day, he would take him to an auction.

Chapter Twenty Six

"Have a good time, Mr Cooper."

Nothing like formality to withhold or make an opinion clear. She didn't like him. He could tell. Ginny Smart offered Michael's hand, which she had been gripping tightly, to Robin. She smiled without parting her lips. She let her smile linger too long. Was she expecting something in exchange for Michael's hand? Ah yes. She was putting her trust in Robin and was waiting for some reassurance. Mirroring her smile was all Robin could muster. He accepted his son's soft hand and experienced an uncanny sensation of isolation and, alongside it, a sudden insight. Was this what it was like for a mother being passed her first baby? "You have a baby boy, Tamsin." No 'Mrs' formality there after the prolonged intimacy of giving birth.

Walking back across the playground, this time gently pressing his son's malleable, pink plump palm, Robin felt slightly chastened. Ginny Smart was only doing her best, had his son's best interests at heart and if overly professional to the point of irritation, then this, surely, was better than being too relaxed and taking risks.

Belted and sitting in the front passenger seat, Michael seemed tranquil. Robin looked down at his son and saw a beautiful boy, his hair still showing bleached highlights after the summer, and his china-smooth skin still bronze.

Pupils from Linbury's First School were filtering on to The High in yew green blazers flashed with yellow. They trotted beside their mums, some of whom were pushing strollers and holding on to even more offspring who toddled and teetered in an effort to keep up with their mothers. The family strings wove in and out between the purposefully striding and the aimlessly dawdling window shoppers, who were scanning the ubiquitous lifestyle shops which had replaced many of the former basic food stores. Since the belated coming of the strongly-protested-against supermarkets on the industrial estate, there were now no butchers, no fish shops nor greengrocers in Linbury. A sign, advertising this Saturday's Farmers' Market, swung and flapped on the ivy clad back wall of the Arts Centre, and on the opposite pavement, the dates of November's auction sale were hard to decipher, as the black and white sandwich board had collapsed outside the auction rooms. A swathe of Virginia creeper, already turning a majestic red, stole across occluded windows behind which forthcoming lots were stacked.

A bluster of wind caught a couple of cans from the overspill of a litter bin and sent them rolling across the road. Robin aimed, steering with a slight swerve, and squashed one with satisfaction. Simultaneously his attention was abruptly diverted to Michael who was deftly fast-forwarding the CD player. He had switched on the radio, turned it to CD mode, and was alternately pausing and fast-forwarding. Robin was startled at his son's nimble skill. Michael stopped, at 'The Wheels On The Bus'. It was on John's advice that Robin had purchased the CD.

"Go round and round." Michael smiled at the dashboard. "Mummy."

"Pardon?"

Michael gave no response, but remained smiling at the dashboard and flicking his fingers, and as he did so he rocked back and forwards.

Robin, who had taken his eyes off the road, braked hard at the zebra crossing. Three people, women, were waiting to cross.

"I am not surprised," he mumbled to himself appraising the first two women, and their relationship, as they stepped onto the crossing. He waved. The women waved back and smiled broadly as they swiftly advanced across the road, one clack-clicking in high heeled peep-toed shoes, and the other padding in trainers; Mollie, a Lindon in the making, and Muriel Lindon, her prospective mother-in-law. Mollie looked back over her shoulder and mouthed, "Thanks." The sexy minx. The third had a walking stick and followed more slowly. "Blimey, where the hell did she come from?" It was Tamsin's mother, Debbie. How long had she been back? Back here, in England, Robin supposed for the NHS to sort out her bloody hip. He was aware that his surmise was cheap, but he was unashamed. Did Tamsin know her mother was back? He would be ringing her later anyway .

He drove on with a puzzled frown and around the traffic island, taking the exit parallel with the river, which then immediately began to veer away from the river. In the pocket of land between the river and the road was Lin Park, still mysteriously shiny with laurel and rhododendron and holly, but tempered by brocades of autumnal shades. There were several parking places along the road, and Robin chose one near the entrance. The intimidating double wrought iron gates were more permitting than welcoming.

Michael did not complain when Robin turned off the

engine and the CD's recital came to a curt finish, but he did touch the *on* button and say, "Don?"

"Don? Oh." Realisation dawned. A double realisation. If Michael could acknowledge John, then it must be Robin's neglect, lack of real contact and interplay which was to blame for Michael's inability to name him, his father.

Robin reached into the back seat for the kite he had bought Michael. "Come on son." He held his son's hand firmly as they walked along the pavement, and wondered if it would be all right to let go once inside the confines of the park, but the paths divided and divided again, as they circled rocks and beds, planted and arranged to mimic miniature landscapes: mountains, wooded glades, and ferny waterfalls, which fed a romantic, manageable ravine. Deciding to risk it, he let go of his son's hand, but had to run after him immediately and grab his hand again, as Michael dashed towards a craggy waterfall's flickering tumble. Maybe Tamsin planned her routes more thoughtfully, ahead of time and need. He had a lot to learn.

Robin jumped back still holding Michael's hand, as Michael kicked out at Robin's legs and cried, "Pour water mummy." Robin pulled, propelling him, and they started to run. A small plane flew low overhead. Michael ducked.

"No, no, Michael. It's all right. Look." They had now reached a large expanse of grass, marked by borders of pruned shrubs, in the middle of which was a sandpit with a tier of granite seats and a tall fountain and pool. "Look, look." Robin undid the kite's packaging, wishing he had done this before, to save time, and thus Michael's frustration. Out of the corner of his eye he saw Michael clap and watch him assemble the kite. With a flourish, Robin whipped the kite into the air and ran. "Come on Michael." The kite became airborne. Robin was elated and turned around. "C… " Michael was not there. He'd completely disappeared. In a panic, Robin loosened his grip on the kite. It looped the loop, dive-bombing at Robin's feet. Spinning around to scan the park Robin saw nothing but Tamsin's horrified face.

"Over there." A laughing man, crossing the wooden, humped bridge spanning the ravine, stabbed the air several times. "There. There." He threw his stripy scarf back over his shoulder before he stabbed the air again. "Look. There." He came running up to Robin. "Kids, eh."

With great deliberation, Robin followed the direction of the pointing finger and still saw no Michael.

"In the fountain."

"Oh, good God. Thanks mate."

Obviously delighted to be able to help, the man said, "No worries. I've had three of my own. All flown the nest now. Thank goodness. Good Luck."

Dragging the kite, Robin went over to the fountain. Michael was sitting, tucked under a stepped cascade of shimmering water which streamed down his face. He was soaked through and as happy as Larry, clapping and blowing.

"Out. Now." Robin looked around to see if anyone was watching them. Michael ignored Robin. Robin was embarrassed and grew cross. "Get out now Michael."

"Shower. Shower."

"Shower?" They had no shower at Brock Cottage. But of course. There must be one at Sticklepath House. Michael heaven. He must install one in the cottage. A power shower. He got down on his knees and stretched across the low wall of the pool and across the water, trying to reach Michael. It was too far. Michael would be getting cold. It was October.

"Right." Robin slipped off his shoes and sweater and jacket, dumped them in a pile and rolled up his trousers. After looking around again he entered the pool. There were walkers and talkers about, but no one was paying any attention to this father and son. Not yet anyway.

When Robin tried to lift him, Michael became as stubborn as stone. A passer-by stared and smiled primly. Would they think he was a child abuser, a paedophile? What if a local child went missing tonight, would the police come to his door? What must it look like? "Oh, what the fucking hell." Robin sat down next to Michael. Water washed over him. It was cold but invigorating. "At this rate mate, both you and me are going to need wet-suits. Not just your mum." Something hard was sticking into his hip. He hunched up his shoulder in order to reach into his pocket where he found the water pistol he'd rescued from Michael's window sill. He filled it and squirted a barrel load at Michael, whose eyes widened like an owl's.

"Mummy. Pour water mummy." Michael double-squinted beneath waterlogged eyelashes.

"Once upon a time there was a daddy called Robin Cooper, and a mummy called Tamsin Cooper, and then there was Michael… "

And then something unusual and unexpected occurred. A fully fledged glance passed between Robin and Michael. Or was it a fluke; a coincidence, an accident of passing glances on a collision course?

"I dunno son. Fucking bonding."

"Fucking bonding. Fucking bonding."

"Michael? Right, young man. It's a choice between pneumonia or child abuse." He picked up dripping, screaming Michael and tucked him under his arm, got out of the fountain and wrapped his soaked-to-the-skin son in his sweater and jacket. He slipped on his shoes and strode towards the park entrance and the car, glaring defiantly at every onlooker. Not one reached for a mobile phone. But of course they might take the car registration number. What the hell. A police cell might be peaceful and take away responsibilities.

Michael pressed the radio button. And was happy again. Robin noticed that he too, was not exactly unhappy. Snug with the car heater on, and elated by his recent, new experience, Robin took perverse pleasure in hoping that God's Gift would be on duty, when they arrived back, dripping and drenched, at Sticklepath House.

Chapter Twenty Seven

And there was her best friend, striding along Harbour Road in the mist towards the sail loft, having parked his car in the square behind Alfie's Chippie.

In this unfamiliar setting Tamsin saw Robin anew, as he emerged from the surrounding mist, clear and separate, yet so familiar, having the family-face, and warming her heart.

Last night when her mother rang to say she was back in Linbury, and had seen Robin with Michael together in the car, Tamsin had wept.

"I'll help too. I won't be much help but I'll do what I can," her mother had said. "Still, I don't expect I can do any worse than you and Robin," she'd added, rather too pertinently for Tamsin's liking. People cutting to the quick was something Tamsin wasn't used to. Did people walk on eggshells around her? But Max bluntly pointing out her mortality, and her mother's comment, were timely. Or was she tuning in more to other people these days: ready to hear what they were saying?

But uppermost in Tamsin's heart was the image of Robin and Michael sitting side by side, and Tamsin had felt an overdue wash of relief. To have Robin by Michael's side meant so much. And together, they would all be a great deal stronger.

With her out of the way in Rival, Robin had got on with it. Maybe at home, with her hovering over his every move and gesture, he had felt a pressure to act in a way he could not. He'd rung and told her about the incidents in the park going from good, to bad, to worse.

"Just another normal day out with Michael then!" She'd laughed and realised that their life was normal: normal for her, Robin and Michael.

Being away from Brock Cottage, being physically distant, even for just a few days, had given Tamsin a broader perspective, a longer view. For Tamsin, being objective was scary. It meant loosening the reins, opening the floodgates to criticism, losing a little control, losing control of something or somebody she still needed to hold close. Robin, she had noticed, had the ability to be both subjective and objective.

In Rival, surprise that Robin had spiritually stayed with her for so long grew and lodged. And it was to Rival that he was coming back, coming back to her physically. Was she waiting for a lover?

That was what it felt like as she faced the door he would enter. She heard him on the outside wooden steps leading up to the loft.

By the window in the sail loft standing side by side but not touching, the couple looked out on to a white blur of sea and sky. Three days ago when Tamsin had been in the sea, autumn had been recalling summer; today it was sniffing winter. They were cocooned.

"I've been thinking," Tamsin said.

"Don't. You think too much. And analyse."

"Do I?"

"Come here." He reached out for her and drew her close, tipping her head slightly until it rested on his shoulder. He stroked her long hair and studied a tanned pattern on her bare feet.

Tamsin felt she ought to say something. "Do you want to go into the bedroom?"

"Do you mean, do I want to go into the bedroom or is it that you want us to go into the bedroom together?"

"Stop playing about Robin, of course I mean us. Dope."

"No. I want to just sit here with you on the sofa." Still holding her, he nodded at the sofa and then guided them across the room.

"These are good." He bent down to scan a scatter of photographs, showing church roof bosses and carved oak bench ends, which lay on the glass coffee table. "Green Men? Oh, and that birdwoman?"

"Yeah. Bertha. And the Green Men are from the church over at Morwenna. I want to use a compilation of designs on a jug when I get back."

"That's great. I am glad the camera's come in useful." He put the photographs down and flopped on to the sofa, leaning back with a contented sigh.

Tamsin followed suit, and in silence they listened to one another's breathing. Tamsin rubbed her feet against each another.

"You're cold. Your feet are cold. Where're your socks?"

Tamsin pulled, from behind a cushion, a pair of angora pink knee-high woolly socks. She let Robin kneel on the beech floorboards and put them on for her. When he had pulled them up to her knees, he took one of her feet and through the wooliness massaged it. Then he did the same with the other foot.

Tamsin felt the weight of a debt. She owed Robin.

"The stronger we are, the stronger we will be for Michael." Robin smoothed the socks to fit her calves.

"That is what I have been saying for years."

"So you have," said Robin, touching her lips.

Tamsin was nervous and wished Robin would get on with whatever they were going to do together. She wanted him. She wanted them to be back together, but as they once had been, not like this new fraught, jumpy, friction-cursed couple. Or was it just her? She recognised that it would be a while before the old, easy passion ran through her veins again.

"I am off the pill, by the way."

"So that's why you think I came?" He smirked to tease her. "Don't worry. I called in at a chemists on the way down. Not, and I repeat, that that is what I came for. You know, after Michael and I had been to the park on our own and sat awash in the fountain, I so wanted to share it with you and have a laugh. I couldn't wait. It was just such a," he hesitated, "mammoth experience for me. Why did I leave it all this time before getting on with it?"

"I think a lot of it was my fault."

"'Fucking bonding'! …Kids."

"I know. Full of surprises."

"I remember my dad saying that kids always picked up the words you didn't want them to pick up."

"Even Michael." Tamsin's level tone held a degree of benign triumph.

"Even our Michael." Robin kissed her on the nose. "You know what I'd really like? Just to be with you. Or to be more accurate, you to be with me."

Tamsin tensed at the slight but implied criticism. "I am getting there. Hang on in there Robin." She stroked his cheek. "I love you. I have always fucking loved you. Do you remember The Dolls' House, The Baby House, your father's? I've brought it downstairs and put it on the chest again in the sitting room. I don't know why I put it away in the first place."

"Yeah, I saw you had done that when I went to the cottage. Thank you darling. Maybe because it didn't do anything for Michael?"

"Yes, but I love it. You love it. And given time Michael might love it. If you tell him your stories. What were you doing at the cottage?"

"Oh, I just called in to pay John for some mowing. And by the way, he has made you something. He's very pleased with it too. Just warning you to be very grateful. What do you think about the school exchanging their piano and suggesting we get rid of ours?"

"It's obvious really. I don't know why we didn't think of it before."

"Often the simplest solutions are the ones that occur to you later, rather than sooner. We'll call in Jaguar to value it. I don't know much about pianos but I think ours has had it."

At the mention of Jaguar, Tamsin glowed. She needed to warn, maybe even threaten Debbie, now that she was back, not to say anything, for Jaguar's and Muriel Lindon's sakes. As a newly discovered half-brother, Jaguar felt like a delicate gift she needed to protect. She would tell Robin and maybe, when the time was right, and no one would get hurt, Jaguar and Mollie.

"Oh," Robin continued, "and I did try singing him stories: after the park and on our way back to Sticklepath. Once upon a time, there was a mummy called Tamsin Cooper and a daddy called… I sang it sort of sing-song because he just stared out of the window when I spoke it. Little snob."

"How did he react? To your singing?"

"Glared at my lips as if I was mad, which means at least I got his attention."

"It means he loved it. Try it with The Dolls' House. At home." Tamsin gripped Robin's hand and squeezed it.

They both jumped. The lifeboat's station's maroon had gone off and as one, they rose from the sofa and dashed to the window, where they heard the swish and crescendoing engine of a lifeboat. But they could not see it in the white mist.

"Those poor people out there."

Tamsin shivered. "Yes."

"Shall I open the wine?" Robin had brought two bottles of red. He went to the kitchen to get some glasses and a bottle opener.

"Bring it to bed." Tamsin was agitated.

"What's the hurry?" Robin faced his wife and lifted her hair, cupped it around her cheeks and let it pool in his palms. "All I really would like to do is sleep by your side, or even just lie by your side and hold you, and you not worry about Michael."

"I am not worried. I like Max. And Poppy. I trust them." Tamsin led the way into the bedroom.

"What about God's Gift?"

"Grr!"

Jointly they discarded some items of clothing and threw them onto the floor. Then they climbed on their knees, like children, into the beech bed with its sky blue cotton quilt, Tamsin in just a T-shirt and her pink socks and Robin in his boxers. Robin held Tamsin close. Tamsin, not instinctively but with a flash of bravado, let her hand wriggle its way into Robin's boxers. "I don't think he just wants to lie there."

"In that case," Robin knelt up, encouraged. "Sit up woman. Arms up." He pulled her T-shirt over her head then gently pushed her back onto the pillow again. "Umm, that's better." He bent towards her feet and, without taking his eyes off her face, very slowly slipped off the pink socks, swinging them around his head before hurling them across the room.

But Tamsin was in a bit of a state. Naked, she cringed and with her hands over her head pulled her body down into a foetal position. It had been such a long time.

"Look at me." Robin tenderly pulled away her hands but her eyes were sparkling with tears. She lunged, and with a sudden jerk, slapped Robin across the face. Robin shut and opened his mouth and eyes in astonishment. Instantly he caught her arm.

"What was that all about?"

"I don't know."

"Mollie?" He thought of telling her about Luke's proposition to Sarah but decided against it. A possible spontaneous combustion needed no extra fuel.

"No. Yes."

Their eyes locked. Opposing faces searched for answers. None came, but Tamsin felt even more exposed than she had done before. But differently, and so vulnerable that she softened and warmed to Robin's touch.

"Well, if that's the way you want it." Robin was holding her firmly. Without hurry he placed one of his wife's arms behind her head and then the other. He stroked the insides of her arms, kissed her eyes, her blotchy wet cheeks and lips. "You have no idea how much I love you, have you?"

"Show me."

Later Robin said, "I am surprised you let me in."
Tamsin smirked. "Oh, was that what I was doing?"

In the morning Tamsin woke and was tearful again. "No, no, Robin, I am happy. I feel wonderful. So much better."

"That's all right then." Robin pointed at a scratch on his upper arm. He leant forward. "I'm really sorry about Mollie." But Tamsin was smiling through tears, like the sun through rain. Robin kissed her on her nose.

"No, no. It's more to do with me really. Me and Michael. Sorry," she said, and was sad that she felt closer to Robin in her head than in the physical reality of the sail loft. She caught Robin's eye and saw a perplexed expression, and guessed he felt the same too.

"Don't worry. It'll all take time. On the other hand, the sex was bloody superb. But just give me a bit of warning next time, so I can sort out some real protection."

Tamsin looked alarmed.

"*You* were protected madam. But me ?" He showed her the raw scratch again on his arm. "What's this then? A love trophy? I'm going to need chain mail."

"Fucking bonding?" Tamsin lay back safe and contented.

"Too right. Bloody, fucking bonding."

This time they made love very slowly, very gently and very deeply.

And afterwards the naked pair went to the window and rested their folded arms on the sill. The white mist had dissolved and the sun had come out and was skimming across the sea.

To their left, onto the slip-way, the lifeboat was unloading its crew and rescued passengers. The crew bounced onto the slip-way, whereas the rescued couple climbed down carefully, with blue blankets draped over their shoulders like shawls. They looked like the pair on the *Elderly People Crossing* road sign.

"Good," said Tamsin and Robin in unison.

Chapter Twenty Eight

Tamsin, Robin, Michael and Jaguar stood around the piano in Brock Cottage like a concert party at twilight getting ready to sing.

Debbie was in the kitchen preparing supper, her slim, willow cane propped against the sink. Tomorrow was her first appointment with the consultant at Linbury General.

"No, not just that. I could have had my hip seen to there, in Brazil. State of the Art hospitals. Quite easily," was her reply to Robin when he had quizzed her on her reason for returning to England. "But when Paula, my best friend's daughter, became pregnant with Ferdinand's baby… and …well …they blamed me!"

Debbie and Robin had been in the car at the time, on their way to the auction. Debbie wanted some bits and pieces for her new home. It was raining and the rhythmic swish of the windscreen wipers gave Debbie's words added emphasis.

"Blame you? Why? There must have been other reasons to make you want to come home, over the years, surely?"

"Home." She smiled at Robin. "Home is where you are wanted. And I was. At first. They, the Cabrals, used to show me off to their friends. An English wife. And then we all got used to one another and I was treated as an outsider again. Sometimes, even, in a nice way. They would tease me, my Englishness. But my word never counted for much. I was a great disappointment to them when, as the years went by, I didn't fall for a child. Then they tolerated me. Disdainful, that's what they were. And started to mock my Englishness and my inability to get pregnant." She snuffled and turned her head to look out of the side window. Robin wasn't sure if she was crying or not.

"But you do have a child."

"I know." Debbie contemplated the rain. "Actually, you were right in a way; when my hip started to give me trouble, I did begin to think about my situation." Robin saw her look around at the confines of the car as though she was measuring its safety. "This sounds strange, I know, but when my hip started playing up, I used to look at my feet. And I wanted to run. To run and run."

"And you didn't have anywhere to run to?"

Debbie smiled. "That's more or less what Ferdinand said, when we rowed about what he had done. His mother said I should stay and help look after the child. Ferdinand even said it was my duty…"

"He said that?"

"My best friend's daughter is having Ferdinand's, my husband's, baby. He's old enough to be her father. The Cabrals went wild. Forgave him instantly. Instantly, though. The idea of a new grandchild, niece, nephew. They went insane. The family, his family, want this baby." Debbie sounded exhausted; bitterly sad.

Robin swung the car into Lindon's yard and parked. Again he waited for Debbie. It didn't seem right to get out of the car straight away.

"It's ironical, isn't it? What goes around, comes around. Isn't that what they say? Oh look, there's Jaguar."

"What do you mean?" Robin felt all at sea. He had been so bound up in his own family's problems for months that Debbie's story was like a delta into another country with troublesome tributaries.

"You think I didn't want Tamsin, don't you? Didn't want to take her with me to Brazil?"

"Well… " Robin was embarrassed. "Tamsin's glad to have you home now."

"Thank you. But I am back to settle. I am lucky she'll have me around but I can help a bit with Michael. He's a little whatsit isn't he? Very difficult." She turned to Robin and put a hand on his arm.

Robin studied Debbie's face in a preoccupied manner, because a similarity had just occurred to him. "I too am back to settle. Like you." And now also recognising the privacy of the car, he forgave his mother-in-law a little. "And he is definitely a whatsit, as you say. We need all the help we can get. So get that operation done Debbie. Quick."

Robin then had swiftly kissed Debbie on the nose, and in response two silent tears had trickled down her pale, dry cheeks.

Since their conversation Debbie had been left in charge of Michael several times, and so far had used her new mobile only once, to call them home, when she'd been unable to release Michael's vice-like grip from the gushing tap in the kitchen.

Tonight Robin turned from the piano in the passageway to see Debbie simultaneously turn from the sink and look longingly at Tamsin by his side. When her eyes caught Robin's interception, she reassembled her gaze into a domestic query.

"Pasta or rice with the chicken?"

"Pasta," called Robin firmly.

"What about Tamsin? And the others?"

"Others? Pasta!" Robin said resoundingly without consulting Tamsin.

Debbie's eyes smiled while her mouth scolded.

"It was a lovely piece, once upon a time. Nice bit of mahogany." Jaguar swayed backwards and forwards examining the piano. He stroked the wood and puckered his lips, then stretched them wide and shook his head. "I think it's almost beyond restoring, which is what it needs, but the cost would be prohibitive Robin. Cost more than a new modern upright. Why not get a keyboard, like the school has done?"

Michael, who was fidgeting and jigging about on the spot, reached forward and stabbed D flat.

"Is this is our little pianist then?" Jaguar ruffled Michael's hair. Michael jumped and butted the air.

"Whoops. Steady on old fellow." Jaguar's hand flew back.

"You're staying, aren't you Jaguar? For a bit of supper?" Debbie turned from the stove and smiled lingeringly and sweetly at Jaguar as she poured pasta into boiling water.

Jaguar appeared not to hear her.

"Don't worry Jaguar, I thought as much, but I needed your opinion, just in case." Robin had polished the mahogany until it was a deep, deep mirror, for Jaguar's inspection. But what he didn't need or understand was Debbie's interruption. Although he was getting used to her, and liked how she was fitting in with the family, her attitude to Jaguar irritated him. When it reared its weird head, and to be fair, it was only occasionally, but when it did, her over-attentiveness was embarrassing, to say the least. He had noticed her engaging Jaguar in trivial chatter in the Black Swan, after the last auction when she'd bid for several items for her intended new home, a terraced town cottage in Linbury High.

"He's so good at his job, isn't he?" she'd said to Robin in a lilting voice.

"And so he should be. He's been doing it for years, for God's sake. And it's in the family. His father before him. I don't suppose you knew him? Cecil Lindon?"

"Oh yes. I knew him." Debbie's tone had had a whimsical put-down quality, in answer to Robin's rather superior one. "But Jaguar's nice." Her voice softened. "Not at all like his father. And what a lot his poor mother had to put up with."

Later, back at Brock Cottage, Robin had said to Tamsin, "What is it with your mother and Jaguar? She talks to him as though they have some mysterious connection. And what does she know about how Cecil and Muriel got on?"

Tamsin was immediately on the defensive but also amused, Robin noted. "Oh, you're imagining things. She's just being familiar. Friendly. She does so want to be part of things again. Around here."

"Over-familiar is what's she's being, if you ask me."

Tamsin laughed. "I'll have a word with her. And you - you stop over-reacting." She'd leaned up to kiss him, or as Robin interpreted it, to shut him up. And for the moment he acquiesced.

"To be honest I don't think it's worth me calling in the real experts. Sorry Robin. It would be good to get it tuned for sing-a-long use, though it'll be a bit of a honky-tonk."

"Don't be. If it's not worth anything, so be it. Then we just want to dispose of it in the best way possible. Find a new home for it. Don't we Tams?"

"Definitely," she said, giving Robin the reassurance he needed, that he was not going it alone or being biased. "Definitely. You think The Good Companions' Club are looking for a piano, Jaguar? They can have it for free, if they take it away."

"Yup. Good idea. They've been checking out the sale room for some months now. Do you think you'll get a keyboard?" Jaguar picked up the walnut burr and feather framed photograph of Robin. "Nice frame."

Both Robin and Tamsin simultaneously breathed in deeply and looked at one another. As Tamsin exhaled she said, "No. Robin's going to get a set of drums to fill the space."

Jaguar looked at Robin as if he were mad, and then crouched down with Michael. "Who's this then young man?" Jaguar held the photograph frame lightly, in his well manicured hands, for Michael's inspection.

"He doesn't always recognise… " started Tamsin, protectively.

Michael suddenly stopped jigging about on the spot and studied the photograph. Tamsin and Robin gave one another a quick look. Now they held their breath and stared down at their son, waiting. Michael touched the glass with one finger, but then Tamsin seemed to change her mind and reached down to take the photograph from Jaguar. Robin immediately remembered Tamsin's birthday and instinctively knew she didn't want him to be hurt, like that, again.

It was absurd to feel hurt. He'd told himself to chill out, measure up. Michael wasn't intending to hurt. Wasn't even capable of intentional hurt. He said, "It's all right, love. Don't worry… " And then in the twilight of the passageway, he heard Michael's softest sing-song voice, as though it were coming out of a cloud.

"This Michael, young man. Once upon a time there was a daddy called Robin Cooper and a mummy called Tamsin Cooper and then there was Michael. There was Michael. Fucking bonding. Fucking bonding."

Robin clutched Tamsin's shoulder to steady himself, and hung on tightly. He'd nearly keeled over, as though a baby had given him a gentle but shattering blow to the stomach.

"Well, well. There's a potted family history if ever there was one." Jaguar stood up with sudden determination, and slapped his tweed thighs. "I think I'd best be off then."

"Oh, you are not going are you?" Debbie limped to the passageway. "I thought you were staying for supper."

"Thank you so much Deborah, but I am meeting Mollie. And I'd better not keep her waiting. She gets more like my darling mother every day." He grinned at Debbie but she glared back at him with distinct displeasure.

"Surely… You could… "

By the piano, Tamsin bent down. Robin released her shoulder, letting his fingers trail down her back to rest on her waist, as she nuzzled Michael. "You clever boy, Michael."

Robin felt as though he had been hit by something sliding slowly out of snow. Submitting to the blow his insides melted like a little death.

Tamsin rose and kissed him, her eyes welling with tears, and then left him there in the passageway, with the piano and Michael. Inconsequentially she started to talk to Jaguar and guide him by holding his elbow as they moved. They moved into the kitchen, but for Robin their backs grew distant, as in a silent film. The sounds inside the cottage were muted and for a moment Robin was keenly aware of the outside world, where only the stream drifted in the November mist. Then he bent down, as Tamsin had done, and stroked Michael's hair. "Michael Cooper. Son. Eh?"

"Cooper," echoed Michael in a whisper.

"Yes," said Robin. "For better or worse."

Chapter Twenty Nine

Only the stream moved. Then a fragile snowflake melted and slowly ran down the outside of the bedroom windowpane. There was a hush and an urge to whisper.

"Robin, come and look."

"I thought we were supposed to be in the middle of climate warming. It's only November." Standing behind her Robin rubbed the top of her head with his chin.

"Don't be so prosaic, Robin. It's beautiful. Do you think they'll come to collect it in this?"

"Yes? Why not?"

A sudden rush of wind in the woods across the lane caused splodges of snow to fall with a huff. He gripped her waist and together they scanned their newly made land: remade in the image of a downy white quilt.

Sam was coming down the hill in his tractor and waved when he saw them at the window. The tractor's engine was muffled, and the snow creaked with satisfaction as the tyres compressed it and lacerated the crisp tread marks John had left after driving off to school in the minibus.

"I don't think it will lie long. But if it does I'll lock up early, come home and we'll make a snowman with Michael, when he gets back from school."

Tamsin dressed quickly, pulling on old jeans and her red, thick, mohair jumper, and ran and slid all the way down to her shed. The kiln was on and giving a good, steady, humming account of itself against the chill and the snow. She went outside again, picked up a handful of snow and pressed the pure iciness against her cheek. Then she took a stick and drew two large heads in the snow. Two Green Leafy Men. Why two? At first she didn't know, as she sketched and wove a profusion of oak leaves in and out of their eyes, ears and then their mouths. And then she knew, for she drew down the mouth of one of the Green Men into a grimace, and drew up the lips of the other into the boldest of smiles. She scratched at the snow, filling in the lips and the eyes, making sure the eyes of one were full of dark pain, and the eyes of the other crinkled with laughter lines. It wasn't easy. Next year she decided she would sculpt more Green Men from clay. Since her encounters with them in the churches over the summer she'd grown increasingly drawn to their symbolic nature of death and resurrection.

A battered old blue van skidded and slithered to a halt by the gate. Tamsin leapt up, kicked the stick into the glassy, jewelled edged stream and began to climb the paddock. Her red jumper dazzled against the snow like a brightly burning ember of coal.

"You're brave, coming today," she called over the gate to the two lads sitting in the front of the van. The stunning cold brought a healthy glow to their cheeks. They jumped down from the van and started throwing snowballs at one another.

"Oh, it's brilliant. Mum said, *No, don't be silly.*" The tallest lad guffawed at his mate and slapped his hands against his thighs. "Snow's the best excuse, isn't it Ollie?"

Ollie appeared more self-conscious than his dare-do friend and tipped his head slightly in agreement while keeping his eyes on Tamsin.

"Coffee? Tea?" Tamsin thought they might prefer to be offered something stronger, with more muscle, but she quickly dismissed the thought as pandering to their youthful manliness.

"Please," they shouted in unison as they scooted along the top of the paddock and stood clapping and blowing by the back door, waiting for Tamsin to catch up and let them into her kitchen and its warmth.

While the kettle boiled Tamsin took the lads into the passageway and showed them the piano.

"It's very kind of you," said Ollie.

"Do you think you can manage it?"

"Yeah. No probs. Sorry, I'm James by the way." He flexed his arms. "Muscle. All muscle. Rugby."

"And I am Tamsin. It was my little boy's." She stroked the mahogany.

"Was?" Ollie looked alarmed.

Tamsin realised she had already moved on to the next stage of life, post-piano, with Michael and Robin. "He won't be needing it any more. He, Michael," she said proudly, "has moved on… to drums," she added dreamily.

"Really?" James' eyebrows rose in puzzlement.

Tamsin decided not to explain and changed tack as they sat at the kitchen table with steaming mugs. "What about you two? You don't work with the pensioners, do you? Sorry, I shouldn't presume. Maybe you do."

"No, we are both doing A levels," Ollie said shyly.

"Uni next year, " added James.

How lovely to be so sure, thought Tamsin.

"No, it's our community minded mothers." He pulled a face and grinned at Tamsin. "They're always volunteering *us* for something or other. Now that we've passed our tests and got our licences, suddenly we're very useful. Not that we mind. We love it. Getting the keys to the van. Your lane was like a bob sleigh run. The van slalomed all the way down."

Tamsin looked nervous. "Well I wish you luck carrying the piano along the top of the paddock. It looks very slippery to me. You will be careful, won't you?"

"Don't worry, Tamsin. Piece of cake. And," blustered James, looking at Ollie, "I think we'll take the long way home. Maybe call at the gym. Have a bit of a workout. Ollie?"

Ollie nodded smiling at their collusion, then shook his head, "No kit. Stoopid."

"Of course." James looked self-conscious and reddened. "Right. Let's get on with it. Direct us, Tamsin."

Tamsin stood to one side by the sink as the boys hauled the piano from the passageway and into the kitchen. Tamsin kicked a rush mat out of their way. Every now and then when the boys rested the piano, single notes donged and unfamiliar chords clashed. It seemed to be protesting.

"It'll need tuning. Especially D flat. You'll tell them that won't you? Jaguar Lindon said it has some life left in it." Suddenly she felt absurdly possessive of D flat. It was their note. Michael's, hers and Robin's. Its significance mysterious.

"Yep." James breathed heavily through his mouth, as they ducked and wrestled the piano through the back door Tamsin was now holding open for them. Once outside his breath rose in baby clouds and the honking piano echoed, eerily flat and tuneless around the snowy terrain, and then the echoes floated away and into the unearthly distance.

Tamsin silently pleaded with it to stop, to be quiet, to refrain from drawing attention to itself and the deed of its removal. But it wouldn't. A little further along the top of the paddock, James stumbled and the piano rippled into the urgent ghost of a tune. They lowered the piano into a bed of snow. It tolled a coda of satisfaction.

"It would be easier if we could get a good grip with our feet." Ollie stamped, grinding his heels into the snow.

"Do you want to leave it for another day?" Tamsin was hopeful.

"No. Not now that we have got this far. Right." James

inhaled a large lungful of air. "One, two, three, lift. You got it Ollie?" They heaved the piano and as they did so, Ollie swayed backwards, still holding on to the piano, so that James lost his balance and tripped forwards, hitting his chin on the lid. "Fucking hell." James floundered, endeavouring to remain upright, but this time grabbing out at thin air to be his saviour. His hands landed on the silky mahogany sides of the piano but slid slowly away, and again flailed at nothing, while a bemused Ollie, now sitting like a slap-stick artist in the snow, looked on. The piano bounced with such a cacophony and James followed it, hitting the ground softly and creating his own minor blizzard.

Tamsin cupped her red cheeks and winced, as she watched the piano start to slide slowly, tentatively, as if it were having second thoughts, over the edge of the slope and then gather speed down the incline.

"I am so very sorry," mumbled James in horror.

"No, no leave it," said Tamsin as Ollie staggered up and was making as if to follow the piano.

The three of them watched helplessly as the piano bucked over the hidden thirteen steps, and the terracing, and then zoomed suddenly where the snow was smooth: a beautiful, shiny sledge intent on its destination. The stream. An instrument capable of partnering fingers into the sublime or ridiculous, an instrument capable of such cooperation, exquisite loyalty, had now, finally, become a wild hooligan, a free spirit taking control of its own destiny.

Tamsin remained riveted to the scene as the piano aimed for the dour Green Man, and erased his grimace. A sign she thought, and was uplifted with delight. Joy sparked in her heart. A new beginning. But then the piano shimmied sideways and swiped the smile off the benign Green Man's face. Tamsin laughed. "So be it." And the piano plummeted into the stream and rose again like some ghostly galleon before it flew apart, scattering yellowed ivory keys and black fingers to sink or swim. Which one was D flat? Tamsin was slightly hysterical. "No idea. God only knows," she said aloud, and turned to the two boys. "Well … "

"We are so sorry … "

"Don't worry. Though I expect you will have quite a bit of explaining to do to your mothers. Those poor pensioners. No piano for Christmas carols. Tch. Ah. Are you okay? Broken anything?"

The two boys looked really sheepish. "We are so sorry Mrs… "

"It's still Tamsin. I should definitely go the long way home. Now boys, are you sure you don't want another hot drink?"

James looked at Ollie. "Ollie?"

"No. We'll be fine. Shall we um… rescue the um… what's left of the piano?"

Tamsin looked towards the stream. "My husband will be home soon. We'll sort it. And my son."

The boys sauntered as casually as they could towards the gate, their fit bodies tightly hunched in an effort to become invisible.

Lightning Source UK Ltd.
Milton Keynes UK

176648UK00001B/2/P